THE BROKEN CODE

WARRIORS

LOST STARS

THE BROKEN CODE

Book One: *Lost Stars*

THE BROKEN CODE

WARRIORS

LOST STARS

**ERIN
HUNTER**

HARPER

An Imprint of HarperCollinsPublishers

Special thanks to Cherith Baldry

Lost Stars

Copyright © 2019 by Working Partners Limited

Series created by Working Partners Limited

Map art © 2019 by Dave Stevenson

Interior art © 2019 by Owen Richardson

Library of Congress Cataloging-in-Publication Data

Names: Hunter, Erin, author.

Title: Lost stars / Erin Hunter.

Description: New York, NY : HarperCollins, 2019. | Series: Warriors: the broken code ; [1] |

Summary: "In the midst of the coldest leaf-bare any warrior can remember, the Clans have lost their connection with their warrior ancestors, and only one ShadowClan apprentice can still hear their voices--or their warning about the new shadow rising within the warrior Clans"-- Provided by publisher.

Identifiers: LCCN 2018055864 | ISBN 978-0-06-282351-9 (hardback) | ISBN 978-0-06-282352-6 (library)

Subjects: | CYAC: Cats--Fiction. | Fantasy. | BISAC: JUVENILE FICTION / Animals / Cats. | JUVENILE FICTION / Action & Adventure / General. | JUVENILE FICTION / Fantasy & Magic.

Classification: LCC PZ7.H916625 Los 2019 | DDC [Fic]--dc23 LC record available at https://lccn.loc.gov/2018055864

Typography by Jessie Gang

19 20 21 22 23   PC/LSCH   10 9 8 7 6 5 4 3 2 1

❖

First Edition

ALLEGIANCES

THUNDERCLAN

LEADER **BRAMBLESTAR**—dark brown tabby tom with amber eyes

DEPUTY **SQUIRRELFLIGHT**—dark ginger she-cat with green eyes and one white paw

MEDICINE CATS **JAYFEATHER**—gray tabby tom with blind blue eyes

ALDERHEART—dark ginger tom with amber eyes

WARRIORS (toms and she-cats without kits)

THORNCLAW—golden-brown tabby tom

WHITEWING—white she-cat with green eyes

BIRCHFALL—light brown tabby tom

BERRYNOSE—cream-colored tom with a stump for a tail

MOUSEWHISKER—gray-and-white tom

POPPYFROST—pale tortoiseshell-and-white she-cat

LIONBLAZE—golden tabby tom with amber eyes

ROSEPETAL—dark cream she-cat
APPRENTICE, BRISTLEPAW (pale gray she-cat)

STEMLEAF—white-and-orange tom

LILYHEART—small, dark tabby she-cat with white patches and blue eyes

BUMBLESTRIPE—very pale gray tom with black stripes

CHERRYFALL—ginger she-cat

MOLEWHISKER—brown-and-cream tom

CINDERHEART—gray tabby she-cat

BLOSSOMFALL—tortoiseshell-and-white she-cat with petal-shaped white patches

IVYPOOL—silver-and-white tabby she-cat with dark blue eyes

EAGLEWING—ginger she-cat

DEWNOSE—gray-and-white tom
APPRENTICE, THRIFTPAW (dark gray she-cat)

STORMCLOUD—gray tabby tom

HOLLYTUFT—black she-cat
APPRENTICE, FLIPPAW (tabby tom)

FERNSONG—yellow tabby tom

HONEYFUR—white she-cat with yellow splotches

TWIGBRANCH—gray she-cat with green eyes

FINLEAP—brown tom

SHELLFUR—tortoiseshell tom

PLUMSTONE—black-and-ginger she-cat

LEAFSHADE—tortoiseshell she-cat

SPOTFUR—spotted tabby she-cat

FLYWHISKER—striped gray tabby she-cat

SNAPTOOTH—golden tabby tom

QUEENS (she-cats expecting or nursing kits)

DAISY—cream long-furred cat from the horseplace

SORRELSTRIPE—dark brown she-cat (mother to Baykit, a golden tabby tom, and Myrtlekit, a pale brown she-kit)

SPARKPELT—orange tabby she-cat (mother to Finchkit, a tortoiseshell she-kit, and Flamekit, a black tom)

ELDERS (former warriors and queens, now retired)

GRAYSTRIPE—long-haired gray tom

CLOUDTAIL—long-haired white tom with blue eyes

BRIGHTHEART—white she-cat with ginger patches

BRACKENFUR—golden-brown tabby tom

SHADOWCLAN

LEADER **TIGERSTAR**—dark brown tabby tom

DEPUTY **CLOVERFOOT**—gray tabby she-cat

MEDICINE CAT **PUDDLESHINE**—brown tom with white splotches

APPRENTICE, SHADOWPAW (gray tabby tom)

WARRIORS **TAWNYPELT**—tortoiseshell she-cat with green eyes

DOVEWING—pale gray she-cat with green eyes

STRIKESTONE—brown tabby tom

STONEWING—white tom

SCORCHFUR—dark gray tom with slashed ears
    APPRENTICE, FLAXPAW (brown tabby tom)

SPARROWTAIL—large brown tabby tom

SNOWBIRD—pure white she-cat with green eyes

YARROWLEAF—ginger she-cat with yellow eyes

BERRYHEART—black-and-white she-cat

GRASSHEART—pale brown tabby she-cat

WHORLPELT—gray-and-white tom
    APPRENTICE, HOPPAW (calico she-cat)

ANTFUR—tom with a brown-and-black splotched pelt

BLAZEFIRE—white-and-ginger tom

CINNAMONTAIL—brown tabby she-cat with white paws

FLOWERSTEM—silver she-cat

SNAKETOOTH—honey-colored tabby she-cat

SLATEFUR—sleek gray tom

POUNCESTEP—gray she-cat

LIGHTLEAP—brown tabby she-cat

CONEFOOT—white-and-gray tom

FRONDWHISKER—gray tabby she-cat

GULLSWOOP—white she-cat

SPIRECLAW—black-and-white tom

HOLLOWSPRING—black tom

SUNBEAM—brown-and-white tabby she-cat

ELDERS

OAKFUR—small brown tom

SKYCLAN

LEADER   **LEAFSTAR**—brown-and-cream tabby she-cat with amber eyes

DEPUTY   **HAWKWING**—dark gray tom with yellow eyes

MEDICINE CATS   **FRECKLEWISH**—mottled light brown tabby she-cat with spotted legs

FIDGETFLAKE—black-and-white tom

MEDIATOR   **TREE**—yellow tom with amber eyes

WARRIORS   **SPARROWPELT**—dark brown tabby tom

MACGYVER—black-and-white tom

DEWSPRING—sturdy gray tom

PLUMWILLOW—dark gray she-cat

SAGENOSE—pale gray tom
APPRENTICE, KITEPAW (reddish-brown tom)

HARRYBROOK—gray tom

BLOSSOMHEART—ginger-and-white she-cat
APPRENTICE, TURTLEPAW (tortoiseshell she-cat)

SANDYNOSE—stocky light brown tom with ginger legs

RABBITLEAP—brown tom

REEDCLAW—small pale tabby she-cat

MINTFUR—gray tabby she-cat with blue eyes

NETTLESPLASH—pale brown tom

TINYCLOUD—small white she-cat

PALESKY—black-and-white she-cat

NECTARSONG—brown she-cat

QUAILFEATHER—white tom with crow-black ears

PIGEONFOOT—gray-and-white she-cat

FRINGEWHISKER—white she-cat with brown splotches

GRAVELNOSE—tan tom

SUNNYPELT—ginger she-cat

QUEENS **VIOLETSHINE**—black-and-white she-cat with yellow eyes (mother to Rootkit, a yellow tom, and Needlekit, a black-and-white she-kit)

BELLALEAF—pale orange she-cat with green eyes (mother to Wrenkit, a golden tabby she-kit)

ELDERS **FALLOWFERN**—pale brown she-cat who has lost her hearing

WINDCLAN

LEADER **HARESTAR**—brown-and-white tom

DEPUTY **CROWFEATHER**—dark gray tom

MEDICINE CAT **KESTRELFLIGHT**—mottled gray tom with white splotches like kestrel feathers

WARRIORS **NIGHTCLOUD**—black she-cat

BRINDLEWING—mottled brown she-cat

LEAFTAIL—dark tabby tom with amber eyes

EMBERFOOT—gray tom with two dark paws

SMOKEHAZE—gray she-cat

BREEZEPELT—black tom with amber eyes

CROUCHFOOT—ginger tom

LARKWING—pale brown tabby she-cat

SEDGEWHISKER—light brown tabby she-cat

SLIGHTFOOT—black tom with white flash on his chest

OATCLAW—pale brown tabby tom

HOOTWHISKER—dark gray tom

FERNSTRIPE—gray tabby she-cat

QUEENS　　**HEATHERTAIL**—light brown tabby she-cat with blue eyes (mother to Breezepelt's kits: Woodkit, a brown she-kit, and Applekit, a yellow tabby she-kit)

FEATHERPELT—gray tabby she-cat (mother to Oatclaw's kits: Whistlekit, a gray tabby she-kit; Songkit, a tortoiseshell she-kit; and Flutterkit, a brown-and-white tom)

ELDERS　　**WHISKERNOSE**—light brown tom

GORSETAIL—very pale gray-and-white she-cat with blue eyes

RIVERCLAN

LEADER　　**MISTYSTAR**—gray she-cat with blue eyes

DEPUTY　　**REEDWHISKER**—black tom

MEDICINE CATS　　**MOTHWING**—dappled golden she-cat

WILLOWSHINE—gray tabby she-cat

WARRIORS　　**DUSKFUR**—brown tabby she-cat

MINNOWTAIL—dark gray-and-white she-cat

MALLOWNOSE—light brown tabby tom

BEETLEWHISKER—brown-and-white tabby tom

PODLIGHT—gray-and-white tom

SHIMMERPELT—silver she-cat

LIZARDTAIL—light brown tom

SNEEZECLOUD—gray-and-white tom

BRACKENPELT—tortoiseshell she-cat

JAYCLAW—gray tom

OWLNOSE—brown tabby tom

ICEWING—white she-cat with blue eyes

SOFTPELT—gray she-cat

GORSECLAW—white tom with gray ears

NIGHTSKY—dark gray she-cat with blue eyes

HARELIGHT—white tom

BREEZEHEART—brown-and-white she-cat

DAPPLETUFT—gray-and-white tom

QUEENS

CURLFEATHER—pale brown she-cat

HAVENPELT—black-and-white she-cat (mother to Sneezecloud's kits: Fogkit, a gray-and-white she-kit, and Splashkit, a brown tabby tom)

ELDERS

MOSSPELT—tortoiseshell-and-white she-cat

THE BROKEN CODE

WARRIORS

LOST STARS

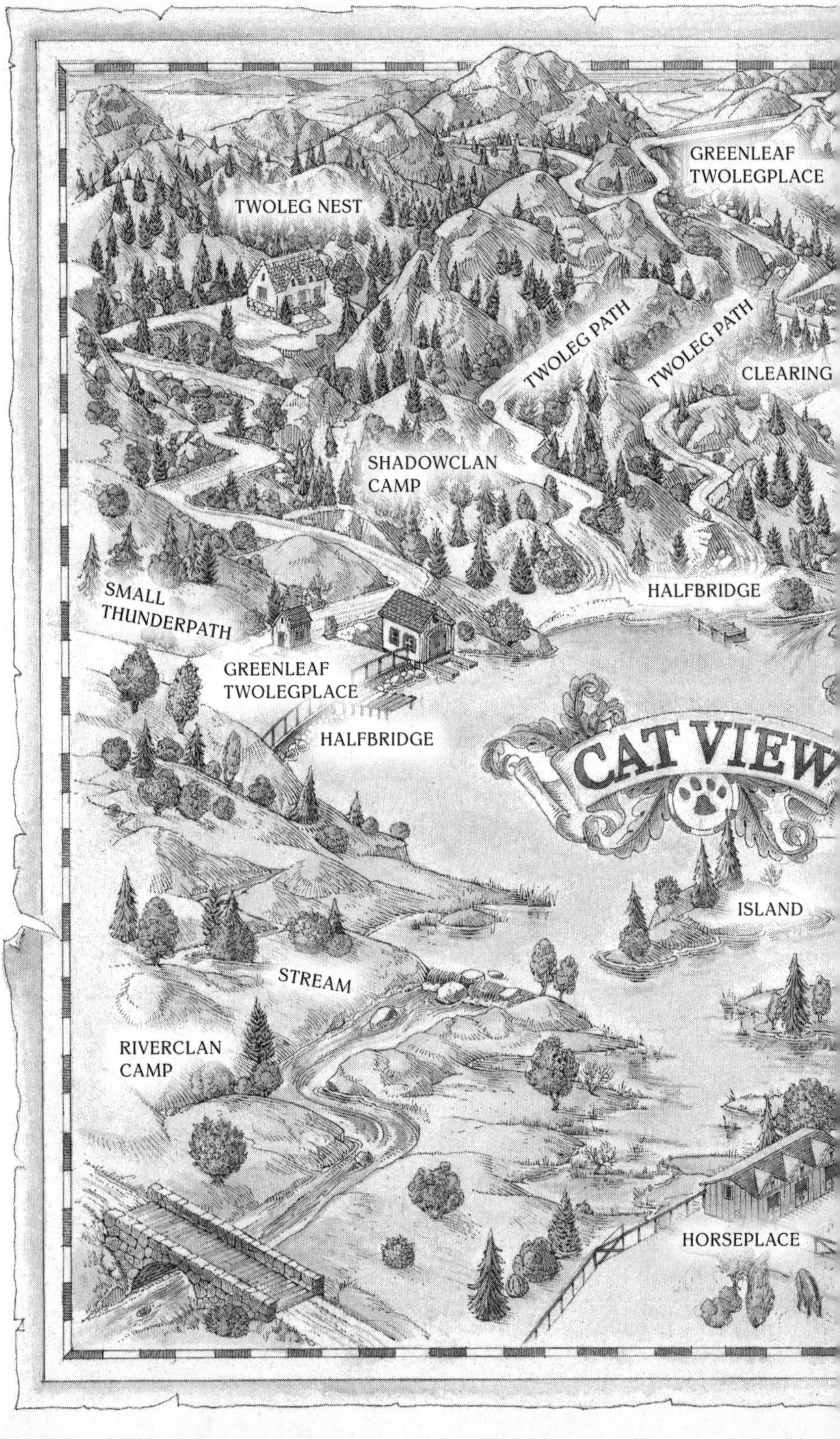

GREENLEAF
TWOLEGPLACE

TWOLEG NEST

TWOLEG PATH

TWOLEG PATH

CLEARING

SHADOWCLAN
CAMP

HALFBRIDGE

SMALL
THUNDERPATH

GREENLEAF
TWOLEGPLACE

HALFBRIDGE

CAT VIEW

ISLAND

STREAM

RIVERCLAN
CAMP

HORSEPLACE

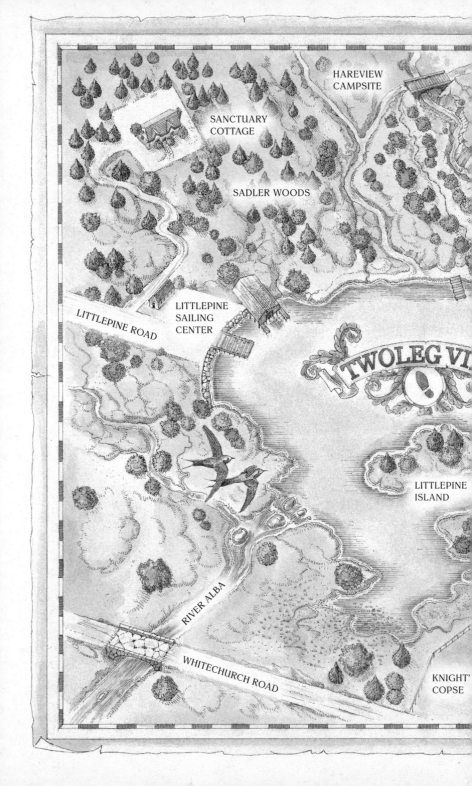

PROLOGUE

♣

From a vast indigo sky, a warrior of StarClan gazed down at the lake and the Clan territories clustered around it. A half-moon floated in the darkness, its light turning the surface of the water to silver and glittering on the snow-covered land. The branches of the trees dipped gently under their weight of snow.

The starry warrior spotted movement at the edge of the trees where forest gave way to the steep slopes of the moor. Two tiny figures toiled upward, their shapes dark against the icy brightness. In the lead was a brown tom with white splotches, while close behind him a smaller tom, a gray tabby with darker stripes, was struggling to make headway, his belly fur brushing the snow. They were both unaware of being observed.

"Puddleshine," the StarClan warrior murmured, recognizing the ShadowClan medicine cat. "And there's his apprentice, Shadowpaw. They must be on their way to the Moonpool for the half-moon meeting."

The spirit cat focused an intense gaze on the tabby apprentice, nodding appreciatively at his determination to keep up with his mentor, and at how his eyes shone with anticipation at the coming meeting, when he would share dreams with StarClan.

"There is no cat like you in all the five Clans, Shadowpaw," the warrior continued. "Now great events are coming, and the Clans will experience far-reaching changes. And you, young apprentice—you will have an important part to play."

The StarClan spirit went on watching as the two medicine cats trudged on up the moorland slope, their figures slowly dwindling into the distance until they crossed the crest of the hill and vanished.

"Yes." The word was breathed out on a sigh of satisfaction. "Shadowpaw, your name will be remembered for as long as the Clans survive."

CHAPTER 1
❧

Shadowpaw craned his neck over his back, straining to groom the hard-to-reach spot at the base of his tail. He had just managed to give his fur a few vigorous licks when he heard paw steps approaching. He looked up to see his father, Tigerstar, and his mother, Dovewing, their pelts brushing as they gazed down at him with pride and joy shining in their eyes.

"What is it?" he asked, sitting up and giving his pelt a shake.

"We just came to see you off," Tigerstar responded, while Dovewing gave her son's ears a quick, affectionate lick.

Shadowpaw's fur prickled with embarrassment. *Like I haven't been to the Moonpool before,* he thought. *They're still treating me as if I'm a kit in the nursery!*

He was sure that his parents hadn't made such a fuss when his littermates, Pouncestep and Lightleap, had been warrior apprentices. *I guess it's because I'm going to be a medicine cat. . . .* Or maybe because of the seizures he'd had since he was a kit. He knew his parents still worried about him, even though it had been a while since his last upsetting vision. *They're probably hoping that with some training from the other medicine cats, I'll learn to control my visions once and for all . . . and I can be normal.*

3

Shadowpaw wanted that, too.

"The snow must be really deep up on the moors," Dovewing mewed. "Make sure you watch where you're putting your paws."

Shadowpaw wriggled his shoulders, praying that none of his Clanmates were listening. "I will," he promised, glancing toward the medicine cats' den in the hope of seeing his mentor, Puddleshine, emerge. But there was no sign of him yet.

To his relief, Tigerstar gave Dovewing a nudge and they both moved off toward the Clan leader's den. Shadowpaw rubbed one paw hastily across his face and bounded across the camp to see what was keeping Puddleshine.

Intent on finding his mentor, Shadowpaw barely noticed the patrol trekking toward the fresh-kill pile, prey dangling from their jaws. He skidded to a halt just in time to avoid colliding with Cloverfoot, the Clan deputy.

"Shadowpaw!" she exclaimed around the shrew she was carrying. "You nearly knocked me off my paws."

"Sorry, Cloverfoot," Shadowpaw meowed, dipping his head respectfully.

Cloverfoot let out a snort, half annoyed, half amused. "Apprentices!"

Shadowpaw tried to hide his irritation. He was an apprentice, yes, but an old one—medicine cat apprentices' training lasted longer than warriors'. His littermates were full warriors already. But he knew his parents would want him to respect the deputy.

Cloverfoot padded on, followed by Strikestone, Yarrowleaf,

and Blazefire. Though they were all carrying prey, they had only one or two pieces each, and what little they had managed to catch was undersized and scrawny.

"I can't remember a leaf-bare as cold as this," Yarrowleaf complained as she dropped a blackbird on the fresh-kill pile.

Strikestone nodded, shivering as he fluffed out his brown tabby pelt. "No wonder there's no prey. They're all hiding down their holes, and I can't blame them."

As Shadowpaw moved on, out of earshot, he couldn't help noticing how pitifully small the fresh-kill pile was, and he tried to ignore his own growling belly. He could hardly remember his first leaf-bare, when he'd been a tiny kit, so he didn't know if the older cats were right and the weather was unusually cold.

I only know I don't like it, he grumbled to himself as he picked his way through the icy slush that covered the ground of the camp. *My paws are so cold I think they'll drop off. I can't wait for newleaf!*

Puddleshine ducked out of the entrance to the medicine cats' den as Shadowpaw approached. "Good, you're ready," he meowed. "We'd better hurry, or we'll be late." As he led the way toward the camp entrance, he added, "I've been checking our herb stores, and they're getting dangerously low."

"We could search for more on the way back," Shadowpaw suggested, his medicine-cat duties driving out his thoughts of cold and hunger. He always enjoyed working with Puddle-shine to find, sort, and store the herbs. Treating cats with herbs made him feel calm and in control . . . the opposite of how he felt during his seizures and the accompanying visions.

"We can try," Puddleshine sighed. "But what isn't frostbitten will be covered with snow." He glanced over his shoulder at Shadowpaw as the two cats headed out into the forest. "This is turning out to be a really bad leaf-bare. And it isn't over yet, not by a long way."

Excitement tingled through Shadowpaw from ears to tail-tip as he scrambled up the rocky slope toward the line of bushes that surrounded the Moonpool hollow. His worries over his seizures and the bitter leaf-bare faded; every hair on his pelt was bristling with anticipation of his meeting with the other medicine cats, and most of all with StarClan.

He might not be a full medicine cat yet, and he might not be fully in control of his visions . . . but he would still get to meet with his warrior ancestors. And from the rest of the medicine cats he would find out what was going on in the other Clans.

Standing at the top of the slope, waiting for Puddleshine to push his way through the bushes, Shadowpaw reflected on the last few moons. Things had been tense in ShadowClan as every cat settled into their new boundaries and grew used to sharing a border with SkyClan. Not long ago, SkyClan had lived separately from the other Clans, in a far-flung territory in a gorge. But StarClan had called SkyClan back to join the other Clans by the lake, because the Clans were stronger when all five were united. Still, SkyClan had needed its own territory, which had meant new borders for everyone, and it had taken time for the other Clans to accept them. Shadowpaw was relieved that things seemed more peaceful now; the brutally cold leaf-bare had given all the Clans more to worry about than quarreling with one another. They were even beginning to rely on one another, especially in sharing herbs when the cold weather had damaged so many of the plants they needed. Shadowpaw felt proud that they were all getting along, instead of battling one another for every piece of prey.

That wasn't a great start to Tigerstar's leadership. . . . I'm glad it's over now!

"Are you going to stand out there all night?"

At the sound of Puddleshine's voice from the other side of the bushes, Shadowpaw dived in among the branches, wincing as sharp twigs scraped along his pelt, and thrust himself out onto the ledge above the Moonpool. Opposite him, halfway up the rocky wall of the hollow, a trickle of water bubbled out from between two moss-covered boulders. The water fell down into the pool below, with a fitful glimmer as if the stars themselves were trapped inside it. The rippling surface of the pool shone silver with reflected moonlight.

Shadowpaw wanted to leap into the air with excitement at being back at the Moonpool, but he fought to hold on to some self-control, and padded down the spiral path to the water's edge with all the dignity expected of a medicine cat. Awe welled up inside him as he felt his paws slip into the hollows made by cats countless seasons before.

Who were they? Where did they go? he wondered.

The two ThunderClan medicine cats were already sitting beside the pool. Shadowpaw guessed it was too cold to wait outside for everyone to arrive, as the medicine cats usually did.

Alderheart was thoughtfully grooming his chest fur, while Jayfeather's tail-tip twitched back and forth in irritation. He turned his blind blue gaze on Puddleshine and Shadowpaw as they reached the bottom of the hollow.

"You took your time," he snapped. "We're wasting moonlight."

Shadowpaw realized that Kestrelflight of WindClan and Mothwing and Willowshine, the two RiverClan medicine cats, were sitting just beyond the two from ThunderClan. The shadow of a rock had hidden them from him until now.

"Nice to see you, too, Jayfeather," Puddleshine responded mildly. "I'm sorry if we're late, but I don't see Frecklewish or Fidgetflake, either."

Jayfeather gave a disdainful sniff. "If they're not here soon, we'll start without them."

Would Jayfeather really do that? Shadowpaw was still staring at the ThunderClan medicine cat, wondering, when a rustling from the top of the slope put him on alert. Looking up, he saw Frecklewish pushing her way through the bushes, followed closely by Fidgetflake.

"At last!" Jayfeather hissed.

He's in a mood, Shadowpaw thought, then added to himself with a flicker of amusement, *Nothing new there, then.*

As the two SkyClan medicine cats padded down the slope, Shadowpaw noticed how thin and weary they both looked. For a heartbeat he wondered if there was anything wrong in SkyClan. Then he realized that he and the rest of the medicine cats looked just as skinny, just as worn out by the trials of leaf-bare.

Frecklewish dipped her head to her fellow medicine cats as she joined them beside the pool. "Greetings," she mewed, her fatigue clear in her voice. "How is the prey running in your Clans?"

For a moment no cat replied, and Shadowpaw could sense their uneasiness. *None of them wants to admit that their Clan is having problems.*

Shadowpaw was surprised when Puddleshine, who was normally so pensive, was the first to speak up. Maybe the cold had banished his mentor's reserve and enabled him to be honest.

"The hunting is very poor in ShadowClan," he replied; Shadowpaw felt a twinge of alarm at how discouraged his mentor sounded. "If this freezing cold goes on much longer, I don't know what we'll do."

The remaining medicine cats exchanged glances of relief, as if they were glad to learn their Clan wasn't the only one suffering.

Willowshine nodded in agreement. "Many RiverClan cats are getting sick because it's so cold."

"In ThunderClan too," Alderheart murmured.

"We're running out of herbs," Fidgetflake added with a twitch of his whiskers. "And the few we have left are shriveled and useless."

Frecklewish gave her Clanmate a sympathetic glance. "I've

heard some of the younger warriors joking about running off to be kittypets," she meowed.

"No cat had better say that in my hearing." Jayfeather drew his lips back in the beginning of a snarl. "Or they'll wish they hadn't."

"Keep your fur on, Jayfeather," Frecklewish responded. "It was only a joke. All SkyClan cats are loyal to their Clan."

Jayfeather's only reply was an irritated flick of his ears.

"I don't suppose any of you have spare supplies of catmint?" Kestrelflight asked hesitantly. "The clumps that grow in WindClan are all blackened by frost. We won't have any more until newleaf."

Most of the cats shook their heads, except for Willowshine, who rested her tail encouragingly on Kestrelflight's shoulder. "RiverClan can help," she promised. "There's catmint growing in the Twoleg gardens near our border. It's more sheltered there."

"Thanks, Willowshine." Kestrelflight's voice was unsteady. "There's whitecough in the WindClan camp, and without catmint I'm terrified it will turn to greencough."

"Meet me by the border tomorrow at sunhigh," Willowshine mewed. "I'll show you where the catmint grows."

"This is all well and good," Jayfeather snorted, "every cat getting along, but let's not forget why we're here. I'm much more interested in what StarClan has to say. Shall we begin?" He paced to the edge of the Moonpool and stretched out one forepaw to touch the surface, only to draw his paw back with a gasp of surprise.

"What's wrong?" Puddleshine asked. One by one, the medicine cats cautiously approached the Moonpool's surface. Shadowpaw sniffed the Moonpool curiously, then reached out a tentative paw. He was stunned when he hit something solid. *What in the stars . . . ?* Instead of water, he had touched ice, so thin that it gave way under the pressure of his pad, the splinters bobbing at the water's edge.

"The Moonpool is beginning to freeze," Kestrelflight meowed, while Shadowpaw licked the icy water from his paw. *That felt really weird!*

"Well, that proves it: the cold is worse than usual," Jayfeather grumbled.

"Has it never happened before?" Fidgetflake asked, his eyes wide.

"I can't recall it happening before," Mothwing replied in an even voice. "There has been ice in the Moonpool from time to time, but I don't remember it freezing all the way through."

"Well, never mind—it's time to share dreams with Star-Clan," Jayfeather announced abruptly. "Maybe they can tell us how long we have to suffer this bitter cold."

"And maybe we'll be able to speak with Leafpool," Willow-shine added, her voice soft with grief.

Shadowpaw had hardly known the ThunderClan medicine cat, but he had heard stories about her and knew how much every cat in the forest admired her. Even though Thunder-Clan had two other medicine cats, they must be feeling the loss of Leafpool as if a badger had torn away one of their limbs. He noticed that Jayfeather had closed his eyes, as if he was struggling with desperate pain, and he remembered that Leafpool had been Jayfeather's mother as well as his mentor.

Suddenly Shadowpaw could forgive all Jayfeather's earlier gruffness. *Dovewing can be really embarrassing at times, treating me like I'm still a kit, but I can't imagine how much it would hurt to lose her.*

Alderheart drew closer to his Clanmate. "She still watches over us from StarClan," he murmured.

"I know." Shadowpaw could hardly hear Jayfeather's low-voiced response. "But even for medicine cats, it's not the same."

Huddling together for warmth, the nine medicine cats stretched their necks out over the Moonpool and lowered their heads to touch their noses to the surface. Shadowpaw's breathing grew rapid from excitement. Within a couple of heartbeats, he knew, he would find himself transported into StarClan; either that, or the StarClan warriors would leave their territory and come to meet with the living cats at the Moonpool.

Instead there was only silence. Then, as the moments crawled by, Shadowpaw heard a confused clamor of cats' voices, faint as if coming from an immense distance. He couldn't make out what the cats were trying to say, or even if there were coherent words in their cries. Alarmed, Shadowpaw looked up to find cloudy images in the sky, like scraps of softly glowing mist. For a few heartbeats, each of the scraps would almost solidify into the form of a cat, then fade and dissolve again into a shapeless blur.

Icy fear flooded over Shadowpaw, and he pressed himself closer to Puddleshine's side. Fighting back panic, he tried to tell himself that he was being stupid. *I haven't been to the Moonpool as many times as the others,* he told himself. *Maybe this isn't unusual.*

But as the misty images faded, Shadowpaw saw that the other medicine cats were staring at one another, shocked and unnerved. "Has this happened before?" he asked, striving to stop his voice from squeaking like a terrified kit.

Kestrelflight shook his head. "I've never seen anything like that before," he replied. "I've never even heard of it, not from any cat."

The other medicine cats murmured agreement.

"What does it mean?" Shadowpaw asked. "It can't be good . . . right?"

"I wouldn't worry about it." Puddleshine pressed his muzzle briefly into Shadowpaw's shoulder, a comforting gesture. "Maybe it's because the Moonpool is freezing over. Once it thaws, the StarClan cats will be stronger presences again."

Shadowpaw wished he could believe his mentor, but the other medicine cats were exchanging doubtful looks, and he wasn't sure that even Puddleshine believed what he had just said. However, no cat spoke to contradict him. None of them seemed ready to talk about what had happened—they just headed back up the slope and out of the hollow, then said their farewells.

Padding at Puddleshine's side on the way back to Shadow-Clan, Shadowpaw still felt a worried tingle in his fur. *If this has never happened before, why is it happening now? What does it mean?* Turning to Puddleshine, he opened his jaws and began, "What do you—"

But Puddleshine's expression had grown somehow remote, as if he was turned in on himself in thought. Shadowpaw didn't know why, but he got the sense that this wasn't the time to bother his mentor with an apprentice's questions.

Remembering the cloudy shapes and the distant voices, Shadowpaw felt a dark cloud hovering over him and all the Clans, as if a devastating storm were about to unleash itself. Once again he tried to tell himself that he was anxious because he didn't have the others' experience. He just needed more time to get used to it.

Surely that's all it is . . . right?

CHAPTER 2

❧

"*Let all cats old enough to* catch their own prey join here beneath the Tallrock for a Clan meeting!"

Hearing Leafstar's voice ring out clearly across the camp, Rootkit poked his head out of the nursery, then scampered out into the open. The SkyClan leader was standing on top of the massive boulder that reared up more than three tail-lengths in the center of the clearing. Its sides were blotched with yellow lichen. A split gaped open at the bottom; in the hollow space beyond it was where the Clan leader had her den.

As Rootkit hurried toward the Tallrock, another cat landed on top of him, carrying him off his paws and rolling him over on the pebbly surface of the camp floor. A joyful squeal sounded in his ear. "Got you!"

Not again, Needlekit! Rootkit thought with a sigh, recognizing his sister's voice and her eyes gleaming a mouse-length from his own. Wriggling free, he gave her a swipe over her ear, keeping his claws sheathed.

"Give up, mouse-brain," he meowed. "I want to hear what Leafstar has to say."

Needlekit sat up, shaking dust and grit from her

black-and-white pelt. "I know what she's going to say," she responded smugly.

"So do I," Rootkit retorted.

Glancing around the camp, he saw more of his Clanmates emerging from their dens. Turtlepaw and Kitepaw pushed their way between the rocks that screened the apprentices' den, then darted across the clearing to join their mentors, Blossomheart and Sagenose. The two warriors had just appeared from their den underneath the spreading branches of a massive hawthorn bush, closely followed by Plumwillow and the Clan deputy, Hawkwing. Frecklewish and Fidgetflake, the two medicine cats, looked up from where they were sorting herbs outside their den between two boulders at the far side of the camp.

"Do you know what day it is?"

Rootkit turned at the sound of his mother's voice to see Violetshine standing a couple of paces away, her body trembling with a purr as she gazed at him with shining eyes.

"Of course I do," Rootkit replied. "Needlekit and I are six moons old. Leafstar is going to make us apprentices."

Excitement rose inside Rootkit as he spoke, but he thrust it down determinedly. Every kit became an apprentice, but he knew that if he wanted to become a warrior, he would have to focus on his training and learn everything his mentor had to teach him.

And I'm going to be the best warrior I can be!

"That's right," Violetshine responded to him. "And just look at you!" she added with a sigh. "Any cat would think you'd been dragged backward through a thorn thicket!"

Rootkit hunched his shoulders while his mother covered him with fierce licks, smoothing down his pelt. Meanwhile Needlekit gave herself a quick grooming and sat with her tail curled neatly around her forepaws.

"Cats of SkyClan," Leafstar began when the whole Clan had assembled in a ragged half circle in front of the Tallrock. "This is an important day in the life of a Clan, when we make new apprentices." She leaped down from the Tallrock and beckoned Rootkit with a swish of her tail. "Rootkit, come here, please."

Suddenly feeling that his legs were wobbly and wouldn't support him, Rootkit tottered forward until he stood in front of his Clan leader. Leafstar rested her tail on his shoulder.

"From this day forward," she announced, "this apprentice will be known as Rootpaw. Dewspring, you are an efficient and loyal cat. You will be Rootpaw's mentor, and I know you will pass your excellent qualities on to him."

Rootpaw ducked his head respectfully to Leafstar and bounded across the circle of cats to join the sturdy gray tom, who waited for him with a pleased expression on his broad face. Stretching up to touch noses with him, Rootpaw mewed, "I'll work really hard, I promise!"

"I'm sure you will," Dewspring responded.

"Rootpaw! Rootpaw!"

Embarrassment flooded through Rootpaw as he heard the Clan acclaim him with his new name, but he felt strangely pleased, too. *This is the real beginning of my life in the Clan.*

He stood beside his mentor while Leafstar called Needle-kit to her and gave her the name Needlepaw, apprenticing her to Reedclaw.

"Needlepaw! Needlepaw!" he yowled with the rest of his Clan.

Gazing around at the cats cheering for his sister, Rootpaw saw excitement in their shining eyes and waving tails, and encouragement for both of them as they stood at the beginning of their warrior training. *This Clan is the best! It's great to belong here!*

Rootpaw's happiness faded as he spotted his father, Tree, sitting at the edge of the circle with his paws tucked under him and an expression of curious, almost amused, detachment.

Isn't he proud of me? Doesn't he care that I've just been made an apprentice?

But Rootpaw reflected that the detached air was just typical of his father. Tree always seemed bemused by Clan life, as though, even after living among them for so many moons, he still didn't really understand them.

"Hey, congratulations!" Kitepaw bounded over to Rootpaw and gave him a friendly shove. "You're one of us now."

Rootpaw ducked his head. "Thanks."

"Yeah, your mother looks really proud," Turtlepaw added, coming to join them with Needlepaw beside her. "Not so much your father, though."

Her tone was teasing, but the comment pierced Rootpaw like a thorn, all the sharper because he had just been thinking the exact same thing. His fur bristled with indignation.

"Tree is proud of us," he insisted. "He just has a funny way of showing it."

Needlepaw's fur was bushing up, too, and she narrowed her eyes as she glared at Turtlepaw. "Not every cat has to be the same," she hissed.

"Keep your fur on," Kitepaw meowed. "Turtlepaw was only joking. You have to admit, your father is weird."

"Weird is good!" Needlepaw flashed back at him. "Tree's the best cat in the forest at settling quarrels." Tree had been designated the Clans' mediator, the only one in all five Clans.

"He hasn't done that lately, though, has he?" Kitepaw asked.

"That's because there haven't been any quarrels," Rootpaw retorted. "We're at peace with the other Clans. And we have Tree to thank for a lot of that."

"If you say so," Kitepaw mewed good-humoredly. "Come on, let's go to our den and we'll help you make nests."

Rootpaw relaxed a little, letting his fur lie flat. He was about to follow Kitepaw and Turtlepaw when he remembered that he ought to ask his mentor for permission first. He turned to Dewspring, but before he could speak, the gray tom gave him a brisk nod.

"When you've done that," he instructed, "help yourself to a piece of fresh-kill, and then come and find me. We'll do your first tour of the territory."

"You too," Reedclaw, who was standing close by, added to Needlepaw. "We'll all go together."

"Great!" Needlepaw squealed, then ducked her head, clearly embarrassed at behaving like a kit.

She bounded across the camp, hard on the paws of Turtlepaw and Kitepaw, and Rootpaw headed after them.

When they had made nests for themselves in their new den, Rootpaw and Needlepaw sat crouched beside the fresh-kill pile. Rootpaw spotted Tree, who finally rose to his paws and strolled toward them. He had to pass the entrance to the nursery, where Bellaleaf and Wrenkit were drowsing in the pale leaf-bare sunlight. Rootpaw noticed that as Tree passed, Wrenkit jumped up, shivering, and pressed herself closer to her mother's side. Bellaleaf wrapped her tail around her kit's shoulders and followed Tree with a hostile green glare as he padded past.

I know what that's about! Rootpaw thought, stifling a groan.

He couldn't blame Bellaleaf for not liking Tree and keeping her kit away from him. Wrenkit was the only one of Bellaleaf's litter who'd survived. The sadness had been felt across the whole Clan, and it had only been made worse when Tree insisted that the two unnamed kits who had died were still close to Wrenkit, watching over her. Wrenkit had been terrified, and the rest of the Clan had been annoyed with Tree.

And I'd never been so embarrassed in my life!

"So, apprentices now," Tree remarked as he joined Rootpaw and Needlepaw and began scanning the fresh-kill pile for a juicy piece of prey.

"Yes, it's great!" Needlepaw, who hadn't spotted Wrenkit's reaction, looked up from the blackbird she was devouring. "We're going to tour the territory when we've eaten."

"Good," Tree mewed. "Remember what I've told you about fighting foxes."

"Yes!" Needlepaw let out a little *mrrow* of laughter. "Don't!"

Rootpaw kept his gaze firmly fixed on his mouse. *Why can't Tree give us some useful advice, like other fathers?*

A moment later he felt a paw prodding him in the side. "What's the matter with you?" Tree asked.

"Nothing," Rootpaw mumbled, taking another bite of fresh-kill.

"And hedgehogs fly," his father retorted. "Come on, tell me."

Rootpaw let out a sigh, knowing that Tree wouldn't give up until he explained himself. "It's just . . . the way Wrenkit acts around you," he muttered. "You shouldn't have told her about seeing her dead littermates. She's so little; it just freaked her out."

"I thought it would help," Tree responded, shaking his head in exasperation. "I thought she'd like to know that they were still close to her, watching over her, until they left to go to StarClan."

"She didn't understand!" Rootpaw snapped. Unable to stop himself, he added, "Other cats don't say weird stuff like that!"

He glanced up at his father and saw a hurt look in Tree's eyes. "I raised you to think for yourself," Tree meowed. "I don't want you just going along blindly with the ways of the Clan. They're good ways, but they're not the answer to everything."

Rootpaw didn't respond, but just gulped down the last

scraps of his mouse. He knew his father was wrong with every hair on his pelt, but he couldn't find the words to explain why. *I hope my apprenticeship goes quickly,* he thought. He couldn't wait to be a warrior and prove that he was totally committed to his Clan. *When they see that I'm not like my father, maybe my Clanmates will stop treating me like I'm weird too.*

Rootpaw scrambled to his paws, shaking drops of dew from his pelt. Strands of mist still floated among the trees, and the grass in the clearing was heavy with moisture.

Not the best morning for Dewspring to show me his fighting moves! We'll get soaked to the bone.

Two days had passed since Rootpaw and Needlepaw had been made apprentices, and Rootpaw had been excited to go out at dawn with his sister and their mentors for their first session of battle training. But it wasn't working out how he had hoped.

"Let's try it again," Dewspring meowed, "and remember what I told you. If a cat has you pinned down, the best way to escape is to go limp. Let your opponent think you've given up. Then explode out of their grip, as fast as you can. Okay?"

Rootpaw nodded. "Okay."

Dewspring leaped at him, knocking him off his paws, then held him down with one paw on his neck and another on his back. Rootpaw let himself go limp. But as he prepared to spring upward, he heard a yowl of triumph from across the clearing. Kitepaw and Turtlepaw were training with their mentors, leaping and twisting in the air. Kitepaw had just managed to knock Turtlepaw's paws from under her and land on top of her with his jaws at her throat.

"Well done," his mentor, Sagenose, praised him.

I'll never be able to do that, Rootpaw thought.

"Whenever you're ready." Dewspring's voice held an edge of irritation. "Your opponent has had time to claw your fur off."

"Sorry," Rootpaw muttered.

He waited for a couple of heartbeats and then powered upward with all his strength. But instead of leaping clear of his mentor, he flopped clumsily back to the ground, jerked downward by Dewspring, who had both his paws firmly fixed on his tail, trapping him.

Just like the other times I tried it, Rootpaw thought, giving his pelt a shake as Dewspring released him. *It's all Kitepaw's fault. I could do it if I weren't distracted.*

He felt even worse as he saw Needlepaw hurl herself into the air, flip Reedclaw away from her, and land on all four paws with a triumphant lash of her tail.

"That's enough for now," Dewspring meowed; Rootpaw could hear the weariness in his voice. "We'll try it again tomorrow when you're ready to pay attention. Meanwhile, you and Needlepaw can practice together."

Rootpaw just nodded, too embarrassed to say anything.

"Hey, Dewspring!" Blossomheart called from the other side of the clearing. "If you've finished your training session, do you want to go hunting?"

"Sure," Dewspring replied, with a glance at Reedclaw. "We're all done here."

His pelt hot with shame, Rootpaw watched as the four mentors went off together. Needlepaw padded up to him and touched her nose briefly to his shoulder. "It'll be okay," she murmured. "Let's practice. You'll get it soon."

"I don't think I'll ever get it," Rootpaw responded bitterly.

"You're waiting too long." Turtlepaw's voice broke into the conversation as she and Kitepaw crossed the clearing to join Rootpaw and Needlepaw. "And you have to be sure that you don't brace your muscles before you leap. That warns your opponent what you're going to do."

Rootpaw gave her a nod of thanks, but before he could reply, Kitepaw interrupted him.

"Or you might just decide to follow a different path in life," the older apprentice added, a sparkle of malice in his eyes.

"What do you mean by that?" Rootpaw asked, his pelt beginning to prickle with hostility.

"Maybe the reason you're having such problems with training is that you're not meant to be a warrior. Maybe you're meant to be the kind of cat who talks to dead cats. After all, your father has his 'ways,' right?" Kitepaw sounded amused.

Fury swelled inside Rootpaw, and he felt his shoulder fur bushing up. He drew his lips back in a snarl. "Don't talk to me like that!"

"Or else what?" Kitepaw taunted him.

Rootpaw took a pace forward. "Or else I'll claw your ears off!"

"Hey!" Turtlepaw shouldered her way between the two

toms. "You'll get in trouble for fighting. And it's not like you'd win," she added sneeringly to Rootpaw.

Her mockery stripped away the last of Rootpaw's self-control. Letting out a furious screech, he launched himself at the tortoiseshell she-cat. He heard Needlepaw yowl his name, but he ignored her, sliding out his claws and stretching his forepaws to swipe at Turtlepaw.

His blow never landed. Turtlepaw sidestepped quickly and hooked Rootpaw's paws out from under him; he thumped to the ground, the breath driven out of his body. Turtlepaw stood over him, her forepaws on his neck and belly.

Rootpaw let out a furious hiss, then went limp, remembering the move Dewspring had demonstrated. But when he tried to leap upward, he only crashed back down, and twisted around to see Turtlepaw with her paws on his tail and a smug expression on her face.

"You should know better than to attack us," she mewed. "We're older than you, and better fighters. And don't lash out at us just because Kitepaw is right. Maybe you should go be weird somewhere else!"

She stood back, letting Rootpaw scramble to his paws. He felt as though his fur were on fire with anger and embarrassment, even though none of the warriors had seen Turtlepaw overpower him.

"I will become a strong warrior," he insisted. "I'll be important to the Clan. I'm not weird." *Not like Tree,* he added to himself.

The two older apprentices exchanged a knowing look.

"Okay, if you want to prove yourself, maybe you can help us," Kitepaw suggested.

"Rootpaw, no!" Needlepaw padded up to his side. "Dewspring told you to practice," she added urgently. "You don't want to get mixed up with these stupid furballs. They'll only trick you somehow."

Part of Rootpaw's mind told him that his sister was right. But he could just imagine the taunts he would receive from the two older apprentices if he backed down now.

"I can take care of myself," he spat. "Okay, Kitepaw, what do you want me to do?"

"We're going on an expedition down to the lake," Kitepaw replied. "There are supposed to be herbs down there that Frecklewish and Fidgetflake need for their stores. If we can get some, we'll show we're ready to be warriors—maybe we'll even be given our warrior names! Are you brave enough to come with us?"

"Sure I am," Rootpaw responded.

"Rootpaw, don't be a mouse-brain," Needlepaw begged. "You'll only get into trouble if Dewspring finds out."

Rootpaw felt a worm of uncertainty stir in his belly. *Dewspring is fed up with me already—I don't want to make things worse.* But then he saw the gleam of mockery in the eyes of the older apprentices. "I don't care," he told his sister. "Besides, Dewspring won't find out. Not unless you tell him."

Needlepaw looked hurt at the idea that she would give him

away. "I won't," she mewed. "But I think you've got bees in your brain."

Turning away, she stalked off in the direction of the camp. For a heartbeat Rootpaw wanted to go after her, to tell her he was sorry for upsetting her. But he knew he couldn't back down in front of the other apprentices.

"Okay, let's go," Kitepaw ordered.

Rootpaw followed the reddish-brown tom as he headed toward the lake, with Turtlepaw bringing up the rear. With every paw step he felt the air grow colder and colder. He couldn't help shivering, as if icy claws were probing deep into his fur.

"Are you a scaredy-mouse?" Turtlepaw teased him. "Do you want to go back to the nice warm nursery?"

"I'm not scared," Rootpaw insisted, glaring at her over his shoulder. "I'm just cold."

"Sure you are," Turtlepaw retorted with a *mrrow* of laughter.

However, though he would have rather died than admit it, Rootpaw couldn't help feeling daunted when he and the other apprentices emerged from the trees and stood on the top of a bank that sloped down toward the lakeshore. A gray waste of water lay in front of him, whipped into waves by the icy wind that swept over it. At the water's edge the gray was turning to white as the lake froze, the ice stretching several tail-lengths from the pebbly beach.

"Right," Rootpaw meowed. "Let's start looking for these herbs."

He flattened himself to the ground and crept forward to look underneath a straggly thornbush where he could spot some surviving green growth, only to halt a moment later at the sound of a snort of laughter from behind him. He wriggled around to face the other apprentices.

"What do you think you're doing?" Kitepaw asked, his tail curling up with amusement. "We haven't told you what we're looking for, so how do you think you're going to find it?"

Another hot wave of embarrassment swept over Rootpaw, almost banishing the chill from the wind. "I'm only trying to be helpful," he protested indignantly, scrambling out from beneath the bush. "If all you can do is mock, you can find your own herbs!"

He spun around, intending to storm off back to camp, but Kitepaw intercepted him.

"What's wrong?" he asked. "Can't you take a bit of teasing? What sort of warrior are you going to be if you get upset at something as trivial as that?"

Rootpaw dug his claws deep into the ground. Every muscle in his body was taut with fury, and he wanted more than anything to hurl himself at Kitepaw and wipe the sneering look off his face. But he realized that the older apprentice was deliberately goading him.

He probably enjoyed seeing me beaten when I attacked Turtlepaw, and he wants to see it again. Well, I'm not going to give him the satisfaction.

Rootpaw's heart was thumping in his chest from tension and fury as he raised his head, summoning every scrap of dignity, and stepped carefully around Kitepaw on his way back to camp. He felt vulnerable, standing up to an older cat, and though he wanted to swipe his claws across Kitepaw's muzzle, he knew that he would lose.

And if Dewspring heard about that, I'd be in trouble for sure!

"That's right!" Turtlepaw called after him. "Sneak back into the nursery! Go and tell your mother that the horrid cats were nasty to you!"

"Are you sure you're smart and brave enough to be a warrior?" Kitepaw added. "Don't you think you'd be better off going to talk to invisible dead cats?"

Hot rage overwhelmed Rootpaw, burning up his resolve of a few moments before. He whipped around. "I'll show you I'm fit to be a warrior!" he yowled, charging straight at the other two apprentices with teeth bared and claws unsheathed.

Kitepaw and Turtlepaw dodged out of his way. Rootpaw was running so fast that he couldn't stop himself; he sped past them and down the bank toward the lake. Struggling to slow down, to halt, he felt his paws patter on the stretch of pebbles at the water's edge, then skid out onto the ice. He tried to dig in his claws as he slid toward the water, but he could only gaze in horror as he saw cracks open up on the surface. He flinched at the freezing touch of dark water welling up around his paws. A heartbeat later he let out a screech of terror as the ice gave way and he plunged down into the lake.

CHAPTER 3

Bristlepaw tasted the air as she followed her mentor, Rosepetal, through the undergrowth. Beyond the edge of the trees she could hear the wash of waves and feel the chilly wind that blew from the lake right into the depths of her fur. *If only we could find some prey!* she thought. *The whole of ThunderClan is going hungry.*

But in spite of her worries, she raised her head and tail with pride at being out on patrol with Rosepetal and two other warriors, especially when one of them was Stemleaf. Watching him now, crouching beside a bush where he thought he had scented a mouse, she admired his sleek orange-and-white fur and the alert angle of his ears as he listened for his prey.

Does he ever notice me? Bristlepaw wondered. *He said I made a great catch when I killed that squirrel yesterday. But I don't just want him to think I'm a good apprentice. I want him to be impressed with me.*

A sudden yowling from the direction of the lake distracted Bristlepaw from her thoughts. At the same moment Stemleaf pounced under the bush and let out a hiss of fury. "Fox dung! I'd have had the mouse, but that racket scared it off."

"Something's wrong!" Rosepetal exclaimed as the yowling continued. "Come on!"

"But that's SkyClan territory," Eaglewing, the fourth member of the patrol, protested as all four cats raced toward the lake.

Rosepetal glanced over her shoulder at the ginger she-cat. "We help cats in trouble, no matter what their Clan," she retorted.

Bristlepaw thought that she could pick up SkyClan scent coming from the direction of the lake, but the bitterly cold wind whipping around her made it hard to be certain. A few heartbeats later, bursting out of the trees, she saw that she had been right. Farther down the shore, beyond the SkyClan border, two cats were running to and fro along the water's edge. The terrified yowling came from them.

Out in the lake, a third cat was trapped in the freezing water. He was clawing frantically at the edge of the ice, but it kept breaking under the weight of his paws, and his struggles seemed to be driving him farther away from the shore. Each time his head dipped under the water, it took him longer to fight his way back to the surface. Soon, Bristlepaw realized, he would vanish beneath the ice for good.

Instinctively, Bristlepaw bounded forward, outpacing her Clanmates. Reaching the edge of the lake, she took a deep breath, bracing herself to stop her limbs from trembling. *StarClan, help me!* she prayed. Aloud she called, "Hang on! I'm coming!"

Rosepetal's voice came from somewhere behind her. "No! Bristlepaw, come back!"

Bristlepaw ignored her. Venturing out onto the ice, she lay

flat and splayed out her legs to spread her weight as much as possible, and she forced herself to ignore the shock of cold penetrating her fur. Pushing herself forward with tiny movements of her claws, she headed for the struggling cat. She could feel the ice straining under her weight, but it held until she could reach the edge and stretch out her neck to grab the SkyClan cat's scruff as he sank under the surface.

Gradually Bristlepaw edged backward, dragging the other cat with her. The ice began to break up around them under their combined weight, but when it finally gave way, Bristlepaw realized that the water was shallow enough for her to stand. She let go of the other cat's scruff and boosted him with her shoulder so that he could stagger to the bank. Bristlepaw let out a gusty sigh of relief as she followed him and collapsed in a heap beside him on the pebbles. She was shivering, and not only from cold.

I'm lucky that I didn't drown, too!

"Bristlepaw, are you completely mouse-brained?" Rosepetal came to stand by her apprentice, her voice as freezing as the wind and her eyes like chips of amber ice. "I told you to come back. I should have you dealing with the elders' ticks for six moons at least." Her voice grew gentler, almost changing to a purr. "I'd do it, too, if you hadn't been so brave."

"I had to," Bristlepaw explained, warmed by her mentor's praise. "I'm the lightest of us. Besides, he would have died if I'd left him there." As she turned to the cat she had rescued, her warmth gave way to sharp irritation. "You stupid furball!" she exclaimed. "What were you doing out there on the thin ice?"

The cat—he looked barely older than a kit—raised his head to gaze at her. His eyes were full of gratitude. "I'm sorry," he gasped. "It was an accident. I'm lucky you came along."

The two other SkyClan cats had approached and were looking down at their Clanmate. Bristlepaw recognized them as two apprentices she had seen at the last Gathering: Kitepaw and Turtlepaw.

"It was partly our fault," Turtlepaw admitted.

"Yeah, we're sorry," Kitepaw added, ducking his head in shame.

"And so you should be," Rosepetal snapped, turning her furious gaze on the two apprentices. "How much help do you think you were, running up and down and yowling like a pair of foxes in a fit?"

The youngest apprentice nodded, and Bristlepaw noticed that, even drenched and shaking, he had summoned a gleam of appreciation at Rosepetal's scolding.

Rosepetal turned to gaze down at him and went on, "Who are you, anyway? I don't think I've seen you at a Gathering."

The apprentice tottered to his paws. "I'm Rootkit," he said, shivering. "I mean—Rootpaw."

Rosepetal tilted her head, studying him. "Are you *Violetshine's* kit?" she asked. "Hawkwing's kin? Look at you—you're shivering so hard, and there's ice in your fur. We'd better get you back to the ThunderClan camp so our medicine cats can take a look at you."

"No!" Rootpaw protested. "We're SkyClan cats."

"But the ThunderClan camp is much closer," Rosepetal insisted. "It makes much more sense to go there."

"But—" Rootpaw began.

Losing patience, Bristlepaw bent over Rootpaw and pushed her face close to his. "Don't be mouse-brained," she hissed. "You would freeze to death before you got back to your own camp."

Rootpaw hesitated a heartbeat longer, then nodded.

"I'll come with you," Kitepaw meowed. "Turtlepaw, you'd better go back to camp and let them know what happened."

Turtlepaw gulped, as if she wasn't looking forward to that. "Okay," she agreed. "We're sorry, Rootpaw." Without waiting for a response, she bounded off through the trees.

Bristlepaw steadied Rootpaw on one side, with Kitepaw on the other, as Rosepetal led the way back across the Sky-Clan border and toward the ThunderClan camp. The young apprentice looked embarrassed that he couldn't walk by himself. *But there's no shame in that,* Bristlepaw thought. *Not after you nearly drowned. Any cat would need help.*

Stemleaf, who was padding just ahead of the three apprentices, glanced back over his shoulder at Bristlepaw. "You did really well," he mewed. "That was so impressive, how you saved Rootpaw."

Bristlepaw dipped her head. "Thanks, Stemleaf." Now that the emergency was over, she was beginning to feel the tingles of unease that she should have felt when she was out there on the ice. *I'll have nightmares about that for moons!*

But she didn't want to seem weak in front of a warrior—especially when that warrior was Stemleaf. "It was nothing, really," she added.

Even though the icy wind was freezing her wet pelt, even though she felt more exhausted with every paw step, Stemleaf's praise warmed her and made her want to go bounding through the forest, yowling out her joy. What Stemleaf had said to her meant more than any cat's praise. More even than Rosepetal's.

Eaglewing had run ahead to warn the ThunderClan medicine cats, so by the time Rosepetal's patrol returned, Alderheart was already waiting for them. He bustled Rootpaw into the medicine cats' den without asking for any more details.

Following them, Bristlepaw poked her head around the bramble tendrils that screened the entrance of the den, to see Rootpaw already flopped down in a nest of moss and bracken. Alderheart was busily licking his fur the wrong way to get his blood flowing and warm him up. She heard Jayfeather's voice coming from the shadows at the back of the den.

"Thyme leaves for shock, and maybe one poppy seed, to be sure he gets some sleep."

Reassured that Rootpaw would be cared for, Bristlepaw withdrew to discover that her littermates, Thriftpaw and Flippaw, had bounded up behind her, their eyes alight with eagerness.

"What happened?" Thriftpaw demanded. "Rosepetal said

you rescued that SkyClan apprentice!"

For a moment Bristlepaw scuffled her forepaws in the earth floor of the camp, briefly embarrassed to tell her denmates about her own bravery.

Flippaw gave her a friendly shove. "Come on! Spit it out!"

Forcing herself to be calm, Bristlepaw told her story, determined not to exaggerate to make herself sound better. She saw her denmates' eyes grow wider and wider as she spoke.

"Wow, that was brave!" Thriftpaw exclaimed when she had finished.

"They should make you a warrior right away," Flippaw declared.

"Not yet, but that was still very impressive." Bristlepaw turned her head at the sound of a new voice joining in, and let out a gasp to see Bramblestar padding up. "Very well done, Bristlepaw," he finished.

Bristlepaw dipped her head respectfully to her Clan leader. "Thank you, Bramblestar."

"I've got another job for you, if you're not too tired," Bramblestar continued. "I'm sending a patrol to SkyClan, to bring Leafstar up to date about Rootpaw's condition. She needs to know that he's being cared for, and that we'll send him home as soon as he's well enough. I'd like you to go with them."

Bristlepaw turned to see Rosepetal and Stemleaf standing side by side a couple of tail-lengths away. All her tiredness fell away from her. She felt as if she could run all the way around the lake, three times, without stopping. *I'll be part of a mission to another Clan—and I'll be with Stemleaf.*

"Oh, yes, Bramblestar!" she replied. "I'd be glad to go."

When Bristlepaw and the two warriors set out through the forest toward SkyClan territory, the wind seemed stronger than ever. Sometimes the gusts were so fierce that they were almost blown off their paws.

"I've had enough of this," Rosepetal muttered when they were almost halfway to the border. "Let's find somewhere to shelter for a bit."

"I don't mind going on," Bristlepaw protested, afraid that her mentor was suggesting a rest for her sake.

Stemleaf flicked her ear gently with his tail-tip. "You don't have to be the bravest cat in the Clan all the time," he mewed teasingly.

At the same moment Rosepetal angled her ears toward a holly bush that grew at the bottom of a steep rise. "Under there would be good. Come on."

I guess it's okay to stop for a little while, Bristlepaw thought as she followed her mentor and wriggled underneath the branches into the warm layer of debris beneath. *And it does feel good to be out of the wind.*

Crouching beside Stemleaf beneath the holly bush, watching dead leaves whirl past, Bristlepaw couldn't remember when she had been this happy. Even the wind bringing light flurries of snow, dappling their pelts with faint blotches of white, couldn't destroy her buoyant mood.

"Will it be this cold every leaf-bare?" she asked Stemleaf.

The orange-and-white tom shrugged. "I don't know," he replied. "I've heard some of the elders say this is the coldest leaf-bare they remember."

Rosepetal, who had been gazing out into the forest, scrambled to her paws. "The wind is dropping," she mewed. "We should get going."

Bristlepaw and Stemleaf followed her out of their shelter into the buffeting wind. Before they had gone very far, Bristlepaw picked up the faint scent of prey, and she spotted a wagtail fluttering to the ground between two massive trees.

"Should I try to catch it?" she murmured to Rosepetal.

Her mentor nodded. "Let's see your hunting moves."

Stemleaf swiped his tongue around his jaws. "The Clan has been fed," he mewed. "No cat will mind if we stop for a little snack."

Bristlepaw dropped into a hunter's crouch and began to creep slowly toward the wagtail, setting each paw down as lightly as she could and keeping her tail tucked in to her side. From the corner of her eye she could glimpse Stemleaf, working his way around in a wide circle to approach the wagtail from the other side. For a moment she was dismayed, wondering if Stemleaf thought she wouldn't make the catch, but then she realized he was only positioning himself to drive the bird toward her. The thought warmed her to the tips of her claws.

The wagtail seemed unaware that danger was close. It was stabbing its beak into debris at the foot of one of the trees, looking for insects. But as Bristlepaw halted, waggling her hindquarters in readiness for her pounce, something alerted her prey. It let out a harsh alarm call and fluttered upward. At the same moment, Stemleaf sprang forward. The wagtail veered away from him, and Bristlepaw was able to leap up and snag it in her claws. Its wings flapped wildly against her chest as she landed, and she killed it with a swift bite behind its head.

"Great catch!" Rosepetal exclaimed.

"Stemleaf helped," Bristlepaw responded, blinking happily at the orange-and-white tom as he padded up. *We make a great team,* she added to herself.

"You've got the makings of a fine hunter," Stemleaf said as all three cats crouched down to share the wagtail. "In fact, between that and your bravery when you rescued Rootpaw, you're going to be quite a strong warrior one day."

At first Bristlepaw couldn't find the words to reply, but delight filled her until she couldn't even feel the cold anymore. Though Stemleaf was young, she knew that the Clan already respected him as a strong and capable warrior.

If he believes in me, then I know I'll be able to achieve my dream.

"I want to be one of the best warriors in ThunderClan," she meowed to Stemleaf.

"I'm sure you will be," he purred.

A picture flickered across Bristlepaw's mind: an imagined future where she and Stemleaf were striding through the forest, warriors and mates, side by side.

We'll be the strongest pair in the whole Clan. . . .

CHAPTER 4

Grassheart's body jerked as cough after cough battered at her. Eventually the pale tabby she-cat collapsed into her nest in the medicine cats' den, where she lay stretched out among the bracken, her eyes closed and her body shaken from time to time by more fits of coughing.

Shadowpaw bent over her limp form, sniffing her carefully from ears to tail-tip. "It's not greencough yet," he reported to Puddleshine when he finished his examination. "But if this cold weather doesn't let up, it could easily change to greencough. She's worse than she was yesterday."

Puddleshine's voice came from the shadows at the back of the den. "An outbreak of whitecough is the last thing we need, much less greencough," he meowed. "We're getting low on catmint, and even whitecough could be dangerous in this StarClan-cursed cold."

Shadowpaw hardly paid any attention to his mentor's grumbling. His mind kept flying back to the half-moon meeting at the Moonpool, and the hazy, indistinct visions of their warrior ancestors. The distant voices, crying out to the living cats, had haunted his dreams ever since, along with an upsetting theory.

I wonder if it was my fault that we couldn't reach StarClan.

The young tom had always been aware that there was something different about him. Since he was a kit, before he was apprenticed to Puddleshine, he had received odd, unusually strong visions, ones even medicine cats couldn't explain. Often these visions were accompanied by seizures. And sometimes they were about cats who had nothing to do with ShadowClan.

It wasn't a bad thing . . . but it was strange. It wasn't how medicine cats' visions usually worked. Did that make him somehow unsuitable to follow the way of a medicine cat? And worse . . . was it upsetting StarClan enough to turn them away?

He felt a heavy weight in his belly at the thought that StarClan might be rejecting him.

"Shadowpaw!"

His mentor's voice, close to his ear, startled Shadowpaw. He turned his head to see that Puddleshine had emerged from the shadows and was standing beside him with an irritated look in his eyes.

"You haven't heard a word I've said, have you?" Puddleshine demanded.

"Er . . . catmint?" Shadowpaw guessed wildly.

"Yes, I said we'll have to go into the Twolegplace to get some," his mentor told him. He hesitated, and then went on.

"Shadowpaw, it isn't like you to be daydreaming. Is something wrong?"

"Wrong—no!" Shadowpaw didn't dare confess his fears. In the past, Puddleshine had been supportive, but he couldn't forget how silent and tense his mentor had seemed after the half-moon meeting. What if Puddleshine agreed with him, and sent him back to the apprentices' den to train to be a warrior? "Everything's fine."

Puddleshine let out a disbelieving snort, but his voice was kind as he mewed, "You can tell me. That's what I'm here for."

Shadowpaw flicked an ear, thinking quickly. "I was thinking about the meeting, when our StarClan ancestors didn't come to speak to us the way they were supposed to," Shadowpaw admitted, stopping short of telling Puddleshine his worst fears. "Does that mean they aren't watching over us anymore?"

Puddleshine shook his head. "No, of course not. StarClan is always with us. It must be the Moonpool—I've never seen it iced over before, so it must be affecting our connection with our ancestors. Once it warms up again, things should get better."

Shadowpaw looked at his paws. He hoped the problem would be that simple. He was reassured to learn that Puddleshine thought so.

Outside in the camp he could hear the cheerful voices of his littermates, Pouncestep and Lightleap; they had obviously just returned from a border patrol.

"I'm starving! I thought we'd never get to the end," Pouncestep announced.

"Me too!" Lightleap agreed. "But we made a good job of those scent markers. SkyClan won't dare set paw over our borders."

Shadowpaw sighed. His sisters sounded much more confident as warriors than he felt as a medicine-cat apprentice.

"We've done all we can here," Puddleshine continued. "I'm going on a foraging expedition to see if I can find some catmint. Why don't you take a break? Talk to your friends, get yourself a piece of fresh-kill."

"What about Grassheart?" Shadowpaw asked, glancing toward the sick she-cat.

"Grassheart will be fine for a while," Puddleshine assured him. "Off you go, and have a mouse ready for me when I get back." He raced off and disappeared down the bramble tunnel that formed the entrance to the camp. .

Shadowpaw followed him as far as the pool at the bottom of the hollow, where he paused to lap at the water. Ice was forming on its edges, too, and Shadowpaw wondered how long it would take to completely freeze, like the Moonpool. Then he spotted his mother, Dovewing, weaving twigs into the branches of the den she shared with Tigerstar.

"Hi," he mewed, bounding over to join her. "Can I help?"

"If you like," Dovewing replied, pushing a few twigs toward him. "We need every defense we can get against this icy wind."

"When will this leaf-bare pass?" Shadowpaw asked his mother as he fitted the flexible twigs into place. "It seems to have gone on forever."

"You've lived through a leaf-bare before," Dovewing told him. "Don't you remember?"

Shadowpaw shook his head. "Not really. I can remember some of the journey from the big Twolegplace, with Spiresight and the other cats, but nothing about the weather."

"It was pretty cold, but not as bad as this," Dovewing meowed. "But this leaf-bare won't last forever, I promise. Even the worst leaf-bares end. Then we'll have newleaf, when the snow disappears and the trees begin to bud again. And then, before we know it, it will be greenleaf, when the air is warm."

"And after that leaf-fall, and then leaf-bare again," Shadowpaw murmured. He understood the seasons, though they hadn't been as pronounced in the Twolegplace. Now he wondered what would have happened if Tigerheart and Dovewing hadn't regretted their decision to leave the Clans and decided to take their family back. *We'd be safe and warm inside the big den. How many more times will I have to go through this?*

Glancing around the camp, he saw that the early patrols had returned, and that most of the Clan was in the clearing, gathered around the fresh-kill pile or gossiping outside their dens. They all looked thin and bedraggled; every cat was hungry, he knew, and would be until the weather grew warmer again.

Still thinking about the journey from the big Twolegplace where he had been born, Shadowpaw noticed that two of the cats from there, Cinnamontail and Blazefire, were nowhere to be seen.

I don't think I've seen them since yesterday, he realized.

He turned to ask Dovewing if she knew where they had gone, but before he could speak, he was distracted by a bout of furious hissing.

Glancing over his shoulder, Shadowpaw spotted Strikestone and Whorlpelt standing nose to nose with lashing tails and bristling fur, their lips drawn back as they hissed defiance at each other. A heartbeat later Strikestone leaped at Whorlpelt, and the two cats began rolling around on the ground in a snarling, clawing knot of fur.

"Great StarClan!" Dovewing exclaimed, racing across the camp toward them.

Shadowpaw followed, and watched his mother stand poised beside the grappling cats until she could swoop forward and give each of them a sharp swipe over the ear. The two warriors broke apart and sat up, shaking earth and debris off their pelts.

"What's going on?" Dovewing demanded.

"He put thorns in my bedding," Strikestone meowed, glaring at Whorlpelt.

"Did not!" Whorlpelt retorted.

Dovewing heaved an exaggerated sigh. "For StarClan's sake, are you kits?" she asked. "If you have so much energy, you should be using it to help your Clan."

For a few heartbeats both cats turned their furious glares on Dovewing. Then Whorlpelt hung his head. "Sorry," he muttered.

"It won't happen again," Strikestone promised Dovewing.

"I should think not!" Dovewing snapped, turning and

padding back toward her den.

Shadowpaw followed, reflecting how irritable the cold weather was making every cat. Now that the skirmish was over, he remembered his uneasiness about the cats from the Twolegplace, and he veered aside to the fresh-kill pile, where his littermates were sharing a vole.

"Have either of you seen Cinnamontail and Blazefire?" he asked.

Pouncestep gulped down a mouthful of prey. "Not a whisker," she replied.

"I haven't, either," Lightleap added. "Not since yesterday."

By now Shadowpaw was becoming even more anxious. Glancing around, he saw that Tigerstar had appeared and was talking to Dovewing outside their den. Shadowpaw raced over to them.

"That is worrying," Tigerstar agreed, when Shadowpaw had told him about his concerns. "I haven't heard of any foxes or badgers moving into our territory, but in this kind of weather, we can't be too careful. I'll send out a search party."

"I'll lead the patrol," Dovewing offered instantly.

"Thanks," Tigerstar responded. "Choose your cats, and start off by going down toward the lake and the halfbridge. The patrol from the far border just returned, so they're unlikely to be up there."

"Can I come with you?" Shadowpaw asked his mother, eager for something to do that would take his mind off the misty StarClan cats at the Moonpool.

His mother shook her head. "It's too cold, and there

could be danger," she told him. "Besides, you're a medicine-cat apprentice, and this is warrior business. But you can tell Puddleshine to prepare in case our missing Clanmates have been injured."

She headed off, calling Whorlpelt and Strikestone with a wave of her tail, and beckoning Snowbird from beside the fresh-kill pile, before leading the way out through the bramble tunnel.

Shadowpaw watched them go with a frustrated twitch of his tail, reminding himself to tell Puddleshine when his mentor returned with the catmint. Then he padded over to join his littermates and choose a blackbird for himself from the pile of prey.

"Cinnamontail and Blazefire are missing. Dovewing has gone to look for them," he reported.

Lightleap blinked nervously. "I hope she finds them. I can't think why they would go wandering off in this weather."

"Tigerstar was talking about foxes and badgers," Shadowpaw murmured unhappily, imagining how dangerous hungry predators would be.

"But I'm sure there aren't any on our territory," Pouncestep meowed, giving her shoulder a quick lick. "Cloverfoot told all the patrols to keep a special lookout, and there hasn't been so much as a sniff."

"Then why aren't Cinnamontail and Blazefire here?" Lightleap asked.

Shadowpaw had no answer to that. He finished his blackbird, then chose a mouse for Puddleshine and carried it to their den, checking on Grassheart while he was there. To his relief, the she-cat seemed to have fallen into a quieter sleep, and he felt confident enough to leave her and head back into the clearing to wait for the patrol to return.

He had barely rejoined his Clanmates when there was a stir of movement at the mouth of the bramble tunnel. Dovewing appeared, with Cinnamontail and Blazefire just behind her and the rest of the patrol following. Puddleshine brought up the rear, a few stalks of catmint in his jaws.

Tigerstar emerged from his den to meet the returning cats in the middle of the camp. Shadowpaw padded up to listen, and several more of his Clanmates gathered around.

"Well?" Tigerstar asked. "What happened?"

"My patrol met these two crossing the border." Dovewing angled her ears toward Blazefire and Cinnamontail. "Crossing back into our territory. They'd been in the Twolegplace."

"I spotted them lurking around a Twoleg den," Puddleshine added, speaking around his mouthful of herbs. "I made them come back to camp with me."

Tigerstar let out a hiss of fury, and glared at the two straying cats with narrowed eyes. "And why were you there?" he demanded.

Cinnamontail scuffled her forepaws in the earth. "Dunno," she mumbled. "We sort of thought it might be a good place to hunt."

"Really?" Tigerstar snarled with a lash of his tail. "Now tell me something I'm going to believe."

Blazefire took a deep breath. "Honestly, we didn't mean to

do it," he began. "We were just walking in the forest, trying to keep warm, and tasting the air for prey—only there wasn't any. And then we picked up this other scent, coming from the Twolegplace. It smelled of food. . . ." His voice died away miserably.

"Have I got this straight?" Tigerstar asked. His voice was soft, but Shadowpaw knew how angry his father was. "You went into the Twolegplace to get Twolegs to give you food?"

"Oh, no!" Cinnamontail protested, her eyes wide. "We would never do that. But you know how they throw food away, delicious food, in scrapcans! We thought we could just . . . It's *almost* like hunting," she finished.

"And we were so hungry," Blazefire added. "You remember, there was always lots of food to be found in the Twolegplace, and even though this Twolegplace isn't as big, we thought it would be stupid to ignore it."

"Scavenging from a Twolegplace is not the way of a warrior," Tigerstar told them, his ears laid back and his pelt bristling with rage. "If that's what you want to do, maybe you should go and be kittypets, or loners living in the Twolegplace! Then you can find all the food you like. I had thought you both were learning to be strong warriors . . . which means *hunting* for your food!"

Cinnamontail and Blazefire exchanged a dismayed glance.

"We don't want that," Blazefire protested. "We love being part of a Clan. Now we know how to defend ourselves properly, and that there are lots of cats who are loyal to us, who look out for us."

"We were just so hungry," Cinnamontail finished.

"Every cat is hungry," Tigerstar growled, "because prey is scarce. That's how it is in leaf-bare. But if you come to rely on finding food in the Twolegplace, you'll forget how to provide for yourselves through hunting. You'll be weaker warriors, and that means a weaker Clan."

"We're really sorry," Cinnamontail mewed, while Blazefire nodded fervently in agreement.

"'Sorry' fills no bellies," Tigerstar snapped.

Cloverfoot, the Clan deputy, who had been listening closely, stepped up to Tigerstar's side. "There's no telling how a cat will react in conditions like these," she pointed out. "And this is Blazefire's and Cinnamontail's first leaf-bare in a Clan. I don't think we should be too hard on them."

Tigerstar nodded slowly and took a moment to ponder, while the two straying cats waited, their tension visible in their working claws and quivering whiskers.

"Please don't send us away!" Blazefire burst out after a few heartbeats.

"No, I won't do that," Tigerstar meowed. "I'm tempted to send you out to scrape fresh earth over the dirtplace, but I won't do that, either. But since you've eaten Twoleg food today, you'll take nothing from the fresh-kill pile until tomorrow. And you'll go out on a hunting patrol every sunrise from now until the next Gathering."

"Oh, thank you!" Cinnamontail exclaimed, her eyes shining in relief.

"We'll never do it again," Blazefire promised.

"You'd better not," Tigerstar retorted. "Because if you ever do behave so selfishly again, you'll wish you'd never left your big Twoleg den. Is that clear?"

Chastened, both cats nodded, and they stood with heads bowed as Tigerstar stalked off.

As the rest of the Clan broke up, Shadowpaw noticed that Puddleshine looked agitated. "What's the matter?" he asked.

"I need to ask Tigerstar if he'll organize extra hunting patrols so that Grassheart can have more food," he replied. "She needs to keep her strength up."

Shadowpaw wasn't sure if his father would agree to that, not after all he had said about prey being scarce, and how important it was for cats not to be selfish. But he said nothing. *There's no harm in Puddleshine asking.*

Still carrying the precious leaves of catmint, Puddleshine bounded after Tigerstar and caught up with the Clan leader.

Curious to hear what his father would say, Shadowpaw drifted after him, closer to Tigerstar's den.

Even before he came within earshot, he could see from Tigerstar's bristling fur and the gruff sound of his voice that he wasn't sympathetic to what Puddleshine was asking. Finally he heard his father meow, "Leaf-bare or not, I can't risk cats overextending themselves on hunts. If I did, the rest of the Clan would end up in your den with Grassheart. And then where would we be?"

Puddleshine dipped his head respectfully; Shadowpaw could see that he wasn't happy with the Clan leader's decision, but he didn't try to argue anymore.

Before his mentor could see that he had been eavesdropping, Shadowpaw headed back to his den, but as he passed the pool in the center of the camp, he spotted his sister Lightleap waving her tail at him.

"Hey, Shadowpaw! Come and play with us," she called.

Intrigued, Shadowpaw trotted over. Pouncestep was there, too; both his littermates sprang to their paws as he joined them.

"We thought we'd have a play fight," Pouncestep meowed. "It'll keep us warm."

"Do you think I'm mouse-brained?" Shadowpaw asked, his tail curling up in amusement. "I'm not trained like you. You'd claw my fur off."

"No, we'll go easy on you, promise," Lightleap assured him. "Come on! It'll be fun."

"I'll be a badger, invading the camp," Pouncestep suggested. "And you two can be warriors trying to drive me out."

"Okay!" Lightleap reared up onto her hind paws and swiped at her sister's muzzle, her claws sheathed. "Get out of here, filthy badger!"

Pouncestep let out a fearsome growl. "I'm a huge, scary badger, and I'm going to eat you!"

Trying to get into the spirit of the fight, Shadowpaw leaped forward and butted his head into his sister's shoulder. Pouncestep whipped around, lashing out at him with one paw, but Shadowpaw dodged to one side, and the blow never landed. Shadowpaw felt pride shimmering from his pelt. *Did I just dodge a trained warrior?*

While she was distracted, Lightleap jumped in and rolled her sister over, battering at her belly with all four paws. Shadowpaw watched Pouncestep trying to shove her off, then crept up from behind Pouncestep's head and slammed both paws down on her shoulders.

"I think we've trapped this badger," he mewed to Lightleap. "What should we do with it?"

"Shove it out of camp," Lightleap replied, beginning to push her sister across the ground toward the camp entrance.

Pouncestep let out yowls of protest, her paws and tail flailing, then managed to struggle free and scramble to her paws. "Wow, that was a good fight!" she exclaimed, shaking her pelt to get rid of the debris that clung to it. "And you did well, Shadowpaw," she added. "You could have been a warrior if you'd wanted."

"Thanks, but I'm happy being . . . ," Shadowpaw began to mew, then let his voice trail off as a fierce shiver ran all through his body, shaking him from ears to tail-tip. Between one heartbeat and the next, the camp vanished, and he found himself standing once again beside the Moonpool.

The half-moon hung in the sky, as though this were an ordinary Moonpool meeting, but this time Shadowpaw was alone. The pool wasn't frozen, but when he looked around him, the shapes of his warrior ancestors were still blurred like mist, glowing with an eerie cold light that gradually faded away.

"Don't go!" Shadowpaw cried out. "Tell me what's happening!"

There was no reply. Instead Shadowpaw's nose twitched as the smell of smoke drifted over him. His pelt began to prickle as he felt the heat of a fire burning close by, though he couldn't see it or hear the crackle of flames. Ash fluttered in the sky, swirling around him and settling in tiny gray flakes on his pelt.

Then the screech of a furious cat split the silence. Shadowpaw spun around to see the ThunderClan leader, Bramblestar. He had some other cat on the ground and was slashing his claws across its belly. Shadowpaw couldn't see who the other cat was, until it threw off Bramblestar and stood up.

Shadowpaw let out a gasp. "Tigerstar!"

His father's dark brown tabby fur was ruffled, and blood was streaming from gashes along his side, but he sprang back undaunted into the fight, cuffing Bramblestar around the ears with both forepaws.

Staring in horror, Shadowpaw couldn't begin to understand why the two Clan leaders—and they were kin, too, he remembered—would be fighting. But before he could spring forward to intervene, or even ask what they were doing, the vision vanished and he found himself in the camp once more, lying on his side and drawing in long, gasping breaths.

Raising his head, he saw his mother and father gazing down at him anxiously, while Lightleap and Pouncestep looked on from a tail-length away, their eyes wide with fear. Tigerstar's fur was sleek and neatly groomed, with no sign of any wounds.

"You've had another seizure," Dovewing mewed, bending her head to give Shadowpaw's ears a worried lick. "I thought you were growing out of them."

So did I, Shadowpaw thought with dismay. *I guess training isn't making me normal after all.*

"You'd better go to your den and let Puddleshine have a look at you," Tigerstar added.

Shadowpaw's legs felt as though they would give way like thawing ice as he scrambled to his paws, leaning heavily on his father's shoulder. He was desperately trying to cling on to the memory of what he had seen. Even though it had been upsetting, the swell of dread in his belly gave him the feeling that somehow his vision might be very important.

CHAPTER 5

Rootpaw paced up and down in the ThunderClan medicine cats' den, feeling the stiffness leave his legs and his whole body start to warm up.

"That's right," Alderheart encouraged him. "That's a good way to keep your blood flowing."

For some reason, Rootpaw felt uneasy, as if a whole nest of ants were crawling through his pelt. He couldn't understand why. In spite of the cold, he felt comfortable, and he was sure he was almost back to his full strength. *And that has to be a good thing, right?*

Then Rootpaw picked up a familiar scent. Bristlepaw! A moment later the gray she-cat slipped around the bramble screen, dipping her head to Alderheart as she entered.

Instinctively, Rootpaw halted. Whenever Bristlepaw visited him in the medicine cats' den, she would always sit close to him, and he found that comforting. He wondered if that had anything to do with his feeling uneasy about recovering so quickly from his dunking in the lake.

Surely I can't be sad that I'll have to leave ThunderClan soon?

During the few days that Rootpaw had been living in the

ThunderClan camp, he kept remembering how Bristlepaw had rescued him from the freezing water.

She was so brave!

And every time he had seen her since, he had felt himself growing stronger and braver, as if Bristlepaw's strength and courage had inspired him.

"How are you today?" Bristlepaw asked, padding up to him and touching her nose to his shoulder.

"Much better," Rootpaw replied. "Thanks to you. Though with such a cold leaf-bare," he added hastily, feeling a bit guilty, "it might be better for me to stay here for a few more days, get a bit more treatment from the medicine cats, until I know for sure that I'm well enough to go back to SkyClan." *Surely another day or two wouldn't hurt?*

"Don't worry," Alderheart put in, looking faintly amused. "Jayfeather and I won't let you go until we're sure you're okay."

"And when you get home," Bristlepaw meowed, "you need to stay away from Kitepaw and Turtlepaw, and definitely don't listen to their so-called bright ideas. They're not your mentor—they're not even warriors—so there's no reason for you to take a risk trying to impress them."

"They're older than me, and bigger," Rootpaw pointed out.

"They're still nasty flea-pelts," Bristlepaw declared. "And if you try to prove yourself to them, you'll end up in even worse trouble. You should just focus on learning to be a good warrior."

Rootpaw was awestruck to hear all this wisdom from another apprentice. "That's so smart!" he breathed out.

Bristlepaw shrugged. "Not really," she mewed. "But I know enough to tell you to keep away from cats who only want to harm you, or make fun of you."

Rootpaw blinked at her happily, only to freeze a moment later as he heard paw steps and a loud, familiar voice coming from outside the camp. *Oh, no!* he thought.

Poking his head out through the bramble screen, he saw his father, Tree, heading toward the den, escorted by the young ThunderClan warrior Plumstone.

"What's the point of all this battle practice?" Tree was asking, flicking his tail toward the center of the clearing, where a few of the warriors were going through their fighting moves. "Do you expect to have to fight in this leaf-bare? Wouldn't hunting practice be more useful?"

Plumstone tried to get a word in, but Tree was oblivious as he went on. "If warriors weren't always practicing their battle skills, maybe there wouldn't be so much fighting around the lake. Think about it."

"That's your father, isn't it?" Bristlepaw asked, peering out of the den beside Rootpaw.

"Yes, it is," Rootpaw replied, rolling his eyes in an attempt to show Bristlepaw that he didn't agree with Tree. But he was aware that he hadn't quite managed it.

Oh, StarClan, Tree is so embarrassing when he's like this.

Even though Tree had lived with the Clans for many moons—longer than Rootpaw had been alive—he still seemed as if he didn't belong there. Even worse, in Rootpaw's view, he seemed quite content not to belong.

If Tree weren't my father, I wouldn't care what he thought. I just don't want any cat to think that I'll end up like him.

"How do you feel?" Tree asked.

Rootpaw was padding through the forest beside his father, heading back toward SkyClan territory. The frostbitten grass felt rough beneath his pads, and the air was so cold that he could see his breath swirling out in a cloud.

"I'm fine," Rootpaw replied; now that there was no chance of his remaining in ThunderClan, he could be honest about having regained his full strength. "Alderheart's treatment was really good, and even though it's leaf-bare, I felt comfortable and warm."

"How did you end up in the lake in the first place?" Tree asked, turning his head to look down at his son.

"Don't you know?" Rootpaw responded, surprised. "I thought Kitepaw and Turtlepaw would have told every cat how stupid I'd been."

Tree shook his head. "They just told Leafstar that the three of you were foraging for herbs, and you fell in the water. They didn't say how. But I thought there must be more to it than that."

Once again, Rootpaw felt a tingle of embarrassment, recalling the events that had led up to his falling through the ice. "Kitepaw and Turtlepaw were teasing me," he admitted to his father. "They called me weird, and said I'd never be strong enough to be a warrior. It made me so angry. . . . I ran at Kitepaw, but he dodged, and I couldn't stop myself from falling in.

I was so furious, I hadn't realized how close I was to the lake."

For a few heartbeats Tree said nothing, but Rootpaw couldn't bear to look at the disappointment in his eyes. *Why should I care?* he asked, angry with himself for being upset. *Let Tree think what he likes. It doesn't matter to me!*

"This is why you should be your own cat," Tree meowed at last. "Like it or not, you have a different ancestry from most of the other young cats in SkyClan. The way of the warrior is not the only way, and you should be grateful for the chance to see that. There's more to life than fighting and showing yourself off as a strong cat. It's not always about who is the biggest and bravest."

Rootpaw wanted to disagree, to come up with a good argument to prove to Tree that he was wrong, but he couldn't find the words. He couldn't trust himself not to blurt out all his frustration with his father.

If you don't believe in the way of the Clans, why do you stay? Why have you stayed so long, for so many moons, in a place where you clearly don't belong? Where you don't even try to belong?

His father didn't have any quarrels to mediate right now, and Rootpaw didn't understand why Tree refused to get involved in the daily life of the Clan—why he had to be aloof, always separate from the other cats.

He tells me to be my own cat, but here he is, living under rules he doesn't believe in. Which of us is being more true to himself?

A heavy sense of guilt gathered in Rootpaw's chest.

I know it's wrong, but sometimes I wish I had a different cat for a father.

* * *

Rootpaw woke to find himself alone in the apprentices' den, though a faint warmth still lingered in his sister's nest, next to his own. Alarm pierced him, cold as the leaf-bare wind, and he scrambled out through the rocks without pausing to yawn and stretch. Spotting his mentor at the other side of the camp, he bounded over to join him.

"Am I late?" he gasped, seeing the annoyed look on Dewspring's broad gray face. "I'm sorry."

"You're not late," Dewspring responded, though the tip of his tail was still twitching to and fro. "We've missed a lot of training time while you were in ThunderClan, that's all."

"Well, I'm looking forward to starting again now," Rootpaw mewed with a respectful dip of his head.

Dewspring's only reply was a grunt. He angled his ears toward the Tallrock, where Kitepaw and Turtlepaw were standing with bowed heads in front of Leafstar and Hawkwing. Rootpaw was too far away to hear what Leafstar was saying, but from her cold expression and bristling fur, he doubted that it was anything the two older apprentices wanted to hear.

"They're being punished for their part in putting you in danger," Dewspring explained. "Leafstar said she would wait until you returned to decide on a suitable punishment."

"That hardly seems fair," Rootpaw objected. "It was my fault too."

Dewspring shrugged. "They're older than you; they should have known better. Mind you," he added, "I'm disappointed in you, Rootpaw. I thought you were smarter than that. You shouldn't have gone along with them in the first place."

"Sorry," Rootpaw muttered.

"We'll say no more about it," Dewspring meowed. "Now, let's get on with your training."

Rootpaw had hoped that now that he was home, he would be able to forget his accident by the lake. But as he returned to camp after his battle training with Dewspring, he couldn't be pleased with himself. He had felt sluggish; he was sure his limbs and his tail weren't moving as smoothly as Dewspring expected.

Maybe I should have stayed longer in ThunderClan.

The thought made Rootpaw's pads tingle with fury, that Tree had come to collect him before he was ready. Then his anger was driven out by embarrassment as he wondered if he was so keen to be near Bristlepaw that he would prefer to be injured.

That's pretty mouse-brained!

When Rootpaw brushed through the narrow gap between two huge boulders that formed the camp entrance, the first cats he spotted were Turtlepaw and Kitepaw. They were heading right toward him. He halted, instinctively sliding out his claws.

"Hi," he mewed, trying not to sound as nervous as he felt.

Kitepaw gave him a curt nod.

An awkward silence followed. Rootpaw wanted to get away from the older apprentices, but at the same time he felt he couldn't just walk off without saying anything. Clearing his throat, which suddenly felt dry, he asked, "How did your punishment go? I hope it wasn't too terrible."

Kitepaw turned away from him with a hiss, as if he was too angry to speak. It was Turtlepaw who replied.

"My paws are so cold I can't even feel them! Leafstar made us go to the dirtplace and claw at the soil to make sure it's soft enough for any cat who wants to make dirt. It was disgusting!"

"I'm really sorry," Rootpaw meowed. "I didn't—"

"Only a foolish cat would fall into the lake like you did," Kitepaw interrupted. "But then, you're the son of the weirdest cat in the Clans, so it's no surprise that you're just that mousebrained." He jerked his head at Turtlepaw. "Come on. Let's go hunt."

Rootpaw watched as the two cats stalked off among the boulders. His pelt was hot with anger and embarrassment as he headed for the fresh-kill pile. Needlepaw was there, gulping down a thrush; she paused and looked up at Rootpaw as he approached.

"What's the matter?" she asked.

"Nothing!" Rootpaw snarled, pulling a shrew out of the pile.

Needlepaw's ears angled upward in surprise. "Who made dirt in your fresh-kill?" she asked. "Whatever, don't take it out on me."

"I'm sorry." Rootpaw sagged to the ground. "But I don't want to talk about it."

"Oh, come on. . . ." Needlepaw shifted closer to her brother and rubbed her cheek against his. "You can tell me."

Rootpaw scuffled his forepaws on the ground. "It's just . . . ," he began reluctantly, then went on more quickly. "I just . . . I wish cats would take me a bit more seriously, that's all. Because our father's not a warrior or a medicine cat, just some weirdo who talks to dead cats—"

"And the mediator for all five Clans," Needlepaw reminded him. "That's important."

"Except there's been nothing to mediate lately," Rootpaw continued. "And the Clans have never had a mediator before. It's just one more way that Tree doesn't fit into regular Clan life, and another reason the other apprentices don't see us as true members of SkyClan."

"Now, *that* is mouse-brained," his sister meowed. "Why would they think that?"

"I can sort of understand it," Rootpaw responded. "When Tree is settling disputes, he's supposed to be impartial, and that means sometimes he'll rule against SkyClan." He paused, lashing his tail, then went on, "It's so frustrating! If other cats feel our father isn't a real Clan cat, it means I have to work twice as hard to convince them that I'm a loyal member of SkyClan. That's what set me off before, charging at Kitepaw and Turtlepaw."

Needlepaw twitched her whiskers. "I have the same father," she pointed out coolly. "But I just tell the other apprentices to keep their paws out of my business, and they leave me alone. They only tease you because you let them see it bothers you."

"I know, but—"

"You should try not to worry what your Clanmates think,"

Needlepaw interrupted. "If you're true to yourself, you'll prove them all wrong." She gave Rootpaw's ear a lick, her voice growing warm and affectionate. "I'm sure of it."

Rootpaw heaved a deep sigh. "I guess you're right."

But even while he admitted that Needlepaw was making sense, he knew that if the two older apprentices went on mocking him, he was likely to lose his temper again.

I can't help it. I know that Tree is a bit weird, and I don't want to stick out so much like him. Whatever I have to do, I'm going to prove that I belong in SkyClan, and I'll be a strong warrior, through and through!

CHAPTER 6

Near the entrance to the stone hollow, Bristlepaw waited for her
mentor to appear from the warriors' den. She felt as if a whole
colony of bees were buzzing around in her belly, and it was
hard for her to stand firmly on all four paws and not start
shaking with anticipation.

Rosepetal had still not appeared when Bristlepaw's littermates, Thriftpaw and Flippaw, broke away from the group
of cats around the fresh-kill pile and raced across the camp
toward her.

"Is it true?" Thriftpaw asked, skidding to a halt in front of
Bristlepaw. "You're really going to take your warrior assessment today?"

Bristlepaw's pelt tingled with a claw-scratch of guilt. Both
her littermates were gazing at her in awe, but Bristlepaw had
to admit that what was happening to her wasn't entirely fair.
All three of them had been made apprentices on the same day,
and she had assumed they would all take their assessments
together, too.

"Yes, it's true," she mewed. "Rosepetal was so impressed
with how I rescued that SkyClan apprentice that she

persuaded Bramblestar to let her assess me. I'm waiting for her now."

"That's great!" Flippaw exclaimed. "I can't wait for your warrior ceremony. I wonder what name Bramblestar will give you."

"Hang on—I haven't passed yet," Bristlepaw pointed out.

"But you will," Thriftpaw assured her. "You're a great hunter, so why wouldn't you?"

Bristlepaw blinked at her littermates, grateful for their confidence in her. All the same, she wished that they wouldn't go on about it with such loud meows that the whole camp could hear them. *They're starting to make me nervous.*

"I wish we could take our assessments today, too," Thriftpaw grumbled, turning her head away to lick her shoulder.

Hoping to comfort her sister, Bristlepaw began, "It won't be long before—" but she was interrupted by the sound of her name being called from across the camp. Turning, she saw her mother, Ivypool, standing just outside the warriors' den. Rosepetal was a pace behind her.

"Come on, Bristlepaw," Ivypool meowed. "It's time."

Excitement surged up inside Bristlepaw, and she bounded across the camp with a last glance at her littermates. *It'll be okay,* she thought. *I'll comfort them later . . . when I'm a warrior.*

Icy wind probed deep into Bristlepaw's fur as she crouched among the roots of an oak tree, her ears pricked to pick up the slightest sound of prey. She couldn't move around to stop herself from shivering, because she knew that she had to keep still and not warn her quarry that a cat was nearby. All she could hear was the creak of branches above her head, and the whisper of wind over dead leaves.

There was no sign of Rosepetal, but Bristlepaw knew that her mentor would be somewhere behind her, watching and assessing every paw step, every twitch of her whiskers.

What happens if there isn't any prey? Bristlepaw wondered. *How can I pass my assessment if I don't catch anything?* She stifled a growl of frustration. *Well, I have to find something, that's all. A good warrior should be able to find prey even in the toughest leaf-bare . . . right?*

As these thoughts passed through her mind, Bristlepaw's excitement drained away, as quickly as rain on dry ground in greenleaf. She began to wish that she weren't having her assessment early; everything would have been much easier in newleaf. She would have been sure to succeed then. Ever since she became an apprentice she had imagined herself returning to camp with so much prey she could barely carry it.

But that's not going to happen now.

Then it occurred to her that maybe the quantity of prey she caught wasn't necessarily the only thing that mattered. Her mentor must give her credit for showing initiative. If the prey wouldn't come to her, she would have to go and look for it. *Besides, I'm sick of crouching under this tree. If I stay here much longer, I'll turn into an ice cat!*

As silently as she could, her paws gliding over the ground, Bristlepaw slithered forward, her gaze darting this way and that. Opening her jaws to taste the air, she almost gagged on the cold claw that rushed into her throat. There was no prey-scent, not even a single mouse, only fat flakes of snow that began drifting down through the leafless branches.

Bristlepaw carried on searching, squeezing under low-growing branches where she thought prey might be hiding, or pausing beside banks where the snow might be covering their dens. She even clambered into a tree to check a gap in the trunk, in case a squirrel or an owl was hiding inside. But there was nothing.

All the while the icy wind was buffeting her, and her paws were so cold she couldn't feel them anymore. Finally, when she was ready to give up, a fresh gust of wind brought her the scent of vole.

For a few heartbeats Bristlepaw was so relieved that she nearly forgot how cold she was. But after she had followed the scent around a bramble thicket and across a clearing, she realized that she had reached the stream that formed the WindClan border. And the scent of vole—so close now that Bristlepaw could almost taste the succulent flesh—was coming from the opposite side.

"Fox dung!" she muttered.

Bristlepaw stood on the bank of the stream, gazing across into WindClan territory. She was almost sure that the vole must be hiding under a hawthorn bush that overhung the icy surface of the water.

Her pads itching with indecision, Bristlepaw glanced swiftly around. There was no sign of Rosepetal, and no movement on the WindClan side of the border. She could pick up the mingled scents of both Clans' border markers, but no fresh WindClan scent. With the stream frozen, she could dart across in a couple of heartbeats, catch the vole, and be back in her own territory before any cat spotted her.

But even though hunger and anxiety about her assessment were urging her on, Bristlepaw hesitated. Stealing prey from another Clan was a serious violation of the warrior code. Besides, even if she made her catch and returned undetected, she would still be leaving her scent on the WindClan side of the border. If a WindClan patrol picked it up, it would lead to conflict with ThunderClan, and no cat wanted that, especially in such a harsh leaf-bare.

At the same time, Bristlepaw wondered what it would mean for her assessment if she returned to camp empty-pawed. *Will Rosepetal fail me? Will I have to do my whole apprenticeship all over again?*

Bristlepaw stood on the bank of the stream for an agonizingly long time, trying to make up her mind. But eventually one thing became clear to her: She couldn't pass her assessment by breaking the warrior code. It would be dishonorable, and an insult to Rosepetal, who hadn't trained her to break the rules.

At last, sighing deeply, Bristlepaw turned away. As she left the border stream behind her, Rosepetal stepped out from behind a clump of bracken and stood quietly waiting for her.

Oh, StarClan! She was watching me all the time!

Moving as quickly and quietly as she could, Bristlepaw headed for her mentor and halted at Rosepetal's side.

"Well done," Rosepetal mewed. "Even though you were disappointed, and you'd given up on finding prey, you still were smart enough to stay quiet, in case there happened to be prey nearby. That shows great instincts—the kind of instincts ThunderClan needs in its warriors."

As her mentor spoke, Bristlepaw began to feel more hopeful. *Maybe this hasn't been such a disaster after all!*

"Besides that," Rosepetal went on, "you didn't give way to temptation and cross the border, even though you're hungry, and even though this is your warrior assessment. You showed honesty and respect for the warrior code."

Bristlepaw let out a happy purr. "Does that mean I passed?"

She watched Rosepetal as her mentor stood still, blinking thoughtfully, making Bristlepaw's pads tingle with hope. Then, regretfully, Rosepetal shook her head. "I'm sorry, but no. You haven't done anything wrong, Bristlepaw, but I can't pass you this time, not without watching you hunt and actually capture prey. We'll try again soon, when the air is warmer and the prey isn't hiding."

A hard lump formed in Bristlepaw's belly, colder than the icy wind, but she managed to dip her head respectfully. "I understand," she choked out.

Rosepetal stretched out her neck and touched her nose gently to her apprentice's ear. "Let's go back to camp," she meowed, "and find you something from the fresh-kill pile."

Bristlepaw followed her, holding her head high and struggling not to let her disappointment show. *I failed for the first time in my life—and it wasn't my fault!* She wondered what she would say to her littermates, after they had been so encouraging, sure she would return to camp a warrior. She was so wrapped up in her own thoughts that she didn't notice movement ahead of her until Stemleaf bounded up to her and flicked her shoulder with his tail.

"Hey, how's our new warrior?" he asked.

Bristlepaw had thought it wasn't possible to feel any worse, but at the orange-and-white tom's friendly greeting she thought her heart was going to burst. She couldn't find words to answer him.

"Bristlepaw didn't pass," Rosepetal told Stemleaf. "She did everything right, but there just wasn't any prey to be had."

"That's really bad luck." Stemleaf blinked sympathetically at Bristlepaw. "But don't worry. It's just this StarClan-cursed snow. You'll pass easily once the warmer weather comes."

Bristlepaw could hardly bear to look at Stemleaf, much less talk to him, especially when he was being so kind and encouraging. *It'll be such a long time now before we can be mates, the strongest pair in the Clan. And there must be lots of other she-cats who would like to be with him.*

As soon as Bristlepaw padded through the thorn tunnel into the stone hollow, she heard Flippaw let out a welcoming squeal. Both he and Thriftpaw came barreling across the camp toward her, only to skid to a halt before they reached her. Bristlepaw guessed that her expression must have shown that something had gone wrong.

"What happened?" Thriftpaw asked, her eyes wide with concern.

Bristlepaw watched Rosepetal padding across the camp on her way to tell Bramblestar about her assessment. "I failed," she replied, not meeting her littermates' gaze. "There wasn't any prey. I looked and looked."

"It's okay," Flippaw murmured, pressing himself against Bristlepaw's side. "You did your best."

"Yeah," Thriftpaw added. "You're still a warrior to us—the best!"

Even though Bristlepaw was still frustrated at how things had turned out, she was grateful for her littermates' comfort. *Today was going to be such a great day,* she thought, *and it's turned out to be a disaster.*

CHAPTER 7

Wind drove the clouds across the night sky, so that the waxing half-moon shed only a fitful light through the gaps. Puddleshine and Shadowpaw huddled together as they trudged forward against the blast, trying to preserve every scrap of warmth in their pelts. Shadowpaw narrowed his eyes against the harsh wind whipping into his face, and snuffed up the scent of more snow to come.

I hope we'll be able to share dreams with StarClan this time, he thought worriedly. *That would prove I'm not keeping them away.*

Since the last half-moon meeting at the Moonpool, life in ShadowClan had gotten even tougher. There was never enough prey; cats were getting sick because of the cold and lack of food, and every cat's nerves were on edge. Sooner or later, Shadowpaw knew, fights between Clanmates would become the norm.

We need StarClan to guide us, even if all they can do is promise us that this terrible leaf-bare will end soon.

The other medicine cats were already huddling for warmth by the Moonpool when Puddleshine and Shadowpaw stumbled down the spiral path.

"Greetings," Mothwing meowed, dipping her head gracefully. "I'm sorry we didn't wait for you outside, it's just so cold. How is the prey running in ShadowClan?"

"It's not running at all," Puddleshine replied with an edge of bitterness to his tone. "I think every mouse and vole in the territory is tucked up in its hole, sniggering at us."

"ThunderClan is just as bad," Alderheart agreed, while Jayfeather simply lashed his tail once and did not speak.

"At least you have shelter from the trees," Kestrelflight pointed out. "Up on the moor, the wind is strong enough to blow cats off their paws. I had to set Larkwing's dislocated shoulder when she lost her balance and fell down into a gully."

"And RiverClan can't fish when the lake is frozen," Willowshine added. "I've almost forgotten what fish tastes like!"

Shadowpaw saw that Frecklewish and Fidgetflake from SkyClan were looking faintly embarrassed. "I know we have it easier," Frecklewish admitted. "The valley shelters our territory, so while prey is scarce, we're clearly not suffering as badly as the rest of you." She cleared her throat. "If we could help you, we would."

Puddleshine let out a snort. "SkyClan's most sheltered area used to be in our territory," he grumbled, his voice low but loud enough to be heard by the SkyClan cats, who stared at their paws and didn't respond. "We'd be in better shape now if we hadn't given it away."

Any more complaints that the medicine cats might have made were silenced by Jayfeather, who glared around from his sightless blue eyes. "If you're quite finished," he snapped, "perhaps we could make contact with StarClan. That is why we're here, yes?"

Exchanging anxious murmurs, every cat began to move toward the edge of the Moonpool. *Oh, StarClan, please don't leave us alone,* Shadowpaw prayed desperately. *We need you so much!*

He hadn't looked at the Moonpool until now, and when he did, he let out a gasp of mingled shock and awe. The stream that fed the pool was frozen into a cascade of icicles that glittered when the uncertain moonlight fell upon them. The whole surface of the pool was frozen, too.

"I'm sure this has never happened before," Mothwing mewed, blinking unhappily at the sheet of solid ice. "Not even in that dreadful leaf-bare when Flametail died."

With the rest of the medicine cats, Shadowpaw stretched out his neck and bent his head to touch his nose to the ice. Cold stabbed through him like a thorn. He closed his eyes, but when he opened them again, he was still crouching in the icy darkness beside the pool. He hadn't been transported to the warm territory of StarClan, and there was no sign that the warriors of StarClan were trying to reach them here. Raising his head to gaze around, Shadowpaw couldn't even see the hazy shapes that had appeared at the previous meeting, or hear their distant voices.

"Oh, StarClan, where are you?" Frecklewish exclaimed, her voice shaking as she echoed Shadowpaw's silent prayer. "Please come to us—we need you!"

Mothwing moved back from the pool and sat with her forepaws neatly together, her amber eyes gleaming. "We can

cope," she assured Frecklewish kindly. "We don't need guidance from StarClan when we still have our common sense.
We'll get through this."

Jayfeather scowled at her. "What a surprise that you're not
worried," he muttered bitterly.

"What does that mean?" Mothwing asked, her eyes wide.

"It means that you've never believed in StarClan, so it's no
loss to you," Jayfeather hissed.

Shadowpaw stared at the ThunderClan medicine cat as
gasps of surprise rippled through the others. Puddleshine
had told Shadowpaw that the RiverClan medicine cat didn't
believe in StarClan, but it had never been spoken of during a
half-moon meeting.

"The rest of us know how important this is. How alone we
are." Jayfeather's voice trembled with emotion, and his sightless eyes flashed with anger and fear.

Mothwing shifted her paws, looking down at the ground,
then back at Jayfeather. "Not that you asked," she meowed
evenly, "but with time to reflect on what happened in the
Great Battle, and everything that happened with Darktail
and the cats we lost . . . I no longer deny that StarClan exists."

"What?" Kestrelflight demanded, lashing his tail as he
turned to face Mothwing.

"You're serious?" Jayfeather asked.

Shadowpaw shifted nervously on his paws. He'd heard
from Puddleshine that Mothwing's lack of belief was a source
of conflict between her and some of the medicine cats.

Mothwing drew herself up straight. "Let me finish," she

said. "I believe StarClan exists, but I don't know that their intentions are good, or that we always benefit from their 'guidance,'" she said.

"How can you say that?" Alderheart asked. "Their advice about SkyClan returning—"

"Led to Darktail's reign," Mothwing interrupted. "And how many cats died?"

Jayfeather huffed. "How many more would have died, if they hadn't warned us?"

Mothwing shook her head. "That's neither here nor there," she meowed calmly. "We'll never know. Anyway, every cat can believe what he or she wants. I just think we don't need to panic."

Shadowpaw couldn't agree with her, and from the worried looks the other medicine cats were exchanging, he could see that they shared his uncertainty.

We don't just have to worry about the cold and the shortage of prey, he thought. *The real problem is why StarClan isn't coming to meet with us. They've sent me visions, so it can't be me. . . . Have the Clans made them angry somehow?*

"Does this mean that the Moonpool is just a sheet of ice?" he asked. "Isn't it a special place anymore?"

Willowshine reached out her tail and touched him lightly on his shoulder. "It won't last," she promised. "Often in leafbare the water near RiverClan territory freezes up, but the ice melts again as soon as the weather turns warmer."

"But usually it's only the edges of the pool that freeze," Mothwing pointed out. "Never the whole thing. It's never been as cold as this before."

Alderheart shook his head sadly. "I've got a horrible feeling," he mewed, "that nothing we remember can prepare us for whatever is going on here. I just don't understand it. We know that when Squirrelflight spent time in StarClan's hunting grounds, they told her we should draw closer to them. How can we, though, if they won't speak with us?"

An ominous silence fell. Shadowpaw gazed at one worried face after another; a bud of fear began to swell inside him as he realized that none of these medicine cats—the cats he respected and looked up to above all others—had any idea why they were suddenly cut off from StarClan. *And my visions aren't exactly* normal, he thought with shame. *What if there is something about me . . . something that keeps them from contacting the medicine cats through the Moonpool?*

"Let's try again," Kestrelflight suggested after a few heartbeats; it was clear he was striving desperately to sound optimistic.

"Like that will be any use," Jayfeather growled, but no other cat objected, and finally even Jayfeather stooped to touch his nose once more to the ice that covered the pool.

But Jayfeather had been right. No starry cats appeared. It was almost as if the Moonpool had never been a special place . . . as if StarClan had never visited.

"Well, it's not as if StarClan appears to us every time," Kestrelflight meowed when every cat had moved back from the water.

Jayfeather glared sightlessly at the WindClan cat, his

whiskers quivering. "Don't be more mouse-brained than you can help," he snarled. "We all know something is going on. We can all feel it."

Shadowpaw swallowed hard. He glanced at Puddleshine, hoping that his mentor could think of some reason to argue with Jayfeather's terrifying words. But Puddleshine merely stared at his paws, and none of the other medicine cats found anything to say.

It was Kestrelflight who broke the silence. "We might as well end the meeting," he meowed. "It's obvious nothing is going to happen tonight. Perhaps we'll have better luck next time—surely the weather will have warmed up by then."

Every cat murmured agreement. Shadowpaw thought that they were all relieved to be leaving that place, where they had once received wisdom from the spirits of their warrior ancestors, and now were met with only cold and silence.

When the other cats had headed off to their own camps, Puddleshine and Shadowpaw padded silently alongside the lake and crossed the border into ShadowClan territory. Shadowpaw felt worry like a dark cloud enveloping him and guessed that his mentor felt the same. The cold had grown even more intense, making his bones ache. The wind had dropped; a thick layer of cloud covered the sky, cutting off the moonlight and the glitter of the stars.

That has to be a bad omen, Shadowpaw thought.

Snow had begun to fall again, growing heavier and heavier until their fur was covered with it, and they slipped and stumbled into hidden dips in the ground. They were still some distance from the camp when thunder rolled out overhead, splitting the silence of the night. Fear gripped Shadowpaw, and he flattened himself to the ground; even Puddleshine flinched.

"Surely there can't be thunder and snow at the same time?" Shadowpaw asked as the sound died away.

"It happens sometimes," Puddleshine responded, casting an uneasy glance upward. "But if I'm being honest, this is all starting to feel bad. . . ."

Shadowpaw shuddered. It was feeling bad to him, too. But worse than the ominous feeling he had was the worry about what could be behind it.

What if it is me?

Shadowpaw sat abruptly upright, shaking off the moss and bracken from his nest in the medicine cats' den. He was certain that some cat had called his name, though he could see the curve of Puddleshine's back, half buried in his bedding, and hear his mentor's gentle snores. Grassheart too was still deeply asleep in her nest.

"Who's there?" Shadowpaw called out softly.

There was no reply. Shadowpaw began to feel pressure building inside his head, as if he were about to have another seizure. Blinking, he took several deep breaths, trying to ride out the sensation and stay conscious.

Gradually the pressure resolved itself into an urgent command. *You have to go back to the Moonpool.*

Shadowpaw flinched. The voice in his head was as clear as

if Grassheart had woken and called to him . . . but he knew this was no living cat. "Why?" he whispered, though he didn't expect an explanation.

He wondered if he ought to wake Puddleshine and tell him what was going on, but as soon as the thought occurred to him, he felt a strong conviction—almost like an order—that he should not.

This is a journey you have to take alone.

A spark of hope lit within Shadowpaw. *I know this is StarClan. And if StarClan is reaching out to me, it must not be me they have problems with.* Maybe he could be a normal medicine cat after all—a medicine cat who received visions from StarClan and used them to help guide all the Clans. Gathering all his courage, he rose to his paws.

As soon as he ventured outside his den, Shadowpaw spotted Stonewing crouching on guard beside the entrance to the camp. The snow was falling more lightly now and the clouds had begun to break up; the tom's pale pelt glimmered in the starshine.

"I'll never get past him if I go that way," Shadowpaw muttered to himself.

Instead he wriggled through the dirtplace tunnel, and once out in the open he crawled forward with his belly fur brushing the snow until he was well clear of the camp. Then he strode out into the forest, heading for the hills and the frozen Moonpool.

* * *

Shadowpaw stumbled with exhaustion as he made his way down the spiral path to the hollow where the Moonpool lay. The journey from ShadowClan territory seemed to have taken twice as long as usual, and he guessed that dawn couldn't be far away.

Fresh snow had fallen on the frozen pool since Shadowpaw's earlier visit; he brushed it away with one forepaw, enough to clear a space of ice where he could lean forward and touch his nose to the surface. He still had no idea why he had been called here.

Is StarClan trying to reach me? Then why don't they appear?

Straightening up again, he looked around, but nothing disturbed the frosty silence of the night. Convulsive shivers shook him; his head felt oddly full and heavy, and a feeling of dread ran through his whole body. He couldn't remember ever having been so tired and cold.

Maybe it was a mistake to come here, he told himself wretchedly. *But I was so sure.*

Overhead, another rumble of thunder interrupted his thoughts. Shadowpaw flinched, looking up, but all he could see was the whirling snow.

Who was I kidding? I'll never be a normal medicine cat. All I get are weird seizure visions that make everybody uncomfortable. I'm not sure I can make it back to camp, alone, in this weather. I must have had bees in my brain to come here.

While he still gazed upward, white light flashed out from the clouds, blazing down on the surface of the Moonpool;

it was so brilliant that for a few heartbeats Shadowpaw was blinded. When his vision cleared, he glanced around to see faint flares of light in the night sky as lightning crackled in the distance. Thunder rolled again, the noise building and building until it seemed as if the whole world would split apart.

Shadowpaw crouched, terrified, under the onslaught. "But what does it all mean?" he yowled.

The only answer was another flash of lightning, brighter and closer than before. Everything went black, and with a last whimper of terror, he sank into its softness and knew nothing more.

Pain throbbed in Shadowpaw's head as he regained consciousness, and he felt as though every muscle in his body, every hair on his pelt, was aching. His vision swam as he struggled to sit up.

Was I struck by lightning? he wondered dazedly.

He could hardly believe it, and yet all around him the snow was melted, showing blackened earth. There were spiky patches on his pelt, prickling his pad when he touched one of them.

As he gradually recovered, Shadowpaw became aware of a voice inside his head. There was no sign of where it was coming from, no star-furred cats approaching him or waiting for him in a sunny clearing. Only the voice, which he realized had been speaking for some time, always repeating the same words.

There is a darkness in the Clans that must be driven out.

Shadowpaw's pain and exhaustion were swallowed up in panic. Scrambling away from the Moonpool, he tottered up the path to the line of bushes that guarded the hollow. He skidded down the rocky slope on the far side, half jumping and half falling, as if he could outrun the ominous voice.

But there was no escape. The voice went on repeating the same words, over and over. *There is a darkness in the Clans that must be driven out. A darkness in the Clans . . .*

CHAPTER 8

❧

The ground under the holly bush was almost free from snow, but Rootpaw still felt wet and miserable as he huddled underneath the branches beside Dewspring. His mentor was testing him by making him recite the warrior code, but Rootpaw was finding it hard to remember.

I can't think of anything but how cold and hungry I am!

Even so, Rootpaw had to admit that SkyClan was lucky to have its camp in this sheltered valley. He had seen for himself, when he was recovering in their camp, how much harder life was for the cats of ThunderClan.

"And what does the code tell you to do when you catch prey?" Dewspring asked.

His words made Rootpaw think of sinking his teeth into a nice juicy mouse. His jaws watered. "Eat it," he replied.

Dewspring sighed. "We give thanks to StarClan for its life," he mewed. "And then we carry our prey to the fresh-kill pile. The Clan must be fed first." His tail-tip twitched in irritation. "Rootpaw, even a kit knows that! You have to concentrate."

"I do know it," Rootpaw grumbled, annoyed with himself.

"But it's hard to concentrate when my belly thinks my throat's torn out."

"I know." Now Dewspring sounded more sympathetic. "We'll hunt later. For now, tell me what your first duty will be when you're made a warrior."

"Keep vigil for—" Rootpaw began, only to be distracted as he saw Frecklewish and Fidgetflake emerge from Leafstar's den in the gap at the base of the Tallrock, followed by the Clan leader herself and her deputy, Hawkwing. They padded across the camp toward the medicine cats' den, their heads together as they talked, and halted a few tail-lengths away from the holly bush where Rootpaw and his mentor were crouching.

". . . but it still worries us both that we can't get in touch with StarClan" were the first words Rootpaw heard, from a clearly anxious Fidgetflake.

Rootpaw's jaws gaped in astonishment. He managed a shocked "Wha—" before Dewspring silenced him with a tail slapped over his mouth.

Frecklewish nodded. "Nothing like this ever happened back in the gorge. Even when StarClan wasn't sending us any visions or signs, we always felt that they were with us. It's different here," she finished sadly.

"I keep wondering if leaving the gorge and coming here has weakened our connection to our ancestors," Fidgetflake continued. "Did we make the wrong choice?"

Leafstar sighed heavily. "Hawkwing and I, and the whole Clan, made the choices we thought were necessary. I don't believe our warrior ancestors will abandon us forever."

"But what happens when a cat dies?" Fidgetflake asked, alarm in his voice and his wide eyes. "They're supposed to go to StarClan. And what if a leader were to die right now, when the connection to StarClan seems lost? Would they be able to come back? Would a new leader get their nine lives?"

"I don't think a leader is likely to die," Hawkwing pointed out. "None of them are sick, and we're not at war with any Clan."

"That's true. Fidgetflake, you shouldn't worry so much," Leafstar meowed briskly. "The only danger we have to face right now is this leaf-bare."

"But that's bad enough," Frecklewish murmured, so softly that Rootpaw could only just make out her words.

"So, you're going to show me your herb stores," Leafstar went on, beginning to move away again. "If you think there's any hope of finding more, we'll send out a patrol. Which cats would be best at searching, do you think?"

The group moved on, and if Frecklewish replied, Rootpaw couldn't hear her. He exchanged a dismayed glance with Dewspring. "StarClan is lost?" he exclaimed, hardly able to believe what he had just heard. "What are we going to do about it?"

"Not get our tails in a twist," Dewspring responded. "Whatever the problem is, we can rely on Leafstar, Hawkwing, and the medicine cats to guide us through it."

Even though he spoke so confidently, he had a worried and distracted air, and Rootpaw could guess that he didn't believe his own words. *He wants to reassure me, but he's just as anxious as I am.*

"But we—" Rootpaw began.

"Enough of lazing around under this bush," Dewspring interrupted with forced cheerfulness. "It's time to go hunting and bring back something for the fresh-kill pile." He rose and led the way into the open.

Even though Rootpaw sprang eagerly to his paws and followed his mentor, he knew it would be a long time before he could forget the conversation he had just heard.

Fresh snow had fallen overnight, still almost unmarked except for the paw prints of the patrols. Here and there Rootpaw spotted the thin scratches of a bird's claws, but no tracks of mice, rabbits, or squirrels. He couldn't pick up the least trace of any prey-scent.

"I guess they're all huddled in their holes," he meowed, discouraged.

"We just have to keep trying," his mentor responded. "Let's go down to the lake."

As they headed in that direction, Dewspring suddenly darted aside into a patch of undergrowth where overhanging fronds of bracken had protected the ground from the worst of the snow. He emerged a moment later with a shrew dangling from his jaws.

"Great catch!" Rootpaw exclaimed.

"No, it's a skinny thing," Dewspring mewed, setting it down at the edge of the patch and scratching earth over it, ready to collect it later. "But it's better than nothing. Thank you, StarClan, for this prey," he added with a sigh.

Rootpaw wondered whether StarClan could hear him. Even if they could, did they care whether a hunter thanked them? But he knew better than to voice his doubts. He followed Dewspring as his mentor continued, but his hopes of catching something himself were rapidly fading.

The trees were thinning out as they approached the lake, the wider stretches of open ground leaving even less space for prey to hide. Rootpaw's legs were getting so tired, each paw step was an effort.

How much longer is Dewspring going to keep us out here, looking for prey that isn't there?

Then, as Rootpaw rounded a clump of hazel bushes, the lake came into view. His eyes widened as he spotted a huge crow, pecking at the ground on top of the slope that led down to the waterside.

Yes!

Instantly Rootpaw dropped into the hunter's crouch. From the corner of his eye he glimpsed Dewspring raise his tail as if to stop him, then take a step back, leaving the prey to his apprentice. Rootpaw gulped, realizing how important this moment was.

I have to make this kill. I have to get food for my Clan!

Paw step by paw step Rootpaw edged forward. The crow had its back to him, moving slowly away as it pecked among the debris at the foot of a beech tree. The wind was blowing from the crow to Rootpaw, so there was no chance that his scent would alert it. His heart pounded as he drew gradually closer.

This bird is so big and scary—but it would be such great prey to take back to SkyClan!

At last Rootpaw halted, barely a tail-length away from his prey. He waggled his hindquarters, then pushed off in a mighty leap and landed on the crow's back with a thump. For a few heartbeats the crow struggled, its wings a black storm around Rootpaw's head, its talons flailing. Rootpaw bit down hard on the back of its neck, and it suddenly collapsed and lay limp on the ground, the breeze from the lake ruffling its feathers. Rootpaw stared down at it, hardly able to believe that he had caught it.

Dewspring came bounding up, his eyes shining. "Hey, that was amazing!" he exclaimed. "Well done, Rootpaw. You were brave to take on a bird as big as that. It just goes to show you have a talent for hunting."

In spite of the cold wind, Rootpaw felt warm from ears to tail-tip at his mentor's praise. "I thought it would fly away for sure," he confessed, then added conscientiously, "Thank you, StarClan, for this prey."

"We'd better get back to camp," Dewspring meowed. "Are you sure you can manage to carry that?"

"I'll be fine," Rootpaw responded proudly, imagining what his Clanmates would say when he brought back such a magnificent addition to the fresh-kill pile. *Let Kitepaw and Turtlepaw try sneering at that!*

Dewspring led the way to the spot where he had left his shrew and collected it before heading back toward the Sky-Clan camp. Rootpaw followed, dragging the crow along between his legs, staggering a little from the weight.

They had almost reached the camp when Rootpaw spotted his father sitting in the snow at the edge of a bramble thicket. Tree was so still that snow had drifted over his back, almost covering his yellow pelt. Rootpaw hoped that his mentor wouldn't spot him, but at the same moment Dewspring halted.

"What is your father doing?" he asked Rootpaw.

Rootpaw's pride in his catch was swallowed up in embarrassment; he felt as though his fur were on fire. "Dunno," he muttered. "Just sitting there, I guess."

Dewspring looked confused. "Well . . . er . . . I suppose he wasn't brought up in a Clan," he mewed, clearly trying hard not to say something insulting. "He must have his own ways. But I wouldn't want to be out here, getting snowed on."

Rootpaw guessed that his mentor was looking at Tree and wondering if this strange cat, who did everything differently and sometimes took other Clans' sides in disputes, was truly loyal to SkyClan.

Why does Tree have to be so peculiar? Rootpaw asked himself, wishing he could be like Needlepaw and just brush off their father's strangeness.

Completely humiliated, struggling to think of something he could say to Dewspring, Rootpaw spotted movement in the snow. A vole was scurrying toward Tree, who lazily stretched out a paw and slammed it down on top of the little creature.

Dewspring's tail curled up in amusement. "Hey, he's hunting!" he exclaimed. Padding over to Tree, he dipped his head and added, "That's a cool trick! Can you teach me?"

Rootpaw had to admit that his mentor was right. But he still wished that Tree would catch prey using the normal warrior hunting moves.

Tree blinked up at Dewspring. "Sure I can," he replied, his voice a friendly purr. "It's not hard. All you have to do is think bush."

Dewspring looked confused. "'Think bush'?"

"Yeah, imagine your legs are branches and your claws are twigs," Tree explained.

"And my ears are leaves, right?" Dewspring meowed, with a wry glance at Rootpaw, who staggered up, dragging his crow.

"You got it," Tree told him. "Then you have to keep really still, and the prey will come to you." He picked up the vole and added it to a small pile beside him; Rootpaw saw that he had already caught a mouse and a shrew.

His happy pride returned a moment later as Tree spotted his crow and asked, "Rootpaw, did you catch that?"

It was Dewspring who replied, a look of approval on his broad gray face. "He did, all by himself. He's going to be an amazing hunter."

Rootpaw looked up at his father to see the same approval gleaming in his eyes. "That's great to know," Tree meowed. "Good job, Rootpaw."

"We'd better be getting back to camp," Dewspring continued, as Rootpaw basked in the older cats' praise. "The sun will be setting soon."

For the first time Rootpaw noticed that the shadows of the

trees were lengthening, blue against the snow. The short leaf-bare day was drawing to an end.

"I'll come with you," Tree meowed, gathering his prey together.

Dewspring leaned in and picked up the shrew. "Here, let me help carry."

On the way back to the camp, Rootpaw didn't feel too embarrassed anymore in his father's presence. Tree had caught several pieces of prey. But he realized he would have felt differently if his father had just been sitting there, freezing to death while he pretended to be a bush.

The rest of the Clan gathered around the hunters as they pushed their way through the camp entrance and into the clearing.

"Rootpaw, did you really catch that?" Needlepaw exclaimed, staring at the ragged feathers of the crow. "That's amazing!"

His mother, Violetshine, said nothing, but her eyes were warm with praise, and she padded beside Rootpaw on the way to the fresh-kill pile, and leaned toward him to give his ears a loving lick. Even Leafstar, standing beside the pile with Hawkwing and Reedclaw, gave him an approving nod.

"The Clan will eat well tonight," she mewed.

Rootpaw ducked his head; he felt embarrassed all over again, but this time he enjoyed the feeling, because he had earned the respect of his Clan. He could see that the fresh-kill pile was bigger than it had been for many days, and no cat in the Clan would go hungry.

"Why don't you take some prey to Fallowfern," Dewspring

instructed him. "Then you can come back and eat."

"Yes, take her this vole," Tree added, pushing the body of his prey over to Rootpaw. "It's pretty plump, considering it's leaf-bare."

Rootpaw willingly agreed, picking up the vole and bounding across the camp to set it down in front of the deaf elder, who was sitting outside her den with her paws tucked under her.

"Thank you," Fallowfern meowed, swiping her tongue around her jaws. "That looks tasty!"

On his way back to the fresh-kill pile, Rootpaw halted as Turtlepaw stepped out in front of him. "That was an awesome catch," she mewed. She couldn't quite meet Rootpaw's gaze, and he was surprised at how shy she sounded.

"I was lucky, that's all," he responded.

Kitepaw was standing a couple of paces behind Turtlepaw, and Rootpaw braced himself for some mocking remark, but the reddish-brown tom said nothing, only giving Rootpaw a respectful nod as he followed him and Turtlepaw to join the rest of the Clan.

By now, most cats had settled down to eat, but no cat had taken Rootpaw's crow. "We're leaving that for you," Tree meowed, flicking his tail toward Rootpaw's prey. "There's enough to eat for every cat, and you might as well enjoy your first big catch."

"You can choose some cats to share it with," Dewspring added.

Rootpaw nodded eagerly. *It's great to be able to feed my Clanmates!*

He beckoned Needlepaw with his tail, then turned more hesitantly toward Kitepaw and Turtlepaw. "Would you like some?" he asked, trying not to feel nervous.

"Thanks!" Turtlepaw meowed, crouching down beside the crow.

Kitepaw looked surprised, but gave Rootpaw a nod of thanks and sat beside his denmate, sinking his teeth into the crow. "Where did you find this?" he mumbled.

"Down near the lake," Rootpaw replied, sitting next to Needlepaw and tearing off a chunk of prey. "Not far from the border with ThunderClan."

Turtlepaw nodded. "That's a good place," she agreed.

Needlepaw gulped down a mouthful. "Dewspring must have been pleased," she mewed.

"He was," Rootpaw replied. "I was beginning to think he'd always be disappointed in me."

"Most mentors are like that," Turtlepaw assured him. "You should have heard Blossomheart when I first became her apprentice. I thought I would never do anything right!"

Rootpaw felt warmed by the older apprentices' friendliness, as if something had suddenly changed. *Maybe they're not so bad after all,* he thought.

"You know," Kitepaw began, "I was impressed by you, that day you fell through the ice. It was a brave thing to do, standing up for yourself and attacking me like that. Stupid," he added, with a gleam of amusement in his eyes, "but brave."

Suddenly happy, Rootpaw let out a small *mrrow* of laughter. He had made a lucky catch to feed his Clan, he might just be beginning to make friends with Kitepaw and Turtlepaw, and even Tree was being slightly less embarrassing than usual. For the first time he began to believe that this terrible leaf-bare would soon pass, and every cat would be fine.

CHAPTER 9

❧

Bristlepaw flexed her paws to bring feeling back into them as she paused in the snow, surveying the moonlit trees and letting her mentor's instructions run through her mind. *Wind direction . . . uneven ground . . . focus . . . This time I'll catch something for sure!*

Tasting the air, she crept forward, setting each paw down as lightly as a falling leaf, and keeping her tail tucked in to her side. Her ears were pricked to pick up the least sound of prey, but long moments dragged by, and still there was nothing.

Flexing her claws, Bristlepaw couldn't help letting out a growl of exasperation. "I don't understand what I'm doing wrong!"

Her mentor, Rosepetal, padded up behind her and briefly rested her tail-tip on Bristlepaw's shoulder. "You're not doing anything wrong," she explained patiently. "Every cat is having trouble hunting."

"But it's been nearly half a moon since I failed my assessment," Bristlepaw protested miserably. "And since then I haven't caught any prey. I'm not helping my Clan at all!"

"But it's not your fault," Rosepetal reassured her. "I promise you, you're doing everything right. You're just having very bad luck in a very bad leaf-bare."

Bristlepaw heaved a deep sigh. "I guess I'll just keep trying."

"No, that's enough for today," Rosepetal responded. "It's getting late; we should be heading back to camp."

Bristlepaw opened her jaws to argue, then realized that her mentor was right. The scarlet light of sunset had faded. Starlight glittered on the snow-covered ground, except where trees and undergrowth cast patches of deep shade. There would be no more hunting until tomorrow. Reluctantly Bristlepaw nodded; her head and tail drooped as she followed Rosepetal back to the stone hollow.

As Bristlepaw emerged from the thorn tunnel into the clearing, she spotted Thriftpaw and Flippaw bounding across the camp toward her.

"Hey, guess what?" Flippaw yowled as he halted in front of her, panting with excitement. "Thriftpaw caught two mice! Two!"

"It was just luck," Thriftpaw meowed. Her eyes shone as she tried and failed to hide how proud she was. "And Flippaw nearly caught a vole."

"I was mouse-brained," Flippaw confessed. "I messed up my pounce. Hollytuft got it, though."

"That's great," Bristlepaw responded. She wanted to be excited for Thriftpaw, but a weight of misery was gathering in her belly. *Obviously there's prey out there,* she thought. *How come Thriftpaw can catch it and I can't?*

Heading farther into the camp, with Thriftpaw and

Flippaw close behind her, Bristlepaw spotted Bramblestar and the Clan deputy, Squirrelflight, with their heads close together, deep in conversation with the two medicine cats. Curious, Bristlepaw drifted nearer so that she could overhear what they were saying.

"Every Clan is having the same problems?" Bramblestar asked, his amber eyes dark with worry. "No cat can make contact with StarClan?"

"That's right," Jayfeather replied. "We haven't met with StarClan at the last two half-moon meetings. And as far as I know, they haven't sent dreams or visions to any cat."

"It'll be a disaster if we're cut off from our ancestors for long," Alderheart added. "What if we don't follow the right path? What if we mess up our own destinies?"

Bristlepaw was glad to think about something other than Thriftpaw's hunting success. "Huh!" she muttered, turning to her littermates with a dismissive flick of her tail. "Thunder-Clan ought to be more worried about the shortage of prey, not whether we can talk to some dead cats in the sky."

Thriftpaw and Flippaw both let out purrs of amusement at their sister's daring. But their purrs broke off a moment later and their eyes widened as they gazed at something behind Bristlepaw.

"What?" she asked.

A voice, icy as the leaf-bare wind, cut across the single word. "What kind of stupid furball are you?"

Bristlepaw spun around to see Jayfeather glaring at her from sightless blue eyes. Alderheart, Squirrelflight, and

Bramblestar stood beside him. Bristlepaw flinched, taking a pace back. She hadn't meant any cat to hear her, except for her denmates. *It would have to be Jayfeather! He's the scariest cat in the forest! And Bramblestar . . . I said something stupid in front of my Clan leader!* "I . . . uh . . . didn't mean—" she began.

"You have no more sense than a kit before its eyes open," Jayfeather snarled. "StarClan holds all the Clans together. If they desert us, we're nothing but rogues. Clearly you're too young and stupid to understand what that means, but an older, wiser cat would know that separation from StarClan is the biggest problem we could have to face."

Bristlepaw glanced around to see that more of her Clanmates had gathered around, gazing at her with worried eyes. She wanted to shrink into a tiny little bug that could hide itself under a twig.

"I'm really sorry—"

"'Sorry' fills no bellies," Jayfeather snapped. "If I were your mentor, I'd confine you to camp for the next six moons, and the only training you'd get would be how to shift the elders' ticks!"

While he was speaking, Bramblestar stepped forward, and he brushed his tail down Jayfeather's side. "Calm down," he meowed. "If we punished apprentices every time they said something foolish, we'd have no time for anything else. I'm sure Bristlepaw didn't mean it." As he spoke, he fixed Bristlepaw with his powerful amber gaze.

"N-no, I really didn't," Bristlepaw stammered. "I was just . . . I wasn't thinking."

"That's clear enough." Jayfeather took a step back.

"We're sorry, too," Flippaw added, while Thriftpaw nod-ded eagerly.

Bramblestar inclined his head, accepting their apologies. "However," he continued, "it's clear that the three of you don't know enough about StarClan. You'd better come with us to the Gathering tonight, and maybe you'll learn more."

As her Clan leader spoke, Bristlepaw felt a churning in her belly, a weird mix of shame at being scolded by her Clan leader and excitement at being chosen to accompany her Clanmates to a Gathering.

"Really?" Jayfeather twitched his whiskers in disgust. "It's like you're rewarding them!" He stalked off toward his den.

"Jayfeather has a point," Bramblestar meowed, his gaze traveling over Bristlepaw and her littermates. "You'd better make sure that tonight you don't put a single claw out of line."

"Oh, we won't!" Bristlepaw assured him fervently, while her brother and sister nodded in earnest agreement.

The frozen lake shone silver under the full moon as Bristle-paw, Thriftpaw, and Flippaw followed their Clan leader along the water's edge toward the Gathering island. The snow had stopped, but the cold felt like huge claws gripping Bristle-paw's body and striking up through her pads. She had never seen the forest looking so desolate, and the stars that glittered overhead seemed remote and uncaring. For the first time, she wondered why the warriors of StarClan might be refusing to communicate with the medicine cats.

Have we done something to make them angry?

But Bristlepaw's fears receded as she and the rest of her Clan arrived beside the tree-bridge to cross to the island. WindClan's cats were already picking their way along the tree trunk, and the mingled scents of the other Clans wafted from the bushes at the far side.

I wonder which cats I'll meet tonight? Maybe Rootpaw, she added to herself. *I hope he's okay—and I hope the silly furball has had the sense to ignore the other SkyClan apprentices.*

Crossing the tree-bridge felt weird. Bristlepaw had been to Gatherings before, and she was used to the way that the lake water would suck at the tree, making her feel that at any moment she would lose her balance and fall in. Tonight the water was frozen, and Bristlepaw guessed that they could have walked across to the island without using the tree.

Leaping down from the trunk at the other side, Bristlepaw raced up the shore and pushed her way through the bushes into the clearing where the Gathering took place. Thunder-Clan was the last to arrive, and the open space around the Great Oak was already crowded with cats. Bramblestar and Squirrelflight headed for the Great Oak; Squirrelflight took her place on the roots, while Bramblestar leaped into the branches and found a spot near Mistystar, the RiverClan leader. Jayfeather and Alderheart headed to join the other medicine cats.

Glancing around, Bristlepaw saw that her Clanmates were already mingling with cats from other Clans. She waved her tail to greet some young WindClan warriors she had met at previous Gatherings, but as she was making her way toward them, she was almost carried off her paws by a small yellow tom who thrust his way out of the crowd and bounced up to her.

"Hi, Bristlepaw!" he meowed.

"Rootpaw!" Bristlepaw exclaimed. "How are you?"

"I'm fine," Rootpaw assured her. "And it's all thanks to you! I'll never forget how you saved my life. Did they give you your warrior name after that? I'm sorry if I shouldn't have called you Bristlepaw."

Bristlepaw winced; the comment stung, even though Rootpaw had no way of knowing about her failed assessment. *And I'm not about to tell him.* "No, I'm still Bristlepaw," she told him.

"I went on this amazing hunt the other day," Rootpaw chattered on, clearly unaware of how Bristlepaw was feeling. "I caught a huge crow, all by myself! Four of us shared it, and we still couldn't finish it."

Bristlepaw tried to force some enthusiasm into her reply. "That's great."

"I love hunting!" Rootpaw exclaimed, his eyes shining. "Don't you love it, Bristlepaw?"

"I'd love it if there were anything to hunt," Bristlepaw snapped. *Of course I love hunting. I'm going to be a warrior, aren't I? What a mouse-brained question!*

Rootpaw didn't seem bothered by her curt tone. "If you're short of prey in ThunderClan, I could bring you some," he offered.

Bristlepaw's irritation flared into pure anger. Stretching out her neck, she hissed into Rootpaw's face. "ThunderClan cats can catch their own prey, thank you very much!"

Rootpaw jerked backward, his eyes wide with distress. "I—I'm sorry," he stammered. "I didn't mean to say you couldn't."

Bristlepaw instantly felt guilty when she saw how much she had upset the younger apprentice. She was trying to find the right words to apologize when the voice of Tigerstar rang out from the branches of the Great Oak.

"Cats of all Clans, it's time for the Gathering to begin!"

Bristlepaw glanced up at his powerful tabby figure poised on a branch, and when she turned back again, she saw that Rootpaw wasn't by her side any longer. She spotted him scurrying into a group of SkyClan cats, including the two apprentices who had been with him beside the lake.

It wasn't my fault, she tried to tell herself, though she couldn't wipe out her feelings of guilt. *He shouldn't have said something so mouse-brained. And he's still hanging out with those two useless lumps of fur!*

The sounds of talk in the clearing gradually died away as the cats settled down to listen to their Clan leaders, crowding into the shelter of the bushes where the ground was almost clear of snow.

"ShadowClan remains strong," Tigerstar announced, "but I must admit we'll all be glad when this leaf-bare is over."

"RiverClan wishes the same," Mistystar agreed, rising to her paws and giving her blue-gray pelt a shake. "The lake and the streams around our camp are frozen. It seems like moons since we've tasted fish."

"WindClan has problems too," Harestar added. "There's so little shelter in our territory, all the prey has fled."

"And yet you're the Clans who got to keep all your territory when we rearranged the borders to make room for SkyClan," Tigerstar pointed out, an edge to his voice. "If you're not happy with it now—"

"You're still complaining about the borders?" Crowfeather, the WindClan deputy, interrupted from his place on the oak roots. His tail twitched in exasperation. "We already fixed that for you!"

"You know perfectly well why we made that decision," Mistystar added, glaring at Tigerstar from eyes like chips of blue ice. "And unless you can persuade the Twolegs to move the Twolegplace between RiverClan and ShadowClan or the horseplace on our border with WindClan, that's the way it has to be."

Tigerstar was obviously ready to make a furious retort when Bramblestar rose and took a pace forward. "That prey has been eaten," he pointed out calmly, "and the new borders were working well for all the Clans until the weather turned so cold. That's our problem, and that's what we should be concentrating on."

Tigerstar gave his shoulders an angry shrug, while Mistystar dipped her head in acknowledgment of what the ThunderClan leader had said. Bristlepaw felt a stab of pride. Her leader was so wise, to know what to say to prevent a useless quarrel.

"I don't know what we're going to do," Harestar continued after a moment's pause. "This is the worst leaf-bare any cat can remember, and the longest that cold weather like this has lasted."

"And the longest that the medicine cats have gone without receiving messages from StarClan," Jayfeather announced from where he sat with the other medicine cats. There was an ominous note in his voice that chilled Bristlepaw far more than the news of prey shortages.

She could see many of the older cats exchanging worried glances at Jayfeather's words, making her realize even more clearly how serious the problem was.

That was such a mouse-brained thing I said, back in the camp!

"But surely that's just a result of the cold and the Moonpool being frozen?" Mistystar meowed. "I'm confident that all we have to do is be patient and wait for the warmer weather."

Leafstar flicked an ear, her expression tense. "We certainly hope so."

Bristlepaw could see that Jayfeather wanted to object, but Harestar continued before he could get a word out.

"Maybe it's time to share some good news, then," he suggested. "WindClan has two new apprentices, Woodpaw and Applepaw."

A chorus of caterwauling broke out in the clearing as the assembled cats called out the names of the new apprentices. Bristlepaw joined in, seeing the two young cats duck their heads in embarrassment, while their mother and father,

Heathertail and Breezepelt, looked on proudly.

"RiverClan has good news, too," Mistystar announced as the clamor died away. "Curlfeather has given birth to three healthy kits."

Again Bristlepaw joined in the chorus of congratulation, though she could see a faint shadow of anxiety on Mistystar's face, and she spotted a few of the RiverClan warriors exchanging worried glances.

This weather and the shortage of prey must be really tough for a mother cat and newborn kits in the nursery, Bristlepaw thought. *Sparkpelt and Sorrelstripe probably feel the same . . . but I haven't noticed, because I've been so focused on my own worries.* A sharp claw of guilt pierced her as she realized how self-centered she had been, thinking only about how the harsh leaf-bare had spoiled her chances of becoming a warrior.

At last the noise died down again and Bramblestar turned to Leafstar. "How are things in SkyClan?" he asked.

Leafstar seemed reluctant as she rose to her paws, padding forward until her branch began to dip gently under her weight. "Life is hard in SkyClan," she reported, "but perhaps not as hard as for the rest of you." Her tone was hesitant, and Bristlepaw guessed she was aware that her news might spark resentment from the other Clans—especially from Shadow-Clan. "Our territory is in a sheltered valley," the SkyClan leader went on, "and there are caves in the hills beside our top border, where we could withdraw if things get any worse."

Bristlepaw could hear muttered comments from some of the warriors in the clearing below, and Tigerstar's shoulder fur began to bristle as if he thought he was facing an enemy.

"How lucky for you," he muttered.

Leafstar turned to him with a lash of her tail. "Let's not start arguing about this again," she mewed. "The new boundaries were agreed on by all the Clans, including ShadowClan."

Tigerstar's only reply was a snort as he sat down on his branch again.

"This is all very well," Jayfeather began again, rising from where he was sitting beside Alderheart, "but none of it really matters. Why aren't we talking about why we've lost our connection with StarClan?"

This time, Jayfeather's words seemed to reach the cats around him; Bristlepaw could hear uneasy murmurs spreading throughout the crowd.

"Why are we cut off?" Crowfeather from WindClan called out. "And will the connection come back again?"

"Who will watch over us now?" some cat added from among the SkyClan warriors. Bristlepaw couldn't see who it was, but she could hear the alarm in the cat's voice.

"Calm down." Mosspelt, the RiverClan elder, rose to her paws and waved her tail to emphasize her words. "The Moonpool is frozen! That must be what's keeping StarClan away. But don't worry. Newleaf will come; it always does."

More yowling broke out, some cats agreeing with Mosspelt and others snarling their objections. Bristlepaw looked in dismay at their bristling fur and extended claws.

They can't start fighting—not at a Gathering!

But before a blow could be struck, a single word rang out

across the clearing. "Enough!"

Every cat turned to look up at the Great Oak. The cat who had called out was Tigerstar, on his paws again and sweeping the clearing with a commanding gaze.

"What Jayfeather says is not quite right," he meowed when the assembled cats were quiet once more. "There is one cat who can still communicate with StarClan."

Jayfeather looked outraged, but before he could speak, Puddleshine nudged a young cat to step forward from the group of medicine cats. Bristlepaw recognized him as Shadowpaw, the ShadowClan medicine-cat apprentice. *He's my kin,* she remembered. . . . His mother, Dovewing, was the littermate of her own mother, Ivypool. He said nothing, but only stood blinking up at his Clan leader.

"Shadowpaw," Tigerstar announced, "has received a message from StarClan."

CHAPTER 10

Shadowpaw gazed at the assembled warriors, who were all staring back at him, as if they couldn't believe what Tigerstar had told them. Something twisted in his belly, like a snake trying to bite him from the inside. Ever since the lightning strike, when he had awoken beside the Moonpool in a puddle of slush, he had felt that something wasn't right with him. And he couldn't find any explanation for it.

"Go on," Tigerstar encouraged him. "Tell the Clans what you told me and Puddleshine."

Gulping nervously, Shadowpaw launched into the story of how he had woken in his den and been compelled to go back to the Moonpool. "Then, when I got there," he continued, "there was a bright flash of light, and I heard a voice. I think I was struck by lightning."

"Struck by lightning?" some cat in the crowd repeated. "Sure, and hedgehogs fly!"

"Are you sure you weren't dreaming?" Reedwhisker, the RiverClan deputy, asked. He sounded sympathetic, but Shadowpaw could sense that he didn't believe a word of his story. "I've seen what lightning strikes can do," the black tom went on. "It wasn't long ago that lightning almost destroyed our camp. If you had really been struck, you wouldn't be here to tell the tale."

Shadowpaw knew that what Reedwhisker said made sense. "I don't know why I'm here," he responded, feeling more and more self-conscious with every passing heartbeat. "I can only tell you what happened."

"So there was a voice," the WindClan warrior Nightcloud meowed. "What did it say?"

Shadowpaw opened his jaws to reply, but Mallownose of RiverClan interrupted, his voice loud and dismissive. "I think this is all very dubious. Why would only a ShadowClan cat— and an apprentice at that—get a message from StarClan?" His glance raked around the crowd. "Does no other cat find that suspicious? After all, how much trouble has befallen the Clans for believing the things ShadowClan says?"

There were a few murmurs of protest at the RiverClan warrior's harsh words, but Shadowpaw saw that most of the gazes resting on him were hostile. Even his fellow medicine cats were giving him uneasy glances.

Shadowpaw had heard some of his Clanmates say that the other Clans didn't trust them, but he had never really understood what that meant until now. When he looked around, all he could see were bristling pelts and eyes narrowed in suspicion.

Do they really think we're bad cats?

To Shadowpaw's relief, Tigerstar seemed to sense how uncomfortable he was, and leaped down from his place in the

Great Oak to stand by his side. "Perhaps the leaders should talk to Shadowpaw alone," he said.

His tone of voice made the suggestion sound more like a command; Shadowpaw was grateful that no cat objected, though Jayfeather twitched his tail-tip and muttered something under his breath.

Tigerstar wrapped his tail around Shadowpaw's shoulders and drew him to one side of the clearing, nodding at Puddleshine to join them. The other leaders leaped down from the tree and padded over to them, while the rest of the cats huddled together in anxious groups, murmuring doubtfully to one another.

"Okay," Tigerstar began when Shadowpaw, Puddleshine, and all the leaders had settled themselves under the spreading branches of an elder bush. "Shadowpaw, tell us about this voice."

"I heard it speaking to me when I recovered from the lightning strike," Shadowpaw explained. He felt less nervous now that he had to tell his story to only a small group of cats, even though they were all Clan leaders. "It said, 'There is a darkness in the Clans that must be driven out.'" His voice shook as he repeated the ominous words. "I've heard it again since then, in my dreams."

The Clan leaders exchanged thoughtful glances. "Is it a voice you recognize?" Bramblestar asked.

Shadowpaw shook his head. "No, I've never heard it before."

"Then are you sure you weren't dreaming?" Mistystar's blue eyes were sympathetic.

"I'm quite sure," Shadowpaw insisted.

"But Mallownose had a point," Harestar interrupted. "Why would StarClan send a message only to ShadowClan?"

Shadowpaw didn't know the answer to that either. He was thankful that none of the leaders were being openly hostile to him, but he could see that they were all worried and suspicious, uncertain whether to believe him.

"Shadowpaw has always been special." Tigerstar defended him, his ears twitching in annoyance. "He has received visions ever since he was a kit."

The other leaders glanced at one another; Shadowpaw struggled with feelings of frustration, guessing that they thought Tigerstar was just a fond father, boasting about his kit.

"That's true, and I've always had seizures along with my visions," he explained. "But not this time."

"Then I wonder if the fact that you're not having seizures means that you're not actually having visions either," Leafstar mewed.

"No, the vision was real," Tigerstar insisted. "And we need to listen to this message. Remember that he foresaw his own near drowning in the flood. If we'd listened to him then, maybe the flood would never have happened."

Bramblestar turned to Puddleshine, who was sitting on the edge of the group, following the discussion without speaking. "What do you think?" he asked. "Is Shadowpaw having true visions?"

For a few heartbeats Puddleshine hesitated; Shadowpaw

felt a hollow place inside him at the doubtful look on his mentor's face.

"There's no question that I believe Shadowpaw," Puddleshine replied at last. "He's had important visions before. But I can't be sure that these are actual messages from StarClan. We've all had visions, but this seems like something else. Leading him to the Moonpool on his own? Striking him with lightning?" He shot an apologetic look at his apprentice. "It's not that I don't believe you, Shadowpaw, but I'm not sure what to make of it."

Once again the Clan leaders exchanged glances. "This is something I must discuss with my deputy and RiverClan's medicine cats," Mistystar meowed.

The other leaders murmured agreement.

"Then you mustn't take too long about it," Tigerstar warned them. "All the Clans must work together to understand this before we act on it."

Bramblestar dipped his head toward Shadowpaw. "Thank you for telling us about this," he meowed. "It took courage to stand up before a whole Gathering like that."

As he spoke, he gave Shadowpaw a friendly nudge. At the touch, a strange sensation shot through Shadowpaw, as if claws were gripping him inside, twisting his belly and chilling his spine like the icy leaf-bare wind. His breath caught in his throat as he looked up at Bramblestar.

That felt so . . . wrong.

CHAPTER 11

"Okay, today we're going to teach you a new battle move," Dewspring announced. "Reedclaw and I will show you first. Are you ready, Reedclaw?"

"When you are," the tabby she-cat replied.

Two sunrises had passed since the Gathering, and although fierce cold still clamped down on the forest, at least there had been no fresh snow. Rootpaw and Needlepaw were training with their mentors in a sheltered hollow where the covering of dead leaves was visible under a light drifting of white.

"Watch carefully," Dewspring told the two apprentices. "I'm going to attack Reedclaw. I'm bigger and heavier than her, but she's going to beat me."

Rootpaw crouched beside his sister, eager to see what the new move would be. Energy was rushing through him, as if he were a stream suddenly released from the grip of frost. "Wait till it's our turn," he whispered to Needlepaw. "I'm going to squash you!"

Needlepaw let out a small *mrrow* of laughter. "You can always try!"

Dewspring reared up on his hind paws and bore down

on Reedclaw, who flattened herself to the ground, gazing up at him with wide eyes, as if she were terrified. But before Dewspring could land on top of her, she launched herself forward, still keeping low, and scooped his hind paws out from under him.

Rootpaw let out a yowl of excitement as Dewspring tumbled onto his side, hitting the ground with a thud. But Reedclaw hadn't finished. As swift as a striking snake, she spun around and leaped on top of Dewspring, pinning him down with one paw on his throat and another at the base of his tail.

"Awesome!" Needlepaw breathed out.

Reedclaw stepped back to let Dewspring scramble to his paws. He stood for a moment, breathing hard and shaking leaf mold out of his pelt. "That's the move," he meowed. "In a battle, you might not get the chance to do the second part, but it's a good way to deal with any creature who attacks you on hind paws. Especially if they think you're scared."

Needlepaw leaped up, bouncing on her paws with excitement. "I want to try! Come on, Rootpaw, attack me." She crouched on the ground and blinked at him. "Oh, you're such a big, strong cat! Please don't hurt me!"

"You furball!" Rootpaw mewed good-humoredly.

He reared up on his hind paws, just as Dewspring had, and stretched out his forepaws, ready to fall on top of his sister. Needlepaw sprang forward, and even though he knew what she was trying to do, Rootpaw was too clumsy to dodge on hind paws alone. The breath was driven out of his body as he hit the ground; he tried to roll out of Needlepaw's way, but she jumped on top of him and pinned him down with all four paws.

This isn't over, Rootpaw thought.

Remembering his first training session, almost a moon ago, he let himself go limp. As Needlepaw looked up and asked, "Was that okay, Reedclaw?" he powered up from the ground, throwing Needlepaw off, and pinned her in turn with a paw on her neck.

"Mouse dung!" Needlepaw hissed.

Rootpaw stepped back and let her get up. He saw that Reedclaw had curled her tail up with amusement, and laughter was glimmering in Dewspring's eyes.

"Well done, both of you," Reedclaw meowed. "Now let's try it again, and Needlepaw, you attack this time."

When the training session was over, all four cats headed back to the SkyClan camp. Rootpaw lagged behind a few paces, his mind turning to Bristlepaw. Every time he thought about the ThunderClan apprentice, he realized all over again what an amazing cat she was. She had saved his life, she was good at everything, and every cat in her Clan liked her and relied on her, even though she wasn't a warrior yet. Rootpaw had seen so much to admire in her, in the time he had spent in the ThunderClan camp.

I wish she'd seen that great fighting move I pulled off!

Then Rootpaw remembered his last meeting with Bristlepaw, at the Gathering. She had seemed chilly and distant. And everything was going so terribly for the other Clans. Rootpaw had noticed how skinny and miserable they all looked, much worse than the cats of SkyClan, who had the advantage of sheltered territory.

They're all short on prey, and it sounds as if things are getting worse. I wish there were something I could do to help.

"Hey, Rootpaw!"

Needlepaw's voice startled Rootpaw out of his musing, and he realized that he had fallen so far behind that the others were almost out of sight. Bounding forward, he caught up with them just before they reached the camp entrance.

Tree was on his way out, and he dipped his head to the two mentors as they passed. He would have continued without speaking, but Dewspring halted and meowed, "We've just had a good training session. Rootpaw and Needlepaw are doing really well."

"Yes, they're working hard," Reedclaw agreed. "And they're always cheerful, even when we tell them to clear out the soiled bedding!"

Tree listened gravely, though Rootpaw couldn't tell whether he was pleased by their mentors' praise. "Thank you for telling me," he murmured at last.

The two mentors continued into the camp, but Tree held his kits back with a gesture of his tail. "Don't be too obedient," he advised them. "It's important to think for yourselves, too."

"I know," Needlepaw responded instantly. "Don't worry; it's not a problem."

Rootpaw couldn't share his sister's easy acceptance of what their father had said. *Why can't Tree behave like the rest of our Clanmates?* he asked himself, trying to hide his irritation. *Doesn't he know how important it is to be part of a Clan?*

Once he had said good-bye to Tree and headed on into camp, Rootpaw's thoughts flew back to Bristlepaw and his time in ThunderClan. The whole Clan had been kind to take care of him, and Bristlepaw had been so brave to save him from drowning. *She's a real Clan cat! I wish Tree were more like her.* He hated to think of her going hungry, even though he understood why she had rejected his offer to find prey for her. *She has her pride—and I respect her so much for that. But I still wish I could help.*

Glancing at the SkyClan fresh-kill pile, Rootpaw realized that although it wasn't full, there was enough to feed every cat. The SkyClan cats around him in the camp looked far healthier than the ones he had seen at the Gathering.

We're very lucky here, he thought. *I wish I could do something to help the other Clans. Especially ThunderClan. Especially Bristlepaw.*

Then an idea crept into Rootpaw's mind. Spotting Leafstar and Hawkwing standing beside the Tallrock, he padded over to them.

"Greetings, Rootpaw," Leafstar meowed as he approached.

Hawkwing gave him a friendly nod. "How is your training going?" he asked.

"Okay, I think," Rootpaw responded, proud that the Clan deputy was his kin and that he had some good news to share with him. "Needlepaw and I learned a new battle move today."

"Excellent," Hawkwing purred.

"There's something I've been thinking about . . . ," Root-paw began. Now that he was actually standing in front of the Clan leader and her deputy, he was beginning to have doubts about the idea that had seemed so brilliant moments before.

"Spit it out, then," Hawkwing meowed after an awkward silence of a few heartbeats.

Rootpaw took a deep breath. "I've been remembering how welcoming ThunderClan was to me after I fell through the ice. They took care of me and were generous with the prey they shared with me, even though their fresh-kill pile was low."

"Yes, they were very kind," Leafstar agreed, her eyes narrowing a little as she gazed at Rootpaw.

"So I thought . . . maybe to thank them for their kindness, I could take Bristlepaw a piece of prey—just one piece, that I catch myself," he said.

Leafstar's whiskers twitched disapprovingly, while Hawkwing gave his leader a doubtful glance. "Rootpaw . . . ," Leafstar began.

"I'd catch it on my own time, not as part of a hunting patrol," Rootpaw added hastily. "Bristlepaw was so brave, saving me when my own Clanmates couldn't. . . . I just don't feel I've thanked her properly," he finished, "especially when ThunderClan was so good to me."

Rootpaw's heart was pounding as he waited for his leader's verdict, but for several moments Leafstar said nothing. Eventually she turned to her deputy. "What do you think, Hawkwing?" she asked.

Hawkwing closed his yellow eyes in a long blink, then opened them again. "It's not usual for Clans to share prey," he replied. "And as we're a new Clan here beside the lake, I think we have to be careful about overstepping boundaries."

Leafstar nodded. "That's true. But ThunderClan was helpful to one of our own, and I don't want to seem ungrateful."

"He has a point," Hawkwing meowed.

Rootpaw dug his claws hard into the ground as Leafstar still hesitated. Finally the Clan leader dipped her head. "I'll allow this, Rootpaw," she told him. "But—"

"Great!" Rootpaw exclaimed, with a little bounce of excitement. "Thank you!" Then he realized that he had interrupted his Clan leader. "Sorry," he muttered, hanging his head.

"But," Leafstar repeated, "as you said, the prey must be caught on your own time, and you must get permission from your mentor."

"And only one small piece of prey," Hawkwing added. "If you catch another massive crow, it's for us, not ThunderClan!"

"I understand," Rootpaw mewed, nodding eagerly.

"Besides that," Leafstar continued, "make sure that our fresh-kill pile is reasonably full before you take anything to ThunderClan."

"Yes—yes, I will." Every hair on Rootpaw's pelt was quivering with impatience to get moving, but Hawkwing held him back with one raised paw.

"Remember, all Clan cats are proud," he warned Rootpaw. "If you want to bring prey to Bristlepaw, you must make clear that it's to say thank you, that you're paying a debt."

Rootpaw nodded gratefully. "I will," he promised. "And thank you—both of you!"

"Off you go, then," Leafstar meowed.

Rootpaw didn't need telling twice. The words were hardly out of the Clan leader's mouth before he raced across the camp, looking for Dewspring to ask permission.

Sunhigh was long past by the time Rootpaw headed toward the ThunderClan border. A small vole was dangling from his mouth. Its enticing scent and taste flooded his jaws, and with every paw step it became harder to resist. It was all Rootpaw could do not to stop and devour the vole himself.

I'm sure Bristlepaw will be pleased that I'm being so thoughtful, he told himself.

Dewspring and Sunnypelt padded along beside Rootpaw. Though his mentor had given him permission, he had insisted on coming with him, and had asked the young ginger she-cat to come too. Rootpaw had protested, but Dewspring had refused to listen.

"You must be totally mouse-brained if you think I'm going to let an apprentice visit a rival Clan's territory on his own," he had meowed.

Now Rootpaw just hoped that he'd still get to have a private chat with Bristlepaw. There were things he wanted to say to her, but not in front of his mentor.

"I think this is weird," Sunnypelt remarked as they drew closer to the ThunderClan border. "Prey is so scarce right now, and here we are giving it away to another Clan."

Dewspring shrugged. "Leafstar approved it, and it's good to see an apprentice thinking about something other than his own belly."

But I am *thinking about my own belly,* Rootpaw thought ruefully. *And if we don't get to ThunderClan soon, I won't be able to stop myself devouring this prey!*

The pungent scent of the ThunderClan border markers cut through the scent of vole in Rootpaw's jaws, warning him that they were approaching the boundary between the two Clans.

"We'll stop here," Dewspring meowed. "A ThunderClan patrol should come along soon."

Rootpaw dropped his prey and sat down beside it in the shelter of a clump of bracken. Looking out into ThunderClan territory, he could see how heavily the snow had fallen outside the protection of the valley, covering the ground and weighing down the branches of the trees. He hadn't been sitting for long before his paws and his hindquarters were freezing cold; he rose again and began to pace up and down in a futile effort to get warm.

To his relief, it wasn't long before he heard rustling on the ThunderClan side of the border, and three ThunderClan warriors appeared from a copse of elder bushes. Rootpaw didn't recognize any of them from his first Gathering a few nights before.

The cat in the lead, a cream-colored tom with a stumpy tail, stalked up to the border and stood nose to nose with Dewspring. "What are you doing here?" he demanded.

"Greetings to you, too, Berrynose," Dewspring responded. "We've come to—"

He broke off as a tortoiseshell-and-white she-cat bounded up to Berrynose's side and thrust out her muzzle toward Rootpaw's vole. "Look!" she exclaimed, her whiskers quivering with outrage. "Prey! Have you been hunting on ThunderClan territory?"

Dewspring rolled his eyes. "Poppyfrost, have you got bees in your brain?" he asked. "Or do you think we're mouse-brained? Given everything that's happened lately, with so many cats hungry and desperate, do you really believe any warrior would be bold enough to start a quarrel over prey?"

"We have every right to be suspicious," Poppyfrost began hotly. "Especially when—"

"No, it's okay, honestly," Rootpaw interrupted eagerly. "I caught the vole on SkyClan's side of the border. I'm bringing it to Bristlepaw to say thank you for saving me when I fell in the lake."

Berrynose and Poppyfrost exchanged a disapproving glance.

"Bristlepaw can catch her own prey, thank you very much," Poppyfrost mewed, her voice as cold as the ice that covered the lake.

Berrynose shook out his long, creamy pelt, clearly insulted. "I don't think this is a thank-you at all," he snorted. "SkyClan is just rubbing our noses in it, that they have so much prey that they're giving it away."

The third member of the patrol, an older tabby tom, took a

pace forward. "Let them come over," he meowed, amusement glimmering in his amber eyes. "We shouldn't discourage an apprentice from doing something generous."

"Oh, Birchfall, you always think you know best," Berrynose responded with a disdainful sniff. He paused for a moment, his gaze raking over the SkyClan cats. "Fine, you can come," he snapped. "Follow us, and don't put so much as a whisker out of line, or we'll have some SkyClan fur to line our nests."

Dewspring led the way across the border; Rootpaw and Sunnypelt joined him in a tight little group as they headed into ThunderClan territory. Berrynose took the lead with Birchfall bringing up the rear and Poppyfrost ranging to and fro on either side.

As soon as the SkyClan patrol emerged from the thorn tunnel into the ThunderClan camp, Rootpaw gazed around eagerly for Bristlepaw, but there was no sign of her. Dismay jolted through him from ears to tail-tip. *I hope she's not out on patrol.*

His pelt tingled with nervousness when he saw that other ThunderClan cats had spotted them and were beginning to drift over in their direction, exchanging curious glances. Rootpaw realized for the first time that they might not be as friendly as they had been when he was sick and needed help. He was glad now that Dewspring had insisted on coming with him and bringing Sunnypelt.

"Poppyfrost, go find Bristlepaw," Berrynose directed. "I'm going to report to Bramblestar."

He bounded across the camp and began scrambling up

a pile of tumbled rocks by the camp wall, leading to a ledge where Rootpaw knew the Clan leader had his den. Meanwhile Poppyfrost padded over to the apprentices' den and stuck her head through the ferns. A moment later Bristlepaw emerged; Poppyfrost led her back to where the SkyClan cats were waiting.

Excitement rose inside Rootpaw as he saw the pale gray she-cat approaching. He remembered once again how angry she had been at the Gathering because she thought he was implying she couldn't manage to feed herself. *I need to be careful what I say.*

Bristlepaw halted in front of Rootpaw. "Well?" she asked.

Rootpaw dropped the vole at her paws. "Bristlepaw," he began, "I've brought you this vole to say thank you for saving me when I was drowning. You were so brave and helpful—and so was ThunderClan while I recovered here in your camp. I wanted to repay that debt by bringing you this prey."

As he finished speaking, Rootpaw realized that he had sounded far too formal, as if he had been making an announcement at a Gathering. *I meant to sound friendly, and I completely messed up!*

Even worse, he saw that Bristlepaw looked embarrassed. She would not meet his gaze as she licked furiously at her chest fur. "There's no need," she mewed. "It's nice of you, but I can't—"

She broke off at a tiny sound from the ThunderClan cats who surrounded the group. She glanced around at her Clanmates. They were all eyeing the vole hungrily, as if every cat wanted to snatch it up and devour it.

"Thank you, Rootpaw," she began again. "I can catch my own prey, but the ThunderClan elders will be grateful to share this vole. It's a really good one."

Rootpaw struggled again with feelings of dismay. He had wanted Bristlepaw herself to eat his vole. But he could see that her pride wouldn't let her do that. He dipped his head. "Thank you, Bristlepaw," he meowed. "I'll never forget what you did for me."

He never knew if Bristlepaw would have replied, because at that moment Bramblestar came shouldering through the crowd, followed by Berrynose. "Greetings," he meowed to the SkyClan cats. "Welcome to our camp. Rootpaw, that was a kind thought, to bring prey for Bristlepaw."

His amber gaze was warm and friendly, but a chill crept over Rootpaw as he returned the Clan leader's gaze. He blinked, then blinked again. It was as though some kind of dark shadow was hanging over Bramblestar, yet no shadows lay in the clearing. Rootpaw glanced around swiftly at the other cats around him, but none of them seemed to notice anything odd.

"I—I was glad to do it," he stammered in reply to the Clan leader, dipping his head respectfully. Inwardly his heart was pounding so hard he thought every cat must be able to hear it.

Is there something wrong with Bramblestar? Rootpaw asked himself. *Or is there something wrong with* me?

While Dewspring said a formal good-bye to Bramblestar, Rootpaw turned to Bristlepaw. "It was good to see you again," he mewed, scuffling his forepaws awkwardly on the ground. "Maybe we'll meet again at the next Gathering."

"Maybe," Bristlepaw responded; she sounded distant, and she didn't say another word while she stood watching Rootpaw and his Clanmates make their final good-byes and leave.

The ThunderClan cats allowed the SkyClan patrol to travel back to their own territory without an escort. Rootpaw trailed miserably behind Dewspring and Sunnypelt. Even though he had done what he had set out to do, somehow it had all felt wrong.

"Well, that was a waste of time and prey," Sunnypelt commented, echoing Rootpaw's own thoughts.

Rootpaw also couldn't forget the weird shadow that had seemed to enfold Bramblestar. He still wasn't sure that he hadn't been seeing things. *Bramblestar's one of the most honorable cats in the forest. There can't be anything the matter with him . . . right?*

"Hey, did either of you notice anything weird about Bramblestar?" he asked his Clanmates.

Sunnypelt just shook her head. Dewspring glanced back over his shoulder and asked, "What do you mean, 'weird'?"

"I don't know . . . like a . . . shadow."

Dewspring huffed out a breath. "Nope. No idea what you're meowing about."

So that's that, Rootpaw thought. *Maybe it is me.*

Then he realized that his father, Tree, knew a lot about weird stuff. Maybe he would listen to Rootpaw and advise him about what he had seen. *I'll ask him about it as soon as we're back in camp!*

But as they approached the SkyClan camp entrance, Root-paw caught the sound of muttering coming from beneath the low-sweeping branches of a pine tree. Dewspring and Sunny-pelt heard it too.

Creeping nearer to check it out, Rootpaw and his Clan-mates spotted Tree, stretched out comfortably on the thick layer of needles underneath the pine. He seemed to be hold-ing a lively conversation with himself. Rootpaw guessed that he was talking to some dead cat—Tree could see, and converse with, dead cats who weren't in StarClan. But even though he understood, he had to admit that Tree looked and sounded pretty peculiar.

Dewspring and Sunnypelt exchanged a glance; Sunnypelt's whiskers riffled with amusement as the two warriors turned away without commenting and padded on.

Rootpaw's tail drooped. *There's no way I'm going to tell him what I thought I saw now!* He believed his father's power was real, but he had no interest in sharing it. *I just want to be a good warrior . . . a good, normal warrior.*

Rootpaw picked up his pace to catch up with his mentor. "Can we learn some more battle moves tomorrow?" he asked.

"Of course," Dewspring purred. "It's good that you're so eager."

His praise made up a little for Rootpaw's disappointment. *I'm going to concentrate on my training,* he thought. *I'm going to be a normal warrior, and StarClan help any cat who says I'm not!*

CHAPTER 12

♣

From her ears to the tips of her claws, Bristlepaw felt hot with embarrassment as she stood watching Rootpaw and the other SkyClan cats leave the camp.

Why does Rootpaw keep showing off to me? she asked herself. *And why did he bring me prey?* She was worried that he thought she couldn't catch fresh-kill for herself. Did every cat know that hunting had been giving her trouble? Maybe news of her assessment had spread to all the Clans, so now she was known as a failed warrior who needed help all the time.

With a growl of annoyance and frustration she grabbed the vole and carried it over to the elders' den.

She found Cloudtail and Brightheart drowsily curled up together, while Graystripe and Brackenfur were talking quietly, side by side in their mossy nests. All four cats looked up as Bristlepaw approached and dropped the vole in front of them.

"Is that for us?" Brackenfur asked. "Wow, great catch, Bristlepaw."

"It is, but I didn't catch it." Bristlepaw couldn't bear to tell the elders where the vole had really come from, but she didn't want to lie about it.

"Thanks for bringing it, anyway," Graystripe mewed, stretching out his neck to give the vole a good, deep sniff.

"You're welcome," Bristlepaw responded as she began backing out of the den. *The sooner the wretched thing is eaten and I can forget about it, the better.* "Enjoy."

Leaving the elders to share the vole, Bristlepaw headed back into the camp, looking around for Rosepetal. She couldn't see her mentor, but before she had gone many paw steps, Stemleaf bounded up to her and fell into step beside her.

Bristlepaw felt her heart start to thump, and every hair on her pelt grew warm at Stemleaf's closeness. She remembered seeing him in the crowd of cats around the SkyClan patrol. *I wonder what he thought about that?*

"I see you have an admirer," Stemleaf meowed. "How long has Rootpaw been padding after you?"

Bristlepaw halted, staring at Stemleaf in shock. "Rootpaw isn't padding after me!" she choked out.

Stemleaf's gaze was teasing but still kind. "Come on—how many cats go out of their way to do nice things for a cat from another Clan?"

Oh, no! Bristlepaw thought, still staring at Stemleaf. *Maybe he's right. Maybe Rootpaw does like me like that!*

"So what if he is, then," she responded, trying to make her voice calm and detached. "He's just a mouse-brained apprentice."

"Well, he can't be that mouse-brained," Stemleaf purred. "No cat could be, when he's chosen a great cat like you."

Bristlepaw blinked, hardly able to believe what Stemleaf

had just said. "Oh . . . uh . . . thanks," she stammered.

Stemleaf just gave her a friendly nod and bounded off toward the fresh-kill pile, where Spotfur and Cinderheart were sharing prey.

Looking after him, Bristlepaw felt as if her paws were floating several tail-lengths above the camp floor. *That's the nicest thing Stemleaf has ever said to me! He must feel for me what I feel for him!*

All her embarrassment over Rootpaw's visit was swept away and forgotten. Instead she felt grateful to the young cat. He had made Stemleaf realize his feelings for her! Once again she pictured a time when she and Stemleaf would be mates, hunting and fighting side by side for their Clan. Only one thing stood in the way now of that dream coming true:

I have to pass my assessment.

When Bristlepaw emerged from her den the next morning, dawn light had barely begun to seep into the sky, and a few stars still glimmered overhead. Thriftpaw and Flippaw remained curled up in their bedding, their whiskers quivering in time with their snores, but Bristlepaw felt her whole body surge with energy.

This is the day!

Outside the warriors' den, Squirrelflight was arranging the dawn patrols. Bristlepaw arched her back in a long stretch as she watched Twigbranch lead out one group and Molewhisker a second; she noticed with satisfaction that Rosepetal wasn't among them.

After the patrols left, Bristlepaw hurried over to the warriors' den and slid through the outer branches. Rosepetal was buried deep in her nest of bracken, only the curve of her cream-colored back visible among the reddish-brown fronds. For a moment Bristlepaw felt nervous about waking her, especially as she wasn't supposed to be in the warriors' den at all, but her determination urged her on. She picked her way over to her mentor, careful not to wake the sleeping Thornclaw as she skirted his nest.

Rosepetal let out a grunt as Bristlepaw prodded her with one paw. "Wha—? Is it badgers?" she muttered.

"No, Rosepetal, it's me," Bristlepaw replied. "Can I do my assessment today?"

Immediately Rosepetal was awake, sitting up and shaking scraps of moss from her pelt. "Are you sure?" she asked. "No cat is judging you for what happened last time, and conditions aren't any better."

"I'm sure," Bristlepaw responded confidently. "I'm ready. I can do it." *And then I can be with Stemleaf.*

Rosepetal hesitated for a moment, then nodded. "Very well. I'll go tell Bramblestar."

Bristlepaw padded back to her own den to wait while her mentor spoke to the Clan leader. Her littermates were just emerging, yawning and shivering in the cold air.

"I'm going to do my assessment again," Bristlepaw announced, beginning to give herself a quick grooming.

Her brother and sister brightened up immediately. "Wow!" Flippaw exclaimed. "Good luck."

"Yeah," Thriftpaw added. "I'm sure you'll do great this time."

"Thanks," Bristlepaw responded. *Some cats would be jealous, but Flippaw and Thriftpaw are so supportive!*

Before Rosepetal returned, Bristlepaw realized that news of her assessment was spreading through the camp. Her parents, Ivypool and Fernsong, padded over to wish her good luck, along with Squirrelflight and Bramblestar himself.

Bristlepaw thanked them all as she padded out of camp with her mentor, but inwardly she had begun to feel nervous, as if her early confidence were leaking out through her pads. She imagined how dreadful it would be if she failed for a second time and every cat knew it. Maybe Stemleaf would believe that it was StarClan's will for her never to become a warrior.

Oh, that would be terrible. . . . He would never be my mate then.

Once out in the forest, Rosepetal turned to her. "Off you go," she mewed, then stepped away with a nod and disappeared around a bramble thicket. Bristlepaw knew, however, that she would be somewhere close by, watching.

The dawn light was strengthening, though clouds covered the sky and no sun could shine through. For a few moments, Bristlepaw stood still, gazing around at the frozen forest and thinking hard. *I'll stay well away from the WindClan border this time,* she told herself. She was determined not to return to camp without catching something, especially the day after a cat from another Clan had embarrassed her by bringing her prey.

Bristlepaw remembered an area of thick undergrowth in a shallow valley not far from where Rosepetal had left her.

There was plenty of shelter there where prey might be lurking. Her ears pricked alertly, her eyes scanning every paw step of the forest, she padded off in that direction.

Around her the forest was white and quiet, the only sound her paws breaking through the hard crust of the snow, and now and then the creaking of a laden branch. Her breath billowed out in a foggy cloud. The air she breathed in felt like claws in her chest, and it held not the slightest hint of prey.

Finally Bristlepaw stood at the edge of the valley, which lay in front of her like an upturned leaf. The bottom was covered with bushes and ferns; here and there the deep green of holly or the brown of bracken poked up above the white covering of snow. And, for the first time, Bristlepaw picked up a tiny trace of mouse.

Yes!

Setting her paws down carefully, remembering that a mouse would feel the vibrations of her steps before it heard or saw her, Bristlepaw slid down into the valley and between the outer branches of the bushes. Only a dim light filtered in from above, and dead leaves covered the earth.

Keeping her tail well tucked in, Bristlepaw flattened herself to the ground and crept forward. The scent of mouse was stronger now, and before she had gone very far, she spotted it nibbling at something among the roots of a gorse bush.

With every paw step Bristlepaw prepared for the mouse to sense her and run, but it had its back to her, intent on the seed or whatever it was eating. The low branches stopped Bristlepaw from rising into the right position for a pounce; instead, when she was close enough, she flung herself forward, feeling the gorse thorns rake along her back, and trapped the mouse between her forepaws. It let out a thin, terrified squeal that broke off as Bristlepaw bit down on its neck.

Huge relief flooded through Bristlepaw as she looked down at her prey. "Thank you, StarClan," she mewed fervently, even though part of her wondered whether she should be thanking StarClan when they were absent. The mouse was a scrawny thing, but at least she wouldn't be going back to camp empty-pawed. *I've got to catch more than this, though,* she thought. *What if Rosepetal doesn't think one mouse is enough?*

However, when Bristlepaw emerged from the bushes, and set the mouse down so she could taste the air for more prey, Rosepetal appeared from behind a nearby tree.

"Well done—you passed," her mentor meowed. "We can go back to camp now."

Bristlepaw hardly knew how to respond. She wanted to let out a triumphant yowl to celebrate passing her assessment, but at the same time she would have liked a more impressive catch to carry back with her. She had always imagined returning to camp loaded down with prey.

"I might find more if I go on hunting a bit longer," she suggested.

Rosepetal flicked Bristlepaw's shoulder with her tail-tip. "You've proved yourself a good hunter," she mewed kindly. "If you can catch prey in these conditions, you must be one of the strongest, most skillful young cats in the Clan. I'll be really pleased to recommend that Bramblestar make you a warrior."

She set out toward the camp; Bristlepaw had no choice but to pick up her mouse and follow. She was looking forward to her warrior ceremony—and the talk with Stemleaf that was sure to follow—but in the midst of her happiness and relief she still had the niggling sense that the mouse wasn't much of a catch, and that she could have done better.

I hope Rosepetal didn't say I passed just because she felt sorry for me.

As Bristlepaw pushed her way through the thorn tunnel into the ThunderClan camp, she was aware of every cat turning to look at her, their ears pricked with interest. Then she heard her brother, Flippaw, let out a yowl.

"Yes! She caught a mouse!"

At once Bristlepaw's Clanmates began to gather around her. "Congratulations!" Ivypool purred, while Fernsong pressed his muzzle into her shoulder, his eyes warm with pride.

Bristlepaw felt almost overwhelmed, especially when Stemleaf padded up to her and dipped his head to give her mouse an approving sniff.

"Good job!" he meowed.

"It's not much of a catch," Bristlepaw protested.

"But just remember how little prey there is out there," Stemleaf pointed out. "One scrawny mouse now is worth the same as a fat squirrel in greenleaf."

Rosepetal had said much the same, but somehow Bristlepaw was much happier to hear it from Stemleaf. "Thank you," she purred.

Meanwhile Rosepetal had fetched Bramblestar from his den; Bristlepaw saw the Clan leader stop a few tail-lengths away from her while the rest of the cats formed a ragged circle around him.

My warrior ceremony is now? Bristlepaw wondered, frantically beginning to groom herself.

The Clan leader threw back his head and let out a commanding yowl. "Let all cats old enough to catch their own prey join here beneath the Highledge for a Clan meeting!"

The four elders emerged from their den and padded up to sit together at one side of the circle. Alderheart brushed past the bramble screen of the medicine cats' den, followed a heartbeat later by Jayfeather. Sorrelstripe and Sparkpelt sat at the entrance to the nursery with Daisy, while the two litters of kits rolled and play wrestled around their mothers' paws.

When all the cats were assembled, Bramblestar beckoned Bristlepaw with his tail. She padded up to him with Rosepetal at her side. She could feel the gaze of every cat on her, and held her head high, though it was hard to ignore the nest of mice that seemed to be chasing one another inside her belly.

"Cats of ThunderClan," Bramblestar began, "one of the most important tasks a Clan leader can perform is the making of a new warrior. And that is the task in front of me today. Rosepetal, has your apprentice, Bristlepaw, learned the skills of a warrior, and does she understand the meaning of the warrior code?"

Rosepetal dipped her head to her Clan leader. "She has, and she does," she replied. "I am proud to bring her before you."

"Then I, Bramblestar, leader of ThunderClan, call upon

my warrior ancestors to look down on this apprentice," the Clan leader continued, glancing up at the sky with an unsettled expression. "She . . . has trained hard to understand the ways of your noble code, and I commend her to you as a warrior in her turn.

"Bristlepaw, do you promise to uphold the warrior code and to protect and defend your Clan, even at the cost of your life?"

Bristlepaw let her voice ring out clearly across the camp. "I do."

"Then by the powers of StarClan I give you your warrior name." Bramblestar paused. "Bristlepaw, from this moment on you will be known as Bristlefrost. I know that StarClan will honor your skill and your determination, and we welcome you as a full warrior of ThunderClan."

Bramblestar stooped to rest his muzzle on Bristlefrost's head, and she gave his shoulder a respectful lick, then took a step backward. As if at a signal, all the Clan burst out in yowls and caterwauls of acclamation.

"Bristlefrost! Bristlefrost!"

Warmth spread through Bristlefrost from ears to tail-tip. Her meager catch was forgotten in her pride and happiness. She was purring too hard to speak as her parents came up to congratulate her again, while her littermates bounced around her.

"You're awesome, Bristlefrost!" Thriftpaw meowed. "But it's our turn next, don't forget!"

"Yes, you'll both be warriors really soon now," Bristlefrost assured them.

More cats pressed up to give her their congratulations, and Bristlefrost thanked them, but her paws were tingling with impatience for the chance to talk to Stemleaf. Finally, as her Clanmates began to move away, she spotted him standing to one side.

"Bristlefrost is a great name," he told her as she padded up to him. "I'm so glad you passed this time."

"Thank you." Bristlefrost took a deep breath, and strove to stop herself from shaking. *It's now or never!* "Stemleaf," she went on, "I really—really—like you. I've always felt that we might be mates someday. And now that I'm a warrior, maybe this is the time for us to start thinking of each other in a new way?"

Stemleaf stared at her, and Bristlefrost saw to her horror that dismay, and not love, was filling his eyes. "I'm sorry," he mewed. "I had no idea you felt like this, Bristlefrost. I like you a lot, but I always thought of you as a friend—a really good friend, almost like another littermate. I've never felt . . . that way about you."

Bristlefrost felt as stunned as if a rock had fallen from the camp wall and hit her on the head. But she wasn't ready to give up yet. "But now that you know how I feel . . . do you think that in time, Stemleaf, you might feel the same way?"

Stemleaf shook his head. His eyes were full of distress, but that wasn't much comfort to Bristlefrost. "I don't think so. Actually, I . . . I like another cat." His gaze traveled across the camp to where Spotfur was playing with Sparkpelt's and Sorrelstripe's kits outside the nursery. "I'm so sorry, Bristlefrost."

"Oh . . . o-of course," Bristlefrost muttered, stumbling over her words. Any awkwardness she'd felt in the past was nothing compared to the horrible embarrassment that flooded through her now. "Don't worry about it. Just forget the whole thing."

Head down, she fled across the camp, and Stemleaf didn't follow. A few cats paused to congratulate her as she passed, but Bristlefrost didn't want to listen. Instead she plunged into the warriors' den and burrowed into the nearest nest, hiding her head under her paws and tail. This should have been such a proud moment, but now she was full of grief and humiliation. She felt as if a fox were tearing out her belly, and all she wanted was to be left alone.

"Bristlefrost?" She recognized her father's voice. "Bristlefrost, what's the matter?"

Bristlefrost didn't respond to Fernsong. *He won't understand. No cat will understand.*

I'll never be happy again.

CHAPTER 13

❧

Shadowpaw shivered as he padded behind Puddleshine down the spiral path to the Moonpool. He could see every breath the other cats took, misting the air above their heads, but he knew that the chill he felt was not only because of the snow. *There's something in the air, and it isn't right.*

He and Puddleshine were the last cats to arrive at the Moonpool meeting, and Shadowpaw realized at once that the others were wary of him. The only ones not to glance at him suspiciously were Alderheart, who greeted him kindly, and Puddleshine, who stayed close to him as they took their places beside the pool.

Shadowpaw didn't know if the other medicine cats had lost their trust in him because of his ominous message or because they believed he had lied at the Gathering about his vision. *Or maybe they think ShadowClan is up to something?* Whatever the reason, Shadowpaw had never felt so uncomfortable at a half-moon meeting.

Shadowpaw almost dreaded looking at the Moonpool, and when he did, he could see that frost had spread across its surface, covering the water in a sheen of icy blue. It looked as solid as rock. *Surely no cat has seen anything like that before!*

The other cats, too, were casting uneasy glances at the frozen surface, and none of them seemed quite sure how to conduct the meeting. Kestrelflight was the first to clear his throat and begin to speak.

"We have a little catmint beginning to grow back, in spite of the frost," he reported. "But it won't flourish unless the weather gets warmer. Cats are bound to get sick, and times ahead will be tough."

Willowshine dipped her head in agreement. "Most of the Clan cats are focused on the lack of prey," she mewed. "But we medicine cats have to look beyond our immediate needs."

A murmur of assent rose from the rest of the cats. "Sick cats can't hunt, so there'll be even less prey," Alderheart added.

An uncomfortable silence fell again, broken by Jayfeather, who asked the question that Shadowpaw knew must be on all their minds. "Has any cat received a message from StarClan?"

All the cats shook their heads. "I dreamed about our old home in the gorge," Frecklewish meowed. "But I'm sure it was only a dream, not a vision."

No cat had anything to add. Shadowpaw knew that this was the time when they should be approaching the Moonpool to share dreams with StarClan, but he could see that every one of them was reluctant to make the first move.

Finally, though no cat spoke, they began to creep closer to the water's edge, their bellies flattened to the ground as if they were stalking prey. Shadowpaw watched carefully as they touched their noses to the eerie blue surface, then followed their lead. He'd always thought he was learning the ways of medicine cats quickly, but now doubt plagued him. *What if I've been doing it wrong this whole time?* he wondered. *What if that's why StarClan isn't meeting with us?*

Shadowpaw stretched his neck out and touched his nose to the ice. He closed his eyes, waiting to catch glimpses of his warrior ancestors, or to find himself in lush grassland lit by stars, but nothing happened. When he drew back, the sky remained dark and empty. There was no sign of StarClan.

The medicine cats exchanged glances with one another, their eyes wide with dismay.

"I'm afraid this isn't just ice," Willowshine meowed. "StarClan has never abandoned us for this long."

Frecklewish nodded grimly. "We have to do something."

"We'll have to tell the Clan leaders what is happening," Alderheart meowed. "They have to understand how we all sense that StarClan has turned away from us. Jayfeather, I know you've had a bad feeling about this, and I'm beginning to think you're right. What if we've angered StarClan somehow? So they don't want us to be close to them anymore?"

Gasps and murmurs of surprise came from the other cats, and Jayfeather rolled his sightless eyes. "At last! It took you long enough."

Alderheart ignored his Clanmate's harsh tone. "What if our connection to StarClan is lost forever?" he mewed somberly.

Shadowpaw felt a twinge in his chest at the ThunderClan cats' words. *What if they're right?*

The twinge spread throughout his body and became a tingling feeling; Shadowpaw sensed that a nearby presence was trying to signal to him. He turned in a circle, looking for it, but he could see nothing except darkness and the cascade of icicles above the frozen Moonpool.

"What are you doing?" Puddleshine asked.

Shadowpaw looked up at his mentor. "I'm not sure," he replied, "but I think we should wait. I sense there's some kind of power here—something trying to get through."

"What?" Fidgetflake exclaimed.

Willowshine lashed her tail. "What do you mean, 'some kind of power'? Have you got bees in your brain?"

"This is ridiculous," Jayfeather snorted. "Why should we listen to this ShadowClan apprentice? His so-called visions are nothing like the way StarClan usually makes contact with us. Does anyone find it suspicious that only *ShadowClan* is getting visions?"

Shadowpaw's first reaction was to take offense at the cranky ThunderClan cat's dismissive tone. But then he started to ask himself if Jayfeather might be right.

Then, to his surprise, Puddleshine spoke up. "Shadowpaw may be only a ShadowClan cat," he meowed somewhat sarcastically, "as am I, but he has received important visions since he was a kit. Visions that we've all seen come to pass. I'm inclined to trust his instincts."

While Puddleshine was speaking, a light snow began to fall, drifting over the cats' fur. Jayfeather gave his pelt an irritable shake. "Snow!" he spat. "Just what the Moonpool needs!" Then he turned back to Puddleshine. "If we run after this foolish cat's flight of fancy, where will that bring us?" he demanded. "Nowhere good, that's for sure."

"But we have nothing else to go on," Puddleshine pointed out calmly. "StarClan isn't here to guide us."

More protests broke out at Puddleshine's words. Shadowpaw found it hard to listen, as the familiar pressure began to build up in his head. But he sensed that the medicine cats didn't want to argue with one another. *They're just unnerved because their connection with StarClan has been broken.*

At last Frecklewish's voice cut through the clamor. "Maybe we don't need to see StarClan to get messages from them," she suggested.

"What do you mean?" Alderheart asked, sounding just as confused as Shadowpaw felt.

"StarClan's messages are all around us, in everything we see," Frecklewish explained. "Look at the patterns in the frost as they spread across the pool. The ice is thick at the edges, but thinner as you look out toward the center. That must mean that times are hard for the Clans right now, but this leaf-bare will be over soon, and things will get back to normal."

"That makes a lot of sense," Mothwing commented, nodding understandingly.

Jayfeather gave a disdainful sniff. "If we start thinking like that, we'll end up seeing signs everywhere and making up what we would like them to mean."

Shadowpaw was inclined to agree with Jayfeather, even though he would have preferred to believe what Frecklewish said. He heard Kestrelflight break in with a heated objection, but he couldn't go on listening, because the pressure in his head was building up until he couldn't bear it anymore. The tingling in his body intensified. He forced his head back to gaze upward; the sky was still dark and starless, but when he closed his eyes, a series of bright images began to flash through his mind: one cat after another, as clear as if they were standing right in front of him.

As images of Twigbranch and Lionblaze flashed before him, a voice echoed inside Shadowpaw's head. "The Clans have forgotten the code," the voice whispered. "It has been broken time and time again, and because of the codebreakers, every Clan must pay a price. They must suffer."

The images continued to flash through Shadowpaw's mind, faster than before. He saw Crowfeather, Squirrelflight, Mothwing, Tree, Jayfeather . . . Each face tightened Shadowpaw's chest and made it harder for him to breathe, until one image stopped his breath completely.

Dovewing?

His mother's face loomed large in Shadowpaw's mind, but he couldn't understand why she was being shown to him. *She can't be one of the codebreakers—can she?*

As swiftly as the images had come, they were gone, and Shadowpaw became aware of Puddleshine prodding him in the side. "Shadowpaw, are you listening?" his mentor demanded.

Shadowpaw shook his pelt, trying to pull himself together quickly so that none of the other cats would realize that he had just had a vision. He wasn't even sure that was what it had been.

If StarClan isn't communicating with the experienced medicine cats, why would they send a vision to me?

Besides, some of the cats he had seen were standing here with him now. Shadowpaw was afraid that if he told them what he had seen and heard, they would think he was accusing them of something. *They already think I'm a stupid furball. What will they say if I call them out as codebreakers? It certainly won't help!*

"Yes, I—I'm listening," he stammered. "I'll do whatever the rest of you think is best."

Alderheart nodded kindly at his words, while Jayfeather merely grunted, but Puddleshine gave Shadowpaw a long look from narrowed eyes. He seemed to realize that Shadowpaw wasn't telling the whole truth, but he said nothing to challenge him.

The rest of the medicine cats didn't make it easy for Shadowpaw either. He saw the uneasy glances they exchanged, as if they knew that something was wrong.

"You're here to learn," Fidgetflake pointed out, "and yet you were staring up into the sky as if you know something the rest of us don't. What are you hiding?"

"Nothing," Shadowpaw protested, but he sensed Jayfeather glaring at him and found it hard to meet that pale, sightless gaze. Jayfeather might be blind, but he still saw things that other cats didn't.

But Shadowpaw wasn't ready to tell the other medicine cats about what had happened. He still didn't know himself what it meant. He clamped his jaws shut and turned his head away to avoid Jayfeather's gaze.

"I think we should follow Frecklewish's advice for now," Mothwing meowed, changing the subject briskly. "We can't rush StarClan, and we should stay alert for any signs they see fit to send us. And I also suggest that we say nothing more to our Clan leaders. We don't want to panic the Clans. We must focus on getting through this difficult time together."

Frecklewish and Willowshine purred their agreement, though there were grunts of annoyance from Jayfeather and Kestrelflight.

"And if they ask?" Kestrelflight prodded. "Do you expect me to lie to Harestar?"

Mothwing lashed her tail. "You can answer honestly without making it seem like a crisis. Tell them that StarClan hasn't said anything specific, or particularly helpful. That won't seem unusual."

Kestrelflight hissed. "Of course you'd say that."

"If you ask me," Jayfeather meowed, raising his voice above the others', "this *is* a crisis. And we should be preparing our Clans for life without StarClan—whatever that means."

Gasps of horror came from the other medicine cats. Their eyes were wide and shocked, as if the terrible future Jayfeather suggested had never occurred to them.

"No cat did ask you," Willowshine retorted tartly. "That's giving in far too soon."

"StarClan can't have abandoned us for good," Frecklewish insisted.

"That's right," Kestrelflight agreed, even though his fur was bristling with apprehension. "Once the ice melts, everything will go back to normal."

Jayfeather made no response, though his sightless eyes glared a challenge. The other medicine cats' objections soon faltered into silence; the thought of life without StarClan was enough to quiet them. Without any formal ending to the meeting they began to pad slowly up the spiral path, their heads and tails drooping in dejection. Once they were out of the hollow, they split up to return to their Clans with only a brief good-bye.

Shadowpaw and Puddleshine plodded back to Shadow-Clan territory in uneasy silence. Shadowpaw sensed that his mentor was open to listening to him, but he didn't ask any questions, and Shadowpaw didn't want to tell him anything.

When they had made their way through the brambles and into the ShadowClan camp, Puddleshine began leading the way to their den, but Shadowpaw halted.

"I want to speak to Tigerstar," he mewed.

Puddleshine turned back to him, his expression disapproving. "We all agreed not to panic the Clans," he warned his apprentice. "What are you going to tell our leader?"

"It's not about that," Shadowpaw replied. "I just want to see my father."

Puddleshine hesitated, then gave a brusque nod. "Remember what Mothwing said. Be careful what you say," he meowed, and continued to his den.

Shadowpaw padded across the camp until he reached the

Clan leader's den beneath the low-growing branches of a pine tree. Tigerstar was there, curled up with Dovewing in a nest of bracken and pine needles. For a moment Shadowpaw didn't want to wake them; then, gathering his courage, he stepped forward and shook his father's shoulder with one forepaw.

Tigerstar raised his head, blinking drowsily. "Shadowpaw? What is it?" He kept his voice low so as not to wake Dovewing, who was still deeply asleep. "Shouldn't you be at the half-moon meeting with the other medicine cats?"

"I just got back." Shadowpaw paused, reluctant to go on. *But I have to,* he thought. *If I can't tell my father, which cat can I tell?*

Tigerstar moved up and made a space in his nest for Shadowpaw to curl up beside him. "Come on, spit it out," he mewed, giving his son's ear an affectionate lick.

"When I was at the Moonpool, I had a vision," Shadowpaw began hesitantly. "I saw images of lots of different cats, and I heard a voice that said they were codebreakers. It said that because of them, all the Clans would have to suffer. And— and the last cat I saw was . . ." His voice trailed off and he glanced toward his mother.

Shadowpaw felt his belly churning as he finished speaking and tore his gaze away from Dovewing to look up at his father. Tigerstar was staring at nothing, as if he was too stunned to speak.

"Is it true?" Shadowpaw asked after a few moments. "Is she a codebreaker?"

Tigerstar turned his head to gaze at the sleeping Dovewing. "In a way, yes," he replied. "But if your mother is a codebreaker, then so am I. And I can't believe that all code-breakers are evil. Sometimes a cat might have good reasons for breaking the warrior code."

"What were your reasons?" Shadowpaw mewed diffidently, afraid that his father would be angry with him for asking such a personal question.

Tigerstar remained calm, his eyes warm as he gazed at his son. "You know that your mother and I came from different Clans, and so we never should have become mates. Dove-wing's sister, Ivypool, was against it from the beginning. But we each knew there could be no other cat for us."

"So is that why you went to the big Twolegplace, where I was born?" Shadowpaw asked.

Tigerstar nodded. "And when we came back, along with you and your littermates, every cat could see that we loved each other. Well, it took some of them a long time to accept it. The real breaking of the code was when Dovewing left Thunder-Clan and came to live in ShadowClan to be with me."

Shadowpaw thought about that for a few heartbeats. "At the time, didn't any of the medicine cats get a message from StarClan about you?" he asked eventually.

"Not a word," his father told him with a sigh. "Not until now. If what we did is so terrible, surely they would have said something at the start?"

"I don't know," Shadowpaw responded. It felt weird to be advising his father and his Clan leader as if he were a full medicine cat. "This is still new to me. I'm trying to under-stand StarClan's ways."

Tigerstar blinked thoughtfully. "Have you told this to Puddleshine?" he asked. "Or any other cat?"

"No."

"Good." Tigerstar gave another look, full of love and concern, at Dovewing's sleeping form. "If there's any chance that this vision would put Dovewing in danger, you must keep it to yourself."

Shadowpaw wasn't sure how he felt about that. It seemed to go against everything he had learned about what it meant to be a medicine cat. And if he didn't tell any cat about his vision, it might put the Clans at risk from the codebreakers.

But StarClan must be mistaken if they think Dovewing is evil, he told himself. *Or maybe I misunderstood the message.*

"Shadowpaw?" his father prompted him gently.

Shadowpaw heaved a deep sigh. "I won't tell any cat," he promised.

Reluctantly, he hauled himself out of Tigerstar's nest, dipped his head respectfully, and headed toward his own den. But he felt that it would be just as hard to sleep as it was to make contact with StarClan.

The heaviness in his head had returned; it was faint, but it felt like a warning. Shadowpaw couldn't shake the feeling that something bad was about to happen.

I only wish I knew what it was.

CHAPTER 14

❧

Rootpaw thrust his way between the boulders and waited for Dewspring to follow as they headed out of the SkyClan camp and into the forest. The clouds had parted to let through the cold sunlight of leaf-bare, and the trees cast long blue shadows over the snow. Already the light was beginning to grow red as the sun went down.

"I must be completely mouse-brained to be going along with this," Dewspring grumbled from behind his apprentice. "We've already hunted today; we're not going to catch anything now."

"We might," Rootpaw argued. "Prey might venture out as it gets darker."

"And hedgehogs fly," Dewspring retorted.

Rootpaw was pleased that he had managed to persuade his mentor to come out on one more hunt. He wanted to bring back enough prey to build up the fresh-kill pile. Then maybe his Clanmates would forgive him for that stupid business with the vole.

He'd been getting along better with Kitepaw and Turtlepaw since he had brought back the crow, but sometimes he caught them glancing at him resentfully over the dwindling fresh-kill pile. He could only assume it was because he had taken food to ThunderClan.

I never know which way to take them. Sometimes they're fine with me, and sometimes they go back to being bullies. Will it still be like that when we all become warriors?

Even worse, Rootpaw had to admit they had a point. Prey had been scarce for so long, and every cat was hungry, even though SkyClan was better off than the other Clans. It must have been hard to see that vole leaving the territory and going to another Clan. Rootpaw wondered whether his Clanmates believed he'd wanted to pay back ThunderClan, or if they knew he was just a lovesick mouse-brain.

Thinking about his visit to ThunderClan made Rootpaw hot with embarrassment all over again. *I made a complete fool of myself in front of Bristlepaw—and I was stupid to think it would have gone any other way.* The memory of her chilly civility and the way she had passed his offering along to the elders still stung.

I've got to stop thinking about a she-cat from another Clan, he decided. Instead, he knew, he had to concentrate on making it up to his own Clan, and the best way to do that was to catch more prey. The trouble was, Dewspring was right—there might not be any to hunt. Even though SkyClan was better off than the other Clans, it hadn't been easy to find the vole he had given to Bristlepaw.

But if my Clanmates are ever going to respect me, I have to try.

Clouds had covered the sun again, the red light fading into

gloom. Rootpaw padded farther into the snowy woods, tasting the air for the least sign of prey. As he had feared, he could smell nothing but cold, earth, dead plants, and the faint traces of his Clanmates' scents from when they had passed that way on earlier patrols.

"I told you this would be pointless," Dewspring meowed after a while. "It's obvious the prey is hiding from the cold, and who can blame them? Let's go back to camp and rest. We'll try again tomorrow."

Rootpaw spun around to face him, deeply disappointed. "At least let me stay out a bit longer," he begged. "Please?"

Dewspring hesitated. "If you must," he responded at last, with a sigh. "But don't stay out once it's full dark. If I have to come looking for you, I'll tell every cat in the Clan to save up their ticks, just for you."

Rootpaw cringed. Tick duty was one of the worst apprentice duties there was. "I won't!" he promised.

Once Dewspring had left, Rootpaw headed farther into the forest, scratching at the ground and sniffing under bushes and among the roots of trees. Eventually he broke out into the open, at the top of a bank that sloped down to the edge of the frozen lake. But for all his efforts, he couldn't pick up a single trace of prey.

Rootpaw was about to give in and return to camp when he caught a different scent in the air. ShadowClan? What is a ShadowClan cat doing here?

A moment later he spotted a small figure making its way

along the edge of the lake, a dark outline against the icy surface. Rootpaw darted down the bank and halted in front of the interloper.

That's Shadowpaw, the apprentice who told that weird story at the Gathering!

"What are you doing here?" Rootpaw demanded.

Shadowpaw looked startled and a little defensive. "I'm not doing anything wrong," he replied. "I'm staying within three tail-lengths of the lake, and I'm not taking prey. Anyway," he finished defiantly, "I'm a medicine cat. I'm allowed to cross territory."

"I never said you weren't," Rootpaw meowed. "But I'd still like to know where you're going."

Now the ShadowClan apprentice looked faintly guilty. "To the Moonpool," he responded.

Rootpaw blinked at him, puzzled. "I know you're training to be a medicine cat," he began, "but you're still only an apprentice. You're not supposed to be going to the Moonpool alone, are you?"

Shadowpaw ducked his head. "Well . . . I sneaked out," he admitted. "But I have a good reason. I just can't tell any cat in my Clan."

His claws raked the pebbly shore as he spoke; Rootpaw felt sympathy welling up inside him as he recognized how stressed and upset the ShadowClan apprentice was.

"I'm not in your Clan," he pointed out. "You can tell me. And I promise that anything you say will stay between the two of us."

Shadowpaw gave Rootpaw a long look, then nodded quickly, as if he had decided to trust him. "Last night was the half-moon meeting at the Moonpool," he began. "I saw some things there, but no one else did, and I'm not sure what they mean. If I tell the rest of the Clan what I saw, cats could get hurt. My father would be furious, and the other cats in the Clan already think I'm weird."

Rootpaw glanced at his paws. He didn't want Shadowpaw to see in his eyes that he had heard that said about him before, from Kitepaw, who had heard it from ShadowClan apprentices at the Gathering. "But if you don't tell any cat, something bad will happen?" Rootpaw looked at Shadowpaw, trying hard to understand.

"I don't know. I thought I would go back to the Moonpool to see if I can make any more sense of it all."

Rootpaw barely understood what the ShadowClan apprentice was talking about. He didn't know much about medicine cats, but he could tell that Shadowpaw was having a hard time. He felt sorry for him, but at the same time oddly comforted.

I thought I was the only one who felt like an outsider, not quite fitting into my Clan. Now here's Shadowpaw, and he's struggling too. It feels . . . sort of good, knowing there's another cat with the same problems.

Besides, it was a relief to realize that Tree wasn't the only Clan cat whose powers made him seem odd.

"I know I can't really help you," he meowed to Shadowpaw, "but I'll walk with you for part of the way, if that would make you feel better."

Shadowpaw blinked at him gratefully. "I'd like that."

The two cats padded along side by side. The cold was deepening as the last of the daylight died, and a chilly breeze rose from the lake. Rootpaw led the way up the bank and into the shelter of the trees.

"You can be more than three tail-lengths from the edge of the lake when you're with me," he assured Shadowpaw.

But they had hardly traveled more than a couple of fox-lengths in the forest when Rootpaw felt a sharp pain stab upward into his pad. He let out a yowl; lifting his paw, he saw a massive thorn sticking into it.

"Just what I need!" he snapped, furious with himself. "Now my Clanmates will think I can't even take a walk without getting hurt."

"They never need to know," Shadowpaw pointed out. "I'm a medicine-cat apprentice. I can treat you—it's the least I can do, when you're keeping me company."

"Okay, thanks." Rootpaw sat down and stuck his paw out.

"Give it a good lick, and get the thorn out," Shadowpaw directed. "I'm going to look for some dock leaves."

Rootpaw did as he was told. Almost the whole of the thorn was buried in his pad, but eventually he managed to grip the shank in his teeth and draw it out. A trickle of blood came with it, and he licked that away.

Meanwhile Shadowpaw returned with a couple of dock leaves in his jaws, and began chewing them up into a pulp. "This should make your paw feel better by the time you get back to camp," he told Rootpaw as he spread the pulp over his pad. "But for now you'd better walk on three legs."

"It feels better already," Rootpaw responded, relaxing as the cool juices sank into his wound. "Thanks, Shadowpaw." *Kitepaw said that Shadowpaw is seriously weird, but I think he's okay.*

By the time Shadowpaw had finished treating him, the leaf-bare gloom was deepening into night. "It's getting late," Rootpaw meowed. "I'll have to get back to camp, or Dewspring will skin my pelt and use it to line his nest."

"That's okay," Shadowpaw assured him. "I'll be fine from here. Thank you for keeping me company."

"Maybe I'll see you at the next Gathering."

"I hope so." Shadowpaw gave him a friendly nod and bounded away, heading back to the edge of the lake.

"Good luck at the Moonpool!" Rootpaw called after him, then turned toward the camp, padding along with his injured paw carefully raised. On the way, he couldn't stop thinking about what Shadowpaw had told him.

Could something bad really happen to all the Clans?

He was so caught up in his thoughts that as he brushed through the rocks at the camp entrance, he ran straight into Reedclaw, who was on watch.

"Where have you been?" the tabby she-cat asked. She gave his fur a deep sniff and added, "And why do you smell of ShadowClan?"

Rootpaw froze. He couldn't tell Reedclaw about his meeting with Shadowpaw. He'd promised not to tell any cat what they had talked about.

"I stayed out a bit longer to hunt," he explained. "I had Dewspring's permission. I must have gotten too close to the ShadowClan border."

Reedclaw gave him a skeptical look from narrowed eyes. "Okay," she mewed. "But get back to your den now. Remember that you and Needlepaw have to take out all the soiled bedding in the morning."

Like I'd forget that!

"I'll go straight there," Rootpaw promised, and padded off, conscious of Reedclaw's gaze following him across the camp. He was relieved that she hadn't questioned him further, and he had been able to keep his new friend's secret.

And I can use all four paws again, he thought. *Shadowpaw is going to be a great medicine cat!*

Remembering the concern on the young cat's face, he added to himself, *I hope he finds what he's looking for at the Moonpool.*

CHAPTER 15

Every hair on Shadowpaw's pelt tingled with apprehension as he pushed his way through the line of bushes at the top of the hollow and emerged above the Moonpool. The last time he had been here alone, he had been struck by lightning—unless the other medicine cats were right, and he'd imagined it somehow.

I must be flea-brained to risk that again, he told himself. *I know I shouldn't be here alone. But what else can I do?*

Stronger even than his fear was Shadowpaw's conviction that he had to find out more about the voice that had warned him about the codebreakers, and especially the vision he had seen of his mother, Dovewing. This vision was different from his other visions that had come true—it hadn't arrived with a seizure. And it had felt less like a vision than a conversation with a cat he knew. *So is it real . . . ?*

He had to know whether the vision was really from StarClan and figure out what it meant.

Gazing down at the Moonpool, Shadowpaw saw that the icy covering was thicker still. Barely a glimmer of light fell on it from the heavily clouded sky. When Puddleshine had first brought him here, he had been overwhelmed by the Moonpool's beauty. Now it seemed ominous, and it took all Shadowpaw's courage to set his paws on the spiral path that led down to the water's edge. But he had to be back in camp before dawn, or risk trouble from his mentor and his Clan leader. He had no time to waste.

The night was dark and silent as Shadowpaw approached the pool. Stretching out one forepaw, he cleared away the loose snow from the frozen surface and closed his eyes as he touched his nose to it.

Cold spread through Shadowpaw's body, gripping every nerve and muscle and seeming to freeze his blood, as if he were slowly turning to ice. He bore it as long as he could, but when finally he sat up again, breaking the contact, there had been no response from StarClan. Shadowpaw wasn't sure whether he was sorry or relieved.

But as Shadowpaw headed for the bottom of the path, ready to give up and go home, the voice spoke once again in his mind. "The codebreakers are still among you. . . ."

Shadowpaw halted, sliding out his claws to dig deep into the hard ground, then stood motionless as if he really had turned to ice.

"StarClan, you must be wrong this time!" he meowed aloud. "The cats you showed me last time are good cats."

An image of Dovewing flashed into his mind: her sleek gray pelt, her green eyes shining with love for him or with defiance against anything that threatened her Clan or her kin.

"My mother is one of the strongest and most heroic cats

in all the Clans," he protested.

"StarClan is never wrong," the voice responded. "And you know it, Shadowpaw. The Clans have a code for a reason. It's supposed to be followed." The speaker's voice had deepened into a growl. *It's a tom,* Shadowpaw realized, and fear shook him from ears to tail-tip. *Who is he? What does he want?*

"Or do you not believe in the code yourself?" the voice continued, mocking. "Some medicine cat you are!"

"I do believe in the code!" Shadowpaw insisted, indignation helping him to control his terror. "But I believe in my mother, too. And if I know she is a good cat, then who's to say the other codebreakers aren't too?"

The voice made no reply, and as the moments dragged by, Shadowpaw wondered if he had said something terrible, something that insulted this ancestral spirit who had spoken to him when all the other starry warriors had fallen silent.

I don't know everything about StarClan yet. Maybe they don't like being questioned or contradicted. If this voice was the only connection the Clans still had to their warrior ancestors, and Shadowpaw had chased it away . . . *If that's true, then every cat will despise me—and they'd be right to.*

Then the voice spoke again. "Fine. Don't listen to the messages at the Moonpool." The tone was so low and menacing that ice trickled down Shadowpaw's spine and every hair on his pelt lifted with the intensity of his fear. "Let the codebreakers live among you, until no cat respects the rules. See what happens then."

The warning shook Shadowpaw's conviction. "But what if

cats aren't setting out to break the code? Or what if they've stopped? Surely StarClan won't punish them too severely. They won't, will they? They can't!"

"The code must always be respected," the voice continued. "The ways of the Clans cannot be scattered to the wind. Soon, Shadowpaw, you will see the consequences that will befall the Clans if cats ignore the code. Bramblestar will get sick, and it will seem that nothing can cure him."

"Bramblestar!" Shadowpaw gasped. "No! He's a great leader. He never did anything wrong."

"Oh, of course not." The voice was mocking. "The wonderful, respected leader of ThunderClan! However, the trouble coming to the Clans will fall on him first."

Shadowpaw gazed up into the darkness, wishing he could see the face of the warrior spirit who was saying these terrible things. He wanted to defy him and reject what he was saying, but he couldn't. He believed every word of it.

"Isn't there anything we can do?" he asked, his voice quavering.

"Yes, there is a way," the voice replied, the mocking tone giving way to reassurance. "Listen carefully, and I'll tell you what you must do. . . ."

Shadowpaw nodded, pricking his ears to take in the StarClan warrior's instructions. But as the plan unfolded, he grew more and more uneasy.

This sounds so dangerous . . . maybe even crazy. But who am I to question StarClan? He was only an apprentice. It would be arrogant of him to think that he knew better.

Still, the thought of going back to the Clans and reporting what he had discovered made Shadowpaw feel a little sick. *Puddleshine and Jayfeather would never go along with this . . . it goes against everything a medicine cat is taught!* He knew that many of the older medicine cats didn't fully trust him. Coming back with a plan like this would only make them more convinced that Shadowpaw was crazy.

Even if I could convince Alderheart and Puddleshine . . . Jayfeather won't go along. He thinks I'm a stupid apprentice, and it's all in my imagination. And now it was happening again. *Why am I the only cat StarClan has given this message? No way will they ever believe me!*

But then Shadowpaw realized something. Bramblestar had seemed strong and healthy the last time Shadowpaw had seen him at the Gathering. If he suddenly got sick, then that would prove that StarClan's warning was important. Then the medicine cats would listen to him. And if Bramblestar didn't get sick, maybe Shadowpaw wouldn't need to say anything.

"Are you a strong cat?" the voice asked him. "Are you ready to carry out my instructions?"

"Yes, I will," Shadowpaw replied. *But before I do,* he added privately to himself, *there's one cat I need to talk to.*

"Then go," the voice ordered. "And remember—the future of the Clans rests on your shoulders."

Shadowpaw flinched. Not too much pressure, there. But he dared not refuse it, and the voice said nothing more. All he could do was obey.

Exhausted by stress and fear, Shadowpaw toiled up the path that led away from the Moonpool, feeling as shaken as he had when Puddleshine had first taken him there. He had hoped that another encounter with the voice would have made him feel better. Instead he had a whole new set of worries.

The journey back to ShadowClan territory had never seemed so long, but there was still no sign of dawn in the sky when Shadowpaw staggered into camp and sneaked back into the medicine cats' den. Puddleshine was asleep, snoring quietly, and Shadowpaw was able to curl up in his own nest without disturbing him.

He sank at once into sleep, but his worries followed him even into his dreams. He was standing in the forest, looking down at Bramblestar, who lay unconscious at his paws. The ThunderClan leader's eyes were closed, and white flakes of snow were settling in his dark tabby fur.

Shadowpaw woke with a jerk. Gray light was shining into the den, and Puddleshine was already up and out somewhere. Gathering his courage, Shadowpaw headed across the camp and halted outside Tigerstar's den.

To his relief, Dovewing wasn't there. Tigerstar was awake and grooming himself when Shadowpaw stuck his head inside.

"Is something bothering you?" Tigerstar asked, looking up and beckoning with his tail for his son to enter the den. Shadowpaw nodded solemnly. "Then come and tell me what it is."

Shadowpaw padded inside and sat next to his father. "Tigerstar," he meowed grimly, "we have to talk."

CHAPTER 16

❧

The last border patrols of the day had just left the camp, and the remaining cats of ThunderClan were milling around outside the warriors' den while Squirrelflight organized them to go hunting. Though the fierce cold still gripped their territory, most of them seemed eager and optimistic, their eyes bright with purpose.

Bristlefrost stood a little way apart, wondering how her Clanmates could act so cheerful. For a short while the sun had broken through the heavy clouds of leaf-bare, but no light had penetrated the darkness of her heart.

"Hey, Bristlefrost!" Twigbranch called to her. "Do you want to hunt with us?"

Normally Bristlefrost would have agreed at once, pleased to have been invited. All she had ever wanted was to be a warrior and hunt for her Clan. But today she couldn't summon up any enthusiasm.

She shook her head. "No, thanks. I . . . er . . . there's a thorn in my bedding and I need to get it out."

Twigbranch's whiskers twitched as if she thought that was a feeble excuse, and Bristlefrost had to admit to herself that her Clanmate was right. She turned listlessly and was about to enter the den when she felt teeth fasten in her shoulder fur and turned her head to see her former mentor, Rosepetal. Ignoring Bristlefrost's cry of protest, Rosepetal dragged her to a secluded spot between the outer branches of the den and the wall of the stone hollow.

"What's going on?" Bristlefrost asked, bewildered.

"What's going on with *you*?" the cream-colored she-cat challenged her. "You've just been made a full warrior, and that was always your dream—or so I thought. So why are you moping around camp like some cat stole your prey?"

Bristlefrost didn't want to reply. She knew Rosepetal would just think she was being ridiculous, mooning over Stemleaf when the Clan had so many more important problems to face. But her feelings were still so sharp, so overwhelming, that to her horror she found herself pouring out everything to her former mentor.

"I really like Stemleaf," she confessed. "And I was sure that we were meant to be mates, just as soon as I became a warrior. But he wasn't thinking about that at all." Her voice shook with misery as she remembered that terrible conversation. "The whole time, he's wanted to be mates with Spotfur. I've been working so hard, and now . . . it feels like it's all been for nothing."

Rosepetal nodded. To Bristlefrost's surprise, her eyes were kind. "I know exactly how you feel," she meowed. "I've been in that position myself."

Bristlefrost's tail shot up in amazement. "You have?" She

found it hard to believe that Rosepetal—such a beautiful, graceful she-cat, with all the skills a warrior needed—had ever pined for something she couldn't have.

"Of course," Rosepetal went on calmly. "Every cat has been there at least once. I know how painful it is when something, or some cat, that you've set your heart on doesn't work out."

"How did you get through it?" Bristlefrost asked.

"I focused on the things I could control," Rosepetal replied. "Like being the best warrior I could be. And you can do the same. All your training isn't a waste if you can use it for the good of your Clan. And maybe one day you'll find the right mate. You're a young cat; there's no rush. Meanwhile, your Clan needs you."

Bristlefrost nodded slowly. Though Stemleaf's rejection still hurt, Rosepetal's words made sense. Maybe she was right. Maybe Bristlefrost just needed to find her purpose within the Clan.

"Thank you," she murmured. "I'll try my best."

"Good." Rosepetal swished her tail with satisfaction. "Now, if you're up to it, your Clanmates are getting ready to hunt. They could really use your help, and if you hurry, there's still time for you to join them."

Bristlefrost nodded, and rushed around the side of the den to where the cats were assembling. Most of them had already left, but one group remained, gathering around the Clan leader.

Seeing that Stemleaf was part of the group, Bristlefrost hesitated, almost changing her mind. Then she remembered what Rosepetal had said and held her head high as she joined the others.

I am a warrior, she reminded herself. *I have a job to do.*

Stemleaf tried to catch her eye, beckoning with his tail in a welcoming gesture, but Bristlefrost wasn't ready to face him yet. Instead she looked away, focusing on Bramblestar, who was issuing some final instructions, with Squirrelflight by his side.

"I know prey is scarce," he meowed. "But you shouldn't bother coming back until you have something to show for your efforts. If you're real warriors, you'll freeze your paws off if you have to, for the survival of your Clan."

As she listened, Bristlefrost grew uneasy at the tone of her leader's words. His voice sounded rougher than usual, not like the calm, measured leader Bristlefrost had always admired.

Squirrelflight seemed to share her misgivings. "Aren't you being a little harsh?" she murmured to Bramblestar. "All the warriors are doing their best under very difficult conditions."

Bramblestar whipped his head around to face her, a hostile light in his eyes. "You would make excuses for them," he snapped. "You always had a soft spot for weak cats."

Squirrelflight stared at him as if she couldn't believe what he had said to her. Bristlefrost heard one or two stifled gasps from the cats around her and saw them exchanging uncomfortable glances.

Every cat knew that not many moons had passed since Squirrelflight and Leafpool had been gravely injured in a rockslide. Leafpool had died, and Squirrelflight had nearly died, her spirit walking in StarClan as her body healed. In part, it was her love for Bramblestar, and his for her, that had drawn her back into the living world.

So why is he being so mean to her now?

A heartbeat later, Bramblestar seemed to realize that he had gone too far. "I'm sorry if I'm being too stern," he mumbled. "It's just that my responsibilities as leader are weighing more heavily on me in these hard times. I can't just stand by and see my Clan starve."

"It's okay," Squirrelflight mewed, touching his shoulder with her tail-tip. "We understand."

Maybe you *do,* Bristlefrost thought. *I'm not sure I could be so forgiving.*

"I'll lead this hunt myself," Bramblestar announced abruptly. Without another word, he stalked off toward the camp entrance. Squirrelflight gathered the remaining warriors with a wave of her tail, and they followed their Clan leader out into the forest.

"Was that weird or what?"

Bristlefrost started as she realized that Stemleaf had fallen into step beside her. For a moment she was so concerned by what she had just heard and seen that she scarcely reacted to having the cat she loved padding along so close to her. She simply nodded, wide-eyed, then slowed her pace until she was trailing behind the rest of the group.

Bristlefrost knew that this leaf-bare had been tough on every cat. They were all getting more irritable than usual. But if even Bramblestar, usually so even-tempered, was being affected, perhaps things were worse than she had realized.

This just shows that Rosepetal is right, she thought. *I have to dedicate myself to being the best warrior I can be. Nothing is more important than ThunderClan's survival—not even my heart.*

The cats padded through the snow-covered forest, their ears pricked for the least sound and their jaws parted to taste the air for the scent of prey. Soon Bristlefrost's paws were so numb she couldn't feel them, and even her thick gray pelt was no protection against the probing claws of cold.

Now and again Bramblestar would signal with his tail for the hunting patrol to halt. They would raise their noses in the air, checking even more carefully for scent on every passing breeze. But however hard they tried, no cat could pick up the least trace of prey.

Moving along after one of these stops, Bristlefrost noticed that there was something strange about the way that Bramblestar was walking. Usually the ThunderClan leader passed through the forest as silent as the wind. Now he slammed his paws down, breaking twigs and crushing dead leaves.

If there is any prey out here, he'll drive it all away, making that racket, Bristlefrost thought.

Squirrelflight was staring uneasily at Bramblestar as he blundered around a tree stump and stumbled over a projecting root.

"Bramblestar," she began, bounding up to him, "are you—"

Bramblestar turned on her savagely. "For StarClan's sake," he hissed, "leave me alone! I'm fine. I don't need—"

He broke off with a choking cry. Bristlefrost watched in horror as his legs buckled and he sank to the ground. He made one attempt to rise, his forepaws scrabbling in the snow, then flopped back into an unmoving heap.

Yowls of consternation came from the nearby cats. Bristlefrost let out a gasp of dismay and raced up to Bramblestar's side. Squirrelflight was already checking on him.

"He's breathing," she meowed, her green eyes wide with fear. "But I can't wake him."

"What do you want us to do?" Bristlefrost asked.

Squirrelflight was clearly making a massive effort to pull herself together. "We have to get him back to the medicine cats' den," she replied. "Jayfeather and Alderheart will know what he needs."

Bristlefrost looked helplessly around her. Some of the warriors were spread out, absorbed in their search for prey, still unaware of what had happened, while others clustered around, gazing in horror at their fallen leader.

"What about the hunt?" Bristlefrost asked. "Bramblestar told us not to go back to camp until we'd caught something."

"He's in no position to give orders right now," Squirrelflight pointed out. "I'll stay behind and finish the hunt with the rest of the patrol. Bramblestar will need something to eat if he's to recover from this . . . whatever it is," she added, a slight tremor in her voice. "Will you and Stemleaf take him back to camp?"

For a moment, Bristlefrost tensed. She hadn't been alone with Stemleaf since that dreadful day she had told him how she felt about him. But she refused to think about that. Their Clan leader needed help; she and Stemleaf had to give it to him.

While Squirrelflight gathered the remaining warriors together, Stemleaf crouched down in the snow beside Bramblestar, and Bristlefrost pushed their leader onto his back. He was so deeply unconscious that he didn't react at all to being moved.

"Uh . . . he's a heavy cat!" Stemleaf gasped as he staggered to his paws. "And he's cold. It feels like I'm carrying a load of snow."

With Bristlefrost walking alongside and steadying Bramblestar on Stemleaf's back, they slowly made their way through the forest. Bramblestar lay limp, his paws dangling; only the slight movement of his whiskers told Bristlefrost that he was still breathing.

When they reached the stone hollow, Thornclaw, who was on watch, took one look at them and raced across the camp to the medicine cats' den. A few moments later he emerged from behind the bramble screen, with Alderheart just behind him.

"What happened?" Alderheart asked, hurrying up to Bramblestar's side.

While Stemleaf carried Bramblestar into the den, Bristlefrost explained how Bramblestar had seemed to lose his focus in the hunt, and then had collapsed and not moved or spoken since.

"That doesn't make any sense," Alderheart murmured.

Bristlefrost felt a jolt of fear at her heart. She had assumed that once Bramblestar reached the medicine cats, they would know what to do. Instead Alderheart was gazing at him with all the confusion and worry that she felt. Of course— Bramblestar wasn't only Alderheart's Clan leader; he was his father too.

At Alderheart's direction, she pulled together moss and bracken from the store in the den to make a nest for Bramblestar. Stemleaf lowered him gently into it.

"He's so cold," Alderheart mewed, stretching out a paw to touch Bramblestar's forehead. "I just don't understand. He was fine when he left for the hunt. How did he get sick so quickly?"

Neither Bristlefrost nor Stemleaf could answer that question.

"Is he losing a life?" Bristlefrost asked.

Alderheart shook his head. "No, not yet. But if we can't give him the right treatment soon, he will."

Leaving his father's side, Alderheart padded to the back of the den where the medicine cats kept their herbs. Bristlefrost lingered, watching him curiously; he was sorting through the various heaps, but he didn't seem to know what he was looking for.

As she watched, the bramble screen at the entrance to the den was brushed back, and Jayfeather appeared. He halted, sniffing, then asked, "Bramblestar's here? What's happening?"

Alderheart came forward again and explained to Jayfeather what Bristlefrost had told him. "Bramblestar needs treatment," he finished. "But I'm not sure what to do for him."

"I'll examine him," Jayfeather began, then broke off and swung around so that he was facing Bristlefrost; she found it hard to believe that he couldn't see her.

"What are you doing, hanging about here like a spare piece of prey?" he demanded. "Out. Now."

"Okay." Bristlefrost turned to go, hearing Jayfeather ask if Alderheart had given Bramblestar anything.

"No, I haven't gotten that far yet," Alderheart replied.

As he spoke, Bristlefrost heard a sudden rustling, and a weak voice calling, "Alderheart?"

Bristlefrost spun around to see Bramblestar struggling to sit up, his amber eyes wide and intense. Alderheart sprang to his side, supporting his father against his shoulder.

"Alderheart . . . I must talk to you." Bramblestar's voice was weak, his words separated by desperate gasps, his chest heaving with the effort of speaking.

"No, you have to rest," Alderheart mewed. "You're here in my den; we'll take care of you."

"No . . ." Bramblestar's tail lashed once and for a moment Bristlefrost caught a glimpse of the strong and positive leader he had always been. "Listen. I had a terrible dream. . . ."

"Let him talk," Jayfeather meowed. "Whatever it is, he needs to get it off his chest."

"I saw the Clans fighting one another," Bramblestar went on, his voice strengthening slightly. "Everything was chaos. The sky was dark—there were no stars, only a thin claw-scratch of a moon. And then even that faded, and I couldn't see the cats anymore. I could only hear their terrible howls and screeches as the battle went on."

Alderheart stifled a gasp, deep trouble in his face. "There were no stars . . . ," he whispered.

"Is it true?" Bramblestar asked. "Has StarClan forsaken us?"

Alderheart glanced up at Jayfeather, then back at his father. At the same moment, Bristlefrost saw Jayfeather's expression change to mingled anger and panic.

"Alderheart!" Jayfeather took a pace toward the younger medicine cat, his tail raised as if to prevent the younger cat from speaking.

Alderheart shook his head slightly. "The time for silence is over," he told Jayfeather. "Yes, it's true," he responded to his father's question. "StarClan still isn't sending us messages, and we don't know why."

Bristlefrost felt a jolt in her belly as if some cat had thrown a rock at her. *I had no idea!* she thought. *Still nothing from StarClan, moons later? Is that why Jayfeather and Alderheart have been looking so stressed lately?*

"The medicine cats decided we would say nothing!" Jayfeather snapped. "Alderheart, you agreed—"

"You can't hide StarClan's abandonment from the leaders!" Bramblestar interrupted him. "It's far too serious. Alderheart, you were right to be honest." His chest heaved again, his back arching, as if he was struggling to stay conscious. His voice rasped as he continued, "I'll remember you were honest, when not many cats were."

And what does that *mean?* Bristlefrost wondered. Jayfeather looked taken aback, as if he didn't understand it, either.

"Action must be taken," Bramblestar went on, still in the same throaty tone. "But Alderheart, you shouldn't be afraid. You've done the right thing by telling me."

"What action?" Alderheart asked, his expression uncertain. "Bramblestar, tell us what you want us to do."

Another spasm shook Bramblestar's body, and his voice had weakened again as he replied, "Fetch Squirrelflight. . . . Tell the leaders. . . . You must get back in touch with StarClan!"

Alderheart looked up and spotted Bristlefrost still standing beside the entrance to the den. "Fetch Squirrelflight," he repeated.

Bristlefrost nodded, but before she could move, another convulsion shook Bramblestar. He reared up out of his nest, all four paws lashing as if he was trying to attack an enemy. His head was thrown back, his jaws stretched wide in a terrible silent wailing. Then he went limp and collapsed to lie unmoving among the moss and bracken.

CHAPTER 17

❧

A blustering wind flattened Rootpaw's fur to his sides and made his eyes water as he gazed down at the medicine cats around the frozen Moonpool. He couldn't believe that he had been chosen to come here and witness this desperate attempt to make contact with StarClan, along with three of the Clan leaders and many senior warriors. He stared in wonder at the icy cascade where a stream had frozen as it poured down into the pool, and at the frosty glitter of icicles hanging from the rocks.

The medicine cats were padding restlessly around the pool. From time to time one of them would stretch out a paw and touch the surface, as if they were testing the ice. Rootpaw noticed that none of them looked happy about what they were doing; Mothwing and Jayfeather especially seemed edgy, their anxiety clear in their twitching tails and whiskers.

Rootpaw's sister, Needlepaw, stood beside him, and just behind them their parents, Violetshine and Tree. They waited at the top of the hollow, inside the line of bushes, at a respectful distance from the pool itself. Alongside, stretching out in a line, were the representatives of the other Clans.

I know this is an honor and all, Rootpaw thought, flexing his claws in a futile effort to keep his paws warm. *But I wish they would get on with it!*

"What are they doing down there?" he asked, not really expecting an answer. "If the water is frozen solid, what can they do? It's not like they can start chipping away at the ice with their claws, right?"

"The leaders have suggested using a thick branch," Tree told him. "If they position it over a rock, they can lever it to hit the ice much harder. They hope that breaking the ice will help the medicine cats contact StarClan."

Rootpaw tried and failed to imagine any cat doing that. *I wonder whose mouse-brained idea that was!*

"I don't understand what point there is in warriors being here at all," Needlepaw mewed, shivering and fluffing out her fur against the cold. "We're not allowed down by the pool, so what good can we do any cat, standing up here freezing our paws off?"

"The medicine cats asked us to come, because they might need help," Violetshine responded. "And it shows StarClan how determined we all are to get in contact with our ancestors again."

"But are warriors even supposed to be here?" Needlepaw asked. "I thought the Moonpool was only for medicine cats."

Tree and Violetshine exchanged a glance. "That's how Fidgetflake sees it, too," Tree replied. "But Frecklewish and some of the leaders feel . . . differently."

"They think that reconnecting with StarClan is more

important than tiptoeing around the Moonpool," Violetshine explained.

"So what will happen if they can't break through the ice?" Rootpaw asked, hoping to change the subject.

A new voice broke into the conversation. "I don't know."

Rootpaw turned to see Bristlepaw standing nearby, at the edge of the group of ThunderClan cats. It was the first time they had met since the embarrassing incident with the vole, and Rootpaw wasn't sure how he should behave around her. He was aware of Needlepaw watching him with a teasing look in her eyes, but he ignored her with a twitch of his tail and padded over to join the ThunderClan apprentice.

Then he noticed that there was something different about Bristlepaw: a sadness in her eyes that hadn't been there before. *I hope it's not because she feels sorry for me.*

"Hi, Bristlepaw," he meowed.

Bristlepaw took a pace forward that brought her to his side. "It's Bristlefrost," she told him. "I'm a warrior now."

"Hey, that's great!" Rootpaw was pleased for her, but even more confused. *If she's just been made a warrior, why doesn't she look happy?* "Congratulations."

"Thanks, Rootpaw. I wanted to see you," Bristlefrost went on, "because I need to tell you how sorry I am for the way I behaved when you brought me the vole. I was rude and ungrateful."

Rootpaw dipped his head. "Don't worry about it," he mewed. "I know it was stupid, and I shouldn't have done it."

"No, you didn't do anything wrong," Bristlefrost insisted. "You did a kind thing for me, and I treated you horribly. Please forgive me, Rootpaw."

"Of course I do!" Rootpaw replied, happiness spurting up inside him. But the feeling quickly died as he saw how sad Bristlefrost looked. "What's wrong?" he asked her. "You look a little down."

Bristlefrost hesitated, staring down at her paws. "Things haven't been going the way I hoped since I became a warrior," she admitted eventually.

"What do you mean?" Rootpaw asked.

"Oh . . . This leaf-bare is hard on every cat, and I don't feel I've done enough to help my Clan. Right now I'm feeling kind of useless."

Rootpaw could understand that, but all the same he didn't feel it was enough to explain the sorrow in Bristlefrost's eyes. Whatever was on her mind, for now at least she was keeping it to herself.

"But you're one of the greatest cats I've ever met," Rootpaw protested, even though he knew the praise might make her squirm. *I still feel the same about her, even after that stupid episode with the vole.* "You saved my life when my own Clanmates were too scared even to try. If it weren't for you, I'd be at the bottom of the lake right now, frozen solid like the medicine cats say the Moonpool is. And you came to check on me every day while I was recovering."

Bristlefrost shrugged; she looked a little embarrassed, but not, Rootpaw thought, angry with him. "Any cat would have done that," she meowed. "But what have I done since?"

"No warrior can do much while this leaf-bare lasts," Root-paw stated firmly. "And once it's over, you'll be one of the warriors who gets your Clan back on its paws. I'm sure of it."

Bristlefrost looked up; her eyes glowed, making Rootpaw's heart flutter weirdly in his chest. For a moment he felt that there was more than gratitude in her gaze.

"Bristlefrost—" he began.

An earsplitting crack from below interrupted Rootpaw. He spun around to stare down into the hollow. It was so much louder than the sound of the ice breaking on the lake when he'd fallen in—it must mean that the medicine cats had bro-ken through. Yet when the echo died away, it was followed by complete silence. The group of medicine cats stood ranged around the pool, gazing down at the surface.

"Do you know what's supposed to happen when the ice breaks?" Rootpaw asked, turning back to Bristlefrost.

The gray she-cat shook her head. "I have no idea," she replied. "Only medicine cats can commune with StarClan, right? Maybe it worked and we just can't see them."

Rootpaw felt every hair on his pelt rising at the thought that warriors of StarClan might be gathered around the Moonpool, invisible. "It's so weird, watching the medicine cats like this," he murmured.

Bristlefrost did not speak for a moment, ears angled down toward the pool. "Listen," she continued. "I can hear the med-icine cats murmuring among themselves. That's probably not a good sign."

Rootpaw nodded agreement as he heard the muted meows drifting upward from the cats around the pool. Glancing beyond Bristlefrost, wondering how the other Clans were reacting, he felt that something wasn't quite right, and it took him a few heartbeats to work out what it was.

"Why are there no ShadowClan cats here?" he asked.

It was Needlepaw who replied. "I overheard Violetshine telling Tree that ShadowClan wasn't invited, because of the weirdness with their medicine-cat apprentice. The other Clans are wondering if he might be the problem."

"You mean they think Shadowpaw is the reason why StarClan isn't communicating?" Rootpaw asked.

"Some cats do," Needlepaw replied.

Rootpaw thought back to his conversation with Shadow-paw in the twilit woods, when the apprentice was on his way to the Moonpool. He had seemed really worried; he had spoken about something bad coming to all the Clans. Rootpaw thought he seemed kind, and clearly Shadowpaw was already a skilled medicine-cat apprentice.

He treated my wounded paw, and it healed really quickly. How could a healer like that be the problem?

Rootpaw wanted to ask Bristlefrost or Needlepaw that question, but he couldn't do so without revealing that Shadow-paw had been sneaking off to the Moonpool on his own. *And I walked part of the way with him when I should have been hunting. No way can I tell that to any cat!*

Lost in his thoughts about Shadowpaw, Rootpaw hadn't noticed that Frecklewish had begun to climb the spiral path toward the waiting warriors. But now he saw that she had reached the top of the hollow and stood facing them. She looked weary and dejected, and Rootpaw realized there had been no communication with StarClan.

"We have dented the ice," Frecklewish announced, "but we haven't hit water yet. The pool may be frozen all the way through."

Murmurs and gasps of consternation came from the Clan cats, and they exchanged glances of dismay.

"We may need your help in breaking the ice after all," Frecklewish added.

"No. We did not agree to that." Jayfeather had climbed the path behind Frecklewish, and now stood at her side, his tabby fur bristling with indignation. "The Moonpool is the special place shown to us by StarClan, and it should only be touched by medicine cats."

"We've already discussed this, Jayfeather," Frecklewish retorted, her pelt too beginning to rise. "The Moonpool is only special because it's the way that we can reach StarClan. And if we can't do that, and they can't reach us either, then isn't it our job to do everything we can to help StarClan get through?"

Jayfeather's only reply was a hiss of indignation as he turned his head away.

Meanwhile, the remaining medicine cats had left the side of the pool and joined the others at the top of the hollow. "What do the Clan leaders think?" Alderheart asked. "Tell us what you want to do."

Leafstar, Mistystar, and Harestar glanced toward Squirrel-flight, the ThunderClan deputy. Earlier she had told the others that Bramblestar couldn't make the journey to the Moonpool because he had hurt his paw hunting.

"What do you think?" Leafstar asked her. "I understand Bramblestar is very concerned that no cat can make contact with StarClan. That's why we started this whole operation."

Squirrelflight looked torn, as if she wasn't sure how to reply. "Yes, Bramblestar is concerned," she began, "but . . ." Her voice trailed off and she looked down at her paws.

"Well, I'm inclined to agree with Frecklewish," Leafstar meowed. "At the gorge, our medicine cats never had any trouble connecting with our ancestors."

Harestar twitched his whiskers nervously. "Yes, I agree too. WindClan has suffered the worst of this harsh weather. Hunting is nearly impossible, and my cats are starving. We need StarClan's guidance, so we must do all we can to restore the connection."

"What do you think, Mistystar?" Leafstar asked, when the RiverClan leader did not speak.

Mistystar shook her head. "I'm not sure . . . ," she responded reluctantly. "I understand that the medicine cats have different feelings about this. So I'd rather leave RiverClan's decision in the paws of my medicine cats."

Mothwing and Willowshine exchanged a glance. "I'm not sure the warriors should help," Willowshine mewed. "But I miss StarClan's advice as much as any cat. I'll go with the majority decision."

"So will I," Mothwing added.

Every cat turned to look at Squirrelflight, who sighed and seemed reluctant to speak. "I must vote with Bramblestar," she stated at last; Rootpaw could see the tension in her gaze. "He believes that we desperately need StarClan's guidance. The warriors should break the ice."

At Squirrelflight's words the medicine cats stood back to allow the warriors to take the spiral path. The Clan leaders led the way, their tails waving as they charged downward to the edge of the pool. Rootpaw was aware of Jayfeather glaring at them, his fur bushed out until the scrawny cat looked twice his normal size.

Rootpaw hung back, a mixture of confusion and despair dragging at his paws. *Is this right?* he asked himself.

Behind him, Tree abruptly stopped. "I don't think I can do this," he said aloud.

A chorus of surprise came from the cats surrounding them. "What does that mean?" Birchfall, from ThunderClan, asked. Rootpaw thought his tone was a little hostile.

Tree didn't look bothered as he stared back at the Thunder-Clan cat. "It doesn't feel right," he said simply. "I don't fully understand all your Clan beliefs, but I know that the Moon-pool is a sacred place. I know that the medicine cats have special powers. I'm not sure we should be intruding."

Rootpaw wished the ground would open up and swallow him whole. *Please stop, please stop,* he wished fiercely. *They already think you're strange enough.*

"You're a warrior now, Tree," Crowfeather, the WindClan

deputy, meowed irritably. "It's not your job to decide what's right. It's your job to obey your leader."

"And Leafstar said yes," Birchfall added.

All eyes turned to Leafstar, who was watching the scene from the bottom of the spiral path, where she stood with Squirrelflight. The SkyClan leader looked torn.

"I'm not a warrior," Tree clarified. "I'm a mediator. And as mediator, it troubles me that ShadowClan was not included in this effort. I believe I made that clear before."

Leafstar's eyes flashed with annoyance. "That was the leaders' decision."

"But why?" Tree asked. "Because their medicine-cat apprentice is a little odd? Who's not?"

Rootpaw cringed. He wondered whether, if he wished hard enough, he might become invisible.

By now Tree's argument was holding up the procession of warriors. Some cats behind him grumbled in annoyance, but others seemed swayed by his argument.

"Maybe we shouldn't be touching the Moonpool," Spotfur, a she-cat from ThunderClan, mewed, looking thoughtful. "I wouldn't want to upset any cat . . . dead or alive."

"The medicine cats have always said the Moonpool is sacred," Stemleaf agreed. "Should we believe that's changed, just because we're desperate to hear from StarClan?"

"Oh, come on." Rootpaw's heart leaped at the sound of Bristlefrost's voice. The ThunderClan warrior swerved around her two Clanmates to continue along the path. "You all heard the leaders. We have to do whatever we can to reach StarClan!"

But Tree, Stemleaf, and Spotfur all still hesitated. Tree's gaze was leveled squarely on his leader.

Leafstar flicked her tail in annoyance. "Very well," she said. "Any SkyClan cat who doesn't feel comfortable touching the Moonpool, turn back. Your objections have been heard."

Tree nodded, satisfied. Then he turned and began walking up the spiral path, pushing his way past a cluster of RiverClan warriors who were still heading down. Rootpaw heard them grumble in annoyance.

He looked at his mother, Violetshine, who watched Tree leave with a bemused expression. Finally she turned to face Rootpaw, who shot her a questioning look. But she shook her head slightly and continued down the spiral path.

"I'm following Tree," Needlepaw said decisively from behind Rootpaw. "I'm not sure this is right." She turned back to follow her father.

"All ThunderClan warriors," Squirrelflight called in a tight voice, "we need you to help break the ice. As your acting leader, I command you to help!"

Rootpaw could hear the grumbles of Spotfur and Stemleaf. His own paws trembled with indecision. *Does Tree have a point? Is this right?*

But then he saw Bristlefrost stroll past him, following Violetshine. She glanced at Rootpaw and winked.

Without another thought, he fell into step behind the

ThunderClan warrior.

I'm in.

"One, two, three!" Crowfeather yelled a few moments later. Rootpaw pressed his forepaws against the back of a huge, long, flat rock, squeezed between the bodies of countless warriors from four Clans. "Now!"

They all heaved forward, grunting, and managed to push the rock up onto the first of two logs. Alderheart, it seemed, had found the rock lying against the wall of the Moonpool cave, and Crowfeather, Hawkwing, and Reedwhisker had worked together to organize the warriors to move it closer to the Moonpool itself. It was the hope of the three deputies, who'd taken charge of the scene, that once the rock was placed across three logs, the warriors could push it to the edge of the Moonpool, then push it in. They all hoped that the rock was heavy enough—and, when turned on its end, sharp enough—to break through the final layer of ice.

Rootpaw's shoulders ached. Even with countless warriors' help, the rock was heavy. Which was exactly why they all hoped it would work.

As Crowfeather and the other deputies ordered the warriors into place for the next push, Rootpaw rose up on his hind legs and stared into the Moonpool. He wasn't sure what he'd been expecting—maybe something deep, clear, shrouded with fog and stars. Something clearly mystical, touched by StarClan. But now, at least, the Moonpool simply looked like a block of grayish-white ice sunk into a dark rocky bank. The medicine cats had made a break in the ice and dug out an uneven chunk, now pushed off to the side. It had left a wide, triangular gash, which only revealed . . . more ice.

How far down does the ice go? Rootpaw wondered. From their whispers and mumblings, he knew many of the other warriors were wondering the same thing. He couldn't see any sign of water beneath. It felt different from the ice on the lake where he'd fallen in. There he'd been able to feel the ice give, to hear the sloshing of life below.

In contrast, the Moonpool felt inert . . . almost dead, Rootpaw thought with despair. *Surely that can't be good.*

He could only hope they'd succeed in bringing it back to life.

"Warriors, places!" Hawkwing yelled. "We're almost there! One, two . . ."

Rootpaw scrambled back into place on the rock. And slowly, together, the warriors pushed the rock onto the logs. Working shoulder to shoulder, they were able to keep the rock on the logs, slide it slowly across, and push it to the edge of the Moonpool.

"Now," Hawkwing yelled, "we all rest for a moment . . . and, on the count of three, we push it over the edge!"

Rootpaw panted, the cold air burning his lungs. He glanced around and caught the eye of Bristlefrost, who was on the outer edge of the group. She nodded at him and purred, and

Rootpaw nodded back, sharing her sense of satisfaction.

Even if it doesn't work, he thought, *at least we're doing something. Maybe that will impress StarClan?*

But then he saw Jayfeather on the other side of the Moonpool, his eyes cast down with a look of utter despair, like he'd lost his only friend.

That is, if they're not horribly offended that we touched the Moonpool . . .

Rootpaw felt heavy inside. Had things always been this horribly complicated?

"All right, everyone," Reedwhisker yelled. "Take your places! . . . One . . . two . . ."

Rootpaw pressed his forepaws against the rock, pushing with all his might. All the warriors around him did the same, letting out a massive groan as the rock inched forward.

"Break!" Hawkwing yelled, and they all went limp, leaving the sharp edge of the rock dangling a few inches over the pool. Rootpaw tried to stretch his muscles. He knew they would all be sore in the morning.

Reedwhisker spoke up again after a few seconds. "Okay, places . . . One . . . two . . ."

They pushed the rock forward some more. Rootpaw's forelegs ached, and he wondered if they would ever succeed. Then, so suddenly he let out a gasp of surprise, Rootpaw felt no resistance. The rock slid over the side of the pool, its sharp end nosing forward into the gash the medicine cats had dug out. There was silence for a few seconds, then a huge crash as the tip of the rock made contact with the ice.

"Hooray!" Breezepelt, from WindClan, yelled.

"Don't be mouse-brained," Bristlefrost snapped at him. "We don't know whether it broke through. . . ."

At her words, all the warriors stepped forward to the edge of the pool to look down. But before he moved, Rootpaw glimpsed Jayfeather's face.

It hadn't changed.

Breezepelt scrambled to the edge and looked down. "It made a big dent. But there's still more ice!"

Rootpaw felt his heart sink.

"It goes at least five tail-lengths down," Bristlefrost added, staring down into the pool. "So much ice . . ."

Crowfeather was looking, too. "I suppose we can try again . . . ," he meowed. But he sounded tired. As tired as Rootpaw felt.

Hawkwing looked even less optimistic. "We can try countless times," he agreed, "but we don't know where the water begins . . . or whether it's frozen solid."

Frozen solid. A shiver went through Rootpaw's body at those words.

He was willing to try again, as hard as it might be . . . to find another rock, to push it into the pool, to hope that it might break the ice. He was willing to work all day, if he had to. All night, too, if he had the strength.

But as he caught Bristlefrost's eye again, he wondered if she was feeling the same despair he was. All the effort in the world wouldn't bring StarClan back if they'd left them on purpose.

What if StarClan has left us for good?

CHAPTER 18

❧

Bristlefrost stood in the shadow of a rock, gazing around the snow-covered clearing; she was alert to pick up any sign of prey. Mousewhisker, who was leading the hunting patrol, had disappeared with Berrynose around a holly bush, but she could still see Snaptooth, his golden tabby pelt standing out against the white of the snowbank where he was crouching.

With all the tensions in the camp, Bristlefrost was finding it hard to concentrate. Bramblestar was still lying motionless in the medicine cats' den, breathing but seeming unaware of anything going on around him. And the attempt to break the ice in the Moonpool, which had briefly given the Clan cats so much hope, had ended in failure. The Moonpool appeared to be frozen solid, and StarClan had remained stubbornly silent.

We could do with some good prey, Bristlefrost thought, though she had nearly given up hope of finding any. *At least we'd all feel better if our bellies were full.*

Almost as soon as the thought went through her mind, Bristlefrost spotted a disturbance ahead of her, where rocks and tussocks of grass jutted out of a shallow, uneven slope. Some of the snow shifted and rolled down the bank in clumps, leaving a dark hole. A nose poked out, a pair of ears . . .

A rabbit!

Bristlefrost's jaws started to water; it had been so long since she'd seen a rabbit, she could hardly believe it was there in front of her. It emerged from its burrow and hopped slowly forward, its forepaws scrabbling at the snow to uncover buried grass and vegetation. It seemed to have no idea of the danger waiting for it only a few fox-lengths away.

Glancing across the clearing, Bristlefrost realized that Snaptooth had spotted the rabbit too. His ears were pricked, his whiskers quivering, and his gaze was fixed on the creature as it nibbled at the frostbitten grass.

Stay where you are! Bristlefrost wanted to yowl the words at her Clanmate, but she knew that their only hope of catching the prey was to stay still and silent until it was too far away from its burrow to dive safely back inside.

Her heart was thumping so hard it was painful, and it took all her self-control not to hurl herself at the rabbit. *What if it turns back, and all I've done is stand here and stare at it?*

Then Bristlefrost noticed that Snaptooth had flattened himself to the ground and begun to creep forward cautiously, working his way around to get between the rabbit and the burrow. The rabbit, too intent on feeding, didn't notice his stealthy movement. *We'll have it trapped!* Bristlefrost thought with delight, her mouth watering.

Once Snaptooth was in position, Bristlefrost lowered herself into the hunter's crouch and prowled toward her prey, testing the ground with every paw step. But before she was close enough to pounce, a gust of wind passed over her. Bristlefrost froze, hoping the wind hadn't been strong enough to carry her scent to her quarry.

The rabbit sat upright, its ears erect and its nose twitching. *Oh, no! Now it knows I'm here!* Spinning around, her prey darted for its burrow, its strong hind legs thrusting it forward in massive leaps. But Snaptooth was waiting. As he bared his teeth and bunched his muscles for a pounce, the rabbit let out a squeal of terror and skidded to a halt in a flurry of snow. It doubled back and raced off at an angle, heading away from where Bristlefrost was waiting to complete the kill.

Fox dung!

Snaptooth gave chase, but the rabbit was outpacing him. Bristlefrost almost despaired, until she remembered something Rosepetal had told her when she was an apprentice: *Don't run to where your prey is; run to where it's going to be.*

Bristlefrost flung herself forward, aiming for a spot a few fox-lengths ahead of the fleeing rabbit. Dread stabbed into her belly at the thought of losing the best prey she'd seen in moons. *If the rabbit changes direction, I've totally messed up!*

But the rabbit kept going. Bristlefrost leaped on top of it; hunter and prey rolled over and over in a whirl of legs, tail, and snow. Then Bristlefrost managed to fix her paw across the rabbit's throat and dug her claws in deep. Blood gushed out and the rabbit went limp.

"Thank you, StarClan, for this prey," Bristlefrost panted as she staggered to her paws and shook snow out of her pelt. *But is there any point in thanking StarClan when they won't talk to us?*

"Hey, great catch!" Snaptooth came bounding up. "It's pretty plump, too."

Triumph surged through Bristlefrost. She felt better than she had since the dreadful day when she was made a warrior. "It's your catch too," she told her Clanmate.

"Yeah, we make a great team!" Snaptooth purred.

His words sent a pang of pain through Bristlefrost as she remembered what she had hoped for with Stemleaf. Even though she knew that Snaptooth meant no more than friendliness, that was a path where she refused to set her paws.

"Let's go and show Mousewhisker and Berrynose," she meowed. "They went this way."

Carrying the rabbit, Bristlefrost padded across the clearing to the holly bush where the two senior warriors had disappeared. Skirting the prickly branches, she halted at the sound of murmuring voices from the other side, and signaled with her tail for Snaptooth to do the same.

Cautiously, Bristlefrost poked her head around the bush and spotted Berrynose and Mousewhisker huddled together in conversation, not even trying to hunt.

"Lazy furballs!" Snaptooth exclaimed, peering over Bristlefrost's shoulder. "Let's show them the rabbit and make them feel really ashamed of themselves."

Bristlefrost shook her head. "No. I want to hear what's so important they have to talk about it in secret."

With Snaptooth just behind her, Bristlefrost crept forward as far as she could while still remaining in the shelter of the bush.

". . . sickness is really bad," Mousewhisker was mewing as Bristlefrost came into earshot. "And it's getting worse. What will happen if Bramblestar dies?"

Berrynose shrugged helplessly. "When Clan leaders die, they go to StarClan and receive wisdom before they take up their next life and return to go on leading their Clan. But what happens if Bramblestar can't reach StarClan? Will he just die, and never come back?"

"And then what happens to ThunderClan?" Mousewhisker wondered. "Squirrelflight would be a good leader, but what if she can't meet with StarClan and receive her nine lives?"

"Then she'll have to be our leader without StarClan," Berrynose growled. "If StarClan is going to abandon us when we need them most, we can show them that we don't need them!"

Mousewhisker looked uncertain; Bristlefrost thought that he wasn't ready to abandon reliance on the spirits of their warrior ancestors. "I wonder if this is what ShadowClan's weird medicine-cat apprentice saw in his vision," he meowed.

Berrynose let out a snort of disgust. "I don't know. Jayfeather thinks he's birdbrained, and you know Shadow-Clan . . . there's a reason we didn't invite them to help with the Moonpool! They're about as trustworthy as a den of foxes," he muttered.

His voice began to die away, and Bristlefrost leaned closer, angling her ears forward to pick up the lower tones. But at that moment, Snaptooth sneezed, and both senior warriors looked up.

Bristlefrost turned her head to glare at her Clanmate.

"Thanks for that!" she hissed through her teeth. "Now we'll never get to hear the rest of it." Then she padded forward with the rabbit and dropped it at Mousewhisker's paws.

"Good job!" Berrynose exclaimed, swiping his tongue over his jaws as he stared at the prey.

Mousewhisker gave Bristlefrost an approving nod. "Rosepetal taught you well," he mewed.

"It was both of us," Bristlefrost responded, flicking her tail toward Snaptooth, who ducked his head, obviously pleased.

Bristlefrost's feeling of triumph had returned, warming her as she headed back toward camp with the rest of the patrol. But at the same time, she couldn't stop thinking about what the senior warriors had said.

What will happen if Bramblestar loses a life?

Bristlefrost crouched beside the fresh-kill pile, sharing a mouse with her mother, Ivypool. Most of ThunderClan was gathered around, devouring the prey from the morning's hunt. Pride bubbled up inside Bristlefrost as she saw the elders, along with Daisy, Sorrelstripe, and Sparkpelt from the nursery, all feasting on the rabbit she and Snaptooth had caught.

No cat will go to their nest hungry tonight. I helped to care for my Clan.

But Bristlefrost was distracted from her feelings of satisfaction as a commotion rose outside the medicine cats' den. Turning her head, she saw Squirrelflight plunge out from behind the bramble screen, then spin around to speak to some cat still inside.

"I don't want to talk about this! Bramblestar will get

better." Her words carried clearly across the camp. "The only reason he hasn't is that you haven't tried everything!"

Alderheart followed the Clan deputy out of the den. Every cat in the Clan had fallen silent at Squirrelflight's outburst, but the medicine cat remained calm. His voice as he responded was so quiet that Bristlefrost couldn't make out the words.

"You and Jayfeather must save your leader!" Squirrelflight snapped back at him. "I have complete faith in you, so there's nothing to discuss." With that she turned away and stalked across the camp to the fresh-kill pile, head and tail held high.

Alderheart's gaze followed her, and Bristlefrost noticed how devastated he looked, his muzzle tight and his tail drooping. She could imagine how difficult it must be for a medicine cat to treat his own father, especially when he wasn't getting better. Especially when that father was Clan leader, too.

Glancing at Ivypool, Bristlefrost was grateful for the reassuring look in her mother's eyes. "Don't worry," Ivypool murmured. But she still rose to her paws and went to sit at Squirrelflight's side.

Bristlefrost finished up the last few scraps of mouse and was thinking about retiring to her den when she spotted movement at the end of the thorn tunnel. Hollytuft and Flippaw, who had been out on border patrol, appeared; Bristlefrost's eyes widened in surprise as she recognized the cats who followed them into the camp.

Tigerstar and Shadowpaw!

Bristlefrost tensed. Could Tigerstar possibly know about the attempt to break through the ice in the Moonpool? Was he here to yell at Bramblestar? *It would be a shame to get under Tiger-star's fur when the attempt didn't even work.* . . . .

Lilyheart, the third member of the patrol, brought up the rear, and Hollytuft led the way across the camp to where Ivy-pool was trying to coax Squirrelflight to eat a thrush.

Squirrelflight rose to her paws and faced Tigerstar where he halted beside the fresh-kill pile. Shadowpaw stood beside him, looking down at his paws; Bristlefrost could see his whiskers twitching nervously.

"Greetings, Tigerstar." Squirrelflight's eyes were wary, but she inclined her head coolly. "What do you want with ThunderClan?"

"I've come with an important message," Tigerstar replied. "I think it would be best for me to speak in private with Bramblestar."

"I'm sorry." Squirrelflight's voice was calm. "Bramblestar isn't available at the moment. He's . . . out hunting. So what-ever you want to say, you can say in front of all ThunderClan's warriors."

For a moment Tigerstar looked taken aback. He hesitated; Bristlefrost guessed he was weighing the tension in Squirrel-flight's expression.

"Very well," he meowed at last. "My message is a strange one: I know that your leader, Bramblestar, is very sick."

Bristlefrost felt her belly clench and heard gasps of amaze-ment rising from her Clanmates around her.

"How do you know?" Lionblaze demanded. The golden tabby tom rose and skirted the fresh-kill pile to stand beside

Squirrelflight. His amber eyes blazed as he glared at Tigerstar. "Who told you?"

Tigerstar gave no sign that Lionblaze's aggressive tone had offended him. "My son, Shadowpaw," he began, "who as you know is a medicine-cat apprentice, told me, after he received a message from StarClan."

"No cat has received a message from StarClan!" Graystripe put in.

Tigerstar's gaze flicked to the elder and away again. "My son has. And, more important, he knows how to cure Bramblestar."

Every cat's gaze turned to Squirrelflight, who stood silent for a long moment, clearly stunned. Then she glanced at Flippaw. "Please fetch Jayfeather and Alderheart," she requested.

The whole Clan waited in silence while the apprentice scurried across the camp and vanished behind the bramble screen at the entrance to the medicine cats' den. Bristlefrost felt so confused that she couldn't move, her mind racing and filling with half-formed questions. She didn't know whether to hope that Shadowpaw really did have the answer to Bramblestar's mysterious illness, or whether this was all some kind of ShadowClan trick to attack ThunderClan when they were vulnerable. *Maybe Tigerstar did find out about the Moonpool, and this is some complicated strategy to get revenge?*

When Bristlefrost felt she couldn't wait a heartbeat longer, Jayfeather and Alderheart appeared from their den and padded over to the fresh-kill pile with Flippaw following them.

"What's all this?" Jayfeather demanded harshly.

Instead of explaining, Squirrelflight turned to Shadow-paw. "All right," she began, "if Bramblestar were sick, how would you cure him?"

Shadowpaw looked up at the ThunderClan deputy; for a moment Bristlefrost could see he was too overwhelmed to speak, until Tigerstar gave him an encouraging nudge.

"W-well . . . ," the apprentice stammered, "Bramblestar's illness is like a—a wildfire. It can't be snuffed out with treatment. It has to be allowed to burn out on its own."

Squirrelflight's green eyes narrowed as she gazed down at him. "And what does that mean?" she asked.

"It's an unusual idea—" Tigerstar began, then broke off and waved his tail at his son for Shadowpaw to continue.

Shadowpaw gathered himself and started to speak again. Bristlefrost felt a twinge of admiration for the young cat; it must take courage to tell a rival Clan what to do, when he was no more than an apprentice, and to stand up to that Clan's suspicious glares while he explained.

"You should take Bramblestar to a cold place on the moor," Shadowpaw told the ThunderClan medicine cats, his voice sounding more confident as he continued. "The colder the better, and somewhere where the wind is strong. Build him a den in the snow, and have him sleep there overnight. The sickness will get worse before it gets better, but when Bramblestar wakes up he will be strong again, and just as healthy as before."

A long, disbelieving silence followed Shadowpaw's words. At last Squirrelflight shook her head, turning to Tigerstar. "Are you serious?" she demanded. "Do you really think I would allow any cat to drag my sick mate—if he were sick—out onto the moor to freeze to death?"

"Maybe he does," Jayfeather growled, turning a hostile expression on the ShadowClan leader. "Shadowpaw, exactly how has Puddleshine been training you? Don't you realize that what you're suggesting could kill Bramblestar? That would leave ThunderClan weak, when we have problems enough as it is. And maybe that's what Tigerstar wants!" he finished with a lash of his tail.

"Nonsense," Tigerstar responded. He closed his eyes briefly and dug his claws into the ground; Bristlefrost could see what a massive effort it took for him to keep his temper in check. "I came here in good faith, to share my son's vision. I didn't have to go to so much trouble."

"I'm not sure where Shadowpaw's visions come from," Jayfeather snapped back at him, "but the medicine cats couldn't even reach our ancestors when we made cracks in the frozen Moonpool. So I know these instructions aren't coming from StarClan!"

Tigerstar's eyes narrowed. "What are you talking about?" he asked Jayfeather. "Who made cracks in the Moonpool? Why would any cat think of doing that to such a special place?"

A long silence followed the ShadowClan leader's questions. Bristlefrost thought she could see a look of deep regret in Jayfeather's eyes, and uncomfortable glances from the other cats standing around. She knew Jayfeather had never meant to give away so much to Tigerstar, after the ShadowClan cats hadn't been invited to help.

Finally Squirrelflight raised her head, as if she was bracing herself for an unpleasant task. "It was necessary . . . ," she mewed. "To see if we could reach StarClan again. All the Clans helped."

"ShadowClan didn't help," Tigerstar retorted, his shoulder fur beginning to bush up in anger. "Why were we left out?"

Every cat stared uncomfortably at Shadowpaw, who kept his gaze fixed on his paws. Bristlefrost felt sorry for the apprentice, her kin, who wasn't much older than her. He even looked a bit like her and her littermates . . . she could see Flippaw in the shape of his eyes, Thriftpaw in the seriousness of his gaze.

What must it feel like, when all the Clans think you're lying?

But at the same time, Bristlefrost could see why the ThunderClan cats were so doubtful about him now. How could any cat believe that his message about putting Bramblestar out in the cold could really be from StarClan? *Why is Shadowpaw so special?* she wondered. *And why would StarClan seek out a ShadowClan medicine cat, and not one from ThunderClan or one of the other clans?*

"I understand now," Tigerstar growled, when it was clear that no cat intended to answer his questions. "I'm sorry I brought my son here, through the cold, for no good reason. If the other Clans don't view ShadowClan as one of them, then ShadowClan will seek its own path. This is the last wisdom from Shadowpaw that I will share with outsiders!" He raked the crowd of cats around him with a last hostile glare. "Come on, Shadowpaw. We're leaving."

Turning, he stormed off across the camp. For a moment, Shadowpaw hesitated, as if he didn't want to follow, until Tigerstar glanced back over his shoulder and snapped, "Shadowpaw!"

The apprentice dipped his head to Squirrelflight and followed his father.

Before the two ShadowClan cats reached the thorn tunnel, Squirrelflight suddenly stepped forward; Bristlefrost saw remorse in the Clan deputy's face. "Wait . . . ," she called out to the cats' retreating tails, her voice weak and uncertain.

Tigerstar checked for an instant, then continued without looking back. Both he and Shadowpaw disappeared into the tunnel.

When they were gone, Squirrelflight heaved a deep sigh, and turned a glare on Jayfeather from narrowed green eyes. Though Jayfeather couldn't see the glare, he certainly seemed to feel it; he shrugged his shoulders uneasily. "We all know what Tigerstar has been like in the past," he mumbled.

Bristlefrost could feel her pelt tingling from the tension in the camp, as if ants were crawling through her fur. She couldn't believe that such a short time ago she'd been sharing prey with her Clanmates and feeling optimistic.

"Maybe Shadowpaw's idea has some merit," Alderheart meowed. His voice was calm, and he was clearly trying to smooth things over.

"What?" Jayfeather spat. "You must have a whole nest of

bees in your brain if you want to do what that delusional little flea-pelt told you!"

"Keep your fur on, Jayfeather," Alderheart told him, resting his tail for a moment on the older medicine cat's shoulder. "That's not what I mean at all. But don't you remember how I once saved Puddleshine from a terrible Twoleg infection by feeding him the flesh of deathberries? At first, it seemed like they would kill him, and he got worse before he got better—just like Shadowpaw said would be the answer to Bramblestar's illness."

His words were met with silence. Every cat in the Clan was staring at Alderheart. Bristlefrost struggled with a surge of fear. *Bramblestar will die if Alderheart leaves him in the snow.*

The silence dragged out until Alderheart lashed his tail in frustration. "We have to do something to save my father!" he blurted out.

"But we don't have to do *this*," Jayfeather retorted. "It's absurd. We may have known Tigerstar for a long time, but don't forget that before he became Clan leader, he abandoned his Clan and his role as deputy."

"He came back," Squirrelflight pointed out.

"Okay, he came back," Jayfeather meowed. "And then he caused more problems when we were trying to adjust the territories to make a home for SkyClan. And that's what worries me: Tigerstar seems to be a cat who changes his mind and his mood very quickly. We can never be sure what Tigerstar's true motives are—except that he thinks of ShadowClan above all else."

"You think he told Shadowpaw what to say?" Ivypool asked. "To attack ThunderClan by killing our leader?"

No cat could be that evil! Bristlefrost thought, horrified.

Jayfeather shook his head. "No, I believe Shadowpaw means well. He truly thinks he is helping. But in my opinion, none of his visions have ever sounded as if they come from StarClan."

"But when has StarClan ever been predictable?" Alderheart demanded, his tone growing heated. "Maybe StarClan has changed their way of reaching us, and will only communicate through Shadowpaw. Maybe, like so many of StarClan's actions, the reason will only become clear with time. And Bramblestar is dying. None of our usual herbs are working! With StarClan cutting us off, mustn't we—now more than ever—do all we can to keep him alive?"

Squirrelflight stepped forward to Alderheart's side. Bristlefrost could see sorrow in her eyes, and knew she was on the brink of making what must be the hardest decision of her life.

"I'm sorry, Alderheart," she mewed at last. "I can't allow this."

For a moment Bristlefrost thought that Alderheart would protest. Then he lowered his head, saying nothing. Squirrelflight gazed at him for a moment more before padding off to the warriors' den.

"Squirrelflight, you should eat something," Ivypool called after her, but Squirrelflight didn't look back.

An awkward silence fell over the camp, as if no cat had any

idea what to say. One or two of the warriors began to drift away toward their den, only to halt as Jayfeather spoke.

"I have an idea," he told Alderheart. "If we could get some borage, we might be able to rouse Bramblestar."

Hope and confusion warred in Alderheart's eyes. "Why borage?" he asked. "We use it to reduce fever. That's hardly necessary right now."

"It might sound odd," Jayfeather agreed, "but Shadowpaw was right about one thing. The longer Bramblestar stays in our den, the more chance there is of his temperature dropping so quickly that he might never recover. But if we gave him something to *make* him colder . . . Would that spur him on to get better, the way Shadowpaw suggested? The way the deathberries seemed to trick Puddleshine into getting better." When Alderheart didn't reply, he added, "It's got to be worth trying, right?"

Alderheart gave his pelt a shake, as if he was rousing himself from deep concentration. "It might be," he agreed. "But all our herb stocks are low, and we're completely out of borage. I don't know where we'll find any more with snow covering the ground."

"There's one place we might get some," Jayfeather told him. "You know that spit of ground that juts out into the lake? I know borage grows right at the far end, but we usually can't get at it because there's such a tangle of brambles and gorse bushes in the way. In normal times it's not worth the effort, when we can get plenty of borage elsewhere. But now that the lake is frozen . . ."

"We might be able to reach it!" Alderheart exclaimed, his eyes flaring with hope at last.

Bristlefrost leaped to her paws. "I'll lead a patrol to go and collect some!" she offered, excitement making her paws tingle. "Who's coming with me?"

"I will," Spotfur responded instantly.

For a moment annoyance overwhelmed Bristlefrost's excitement. *You would,* she thought sourly. *Showing off in front of Stemleaf.*

Then Bristlefrost realized that she was wrong. Spotfur was a loyal Clan cat, stepping up when her Clan and her leader needed her. Even though Bristlefrost was still upset about Stemleaf, she was impressed by Spotfur's courage.

"Thank you," she meowed, dipping her head toward the spotted tabby she-cat.

Poppyfrost, Stemleaf, Cherryfall, and Flywhisker all stepped forward to volunteer, and Bristlefrost found herself at the head of a patrol.

My first time leading a patrol for my Clan!

"All right," she meowed, filled with a new sense of purpose. "Let's go."

CHAPTER 19

❧

With her patrol following in her paw steps, Bristlefrost broke out of the trees and stood at the top of the bank leading down to the lake. The spit of land where the borage grew curved out into the lake like a cat's tail. Bristlefrost could see the dark tangle of thorns that barred the way from the shore. At the far end, many fox-lengths away, the ground became clearer; Bristlefrost could make out a few frozen stalks sticking up out of the snow.

That must be the borage.

Cherryfall padded up beside her. "We don't know whether the lake is frozen solid," she pointed out. "If we walk out too far, we could fall through the ice. Remember what happened to that SkyClan apprentice."

As if I'm likely to forget it!

The memory returned to Bristlefrost in vivid focus, bringing a mixture of emotions with it. She had been terrified for Rootpaw, and so proud that her rescue of him had impressed Stemleaf. She struggled with another ache of regret at the knowledge that her courage hadn't mattered at all. Stemleaf had already set his heart on another cat as his mate. Bristlefrost couldn't resist a quick glance at Spotfur, wondering what it was about her that Stemleaf preferred.

Icy wind blew into Bristlefrost's face, carrying with it even more memories: the waves of cold wafting off the ice as she stood there reaching out to Rootpaw, and the exposed lake water welling up around her forelegs.

I saved the stupid furball, but I was more frightened than I've ever been in my life. And now I'm thinking about stepping out onto the ice again? On purpose?

"Bramblestar is very sick," Poppyfrost responded to Cherryfall's warning. "I know it's a risk, but it's worth it, to save him."

Spotfur murmured agreement. "We have to take the risk, or why are we here? But we have to be careful, too. We should go slowly, and circle around to find other routes if the ice seems thin."

Who's in charge of this patrol, you or me? Bristlefrost thought, then forced herself to be more generous toward the spotted tabby she-cat.

"Good idea," she meowed. "Follow me, but not too close, to spread our weight out."

Bristlefrost led the way out onto the ice, hugging the side of the spit of land, where the ice was thickest. Her patrol was stretched out behind her, keeping well separated as she had ordered.

At first they made good progress. Though Bristlefrost cringed as the ice made her pads ache, then grow numb, it felt solid under her paws. But before long the gorse and brambles grew thicker, overhanging the lake so that the cats had to move farther away from the shore. Bristlefrost could feel the ice bouncing gently under her weight. After a few more paw steps, she thought she heard an ominous creaking; she raised her tail to signal the others to halt.

"Maybe we should go back," Flywhisker called out to her. "We could try around the other side. It might be safer there."

Bristlefrost twitched her tail-tip back and forth in frustration. Because of the way the spit of land curved around, she could see the clearer area with the stalks of borage just a few tail-lengths ahead. Only a narrow stretch of ice separated the patrol from the life-giving herb.

What if that stalk of borage could save Bramblestar? Surely it would be worth the risk then!

"We're so close," she meowed. "Maybe if one cat went alone, very fast, so their paws hardly touched the ice . . ."

"No!" Spotfur protested. "It's too dangerous. If one cat fell in, how would the others even get them out?"

"You're right, we should turn back." Poppyfrost shuddered. "I remember when Flametail fell through the ice. No cat should have to go through that."

Bristlefrost remembered hearing that story from the elders when she was a kit. Flametail had been a ShadowClan medicine-cat apprentice and had drowned in the lake when the ice gave way during another hard leaf-bare. She shivered at the thought of something so terrible happening again.

But the ice must be thicker now. . . . Every cat says there's never been a leaf-bare as bad as this.

Bristlefrost gazed across the ice at the borage stems. They were so close, and yet they might as well have been countless fox-lengths away.

Without giving herself time to think, she leaped forward, sprinting across the ice so fast that her paws only skimmed the surface. She held her breath, determined to keep her nerve, and a few heartbeats later she sprang off the ice and across a scatter of rocks to where the borage grew.

"I made it!" she yowled triumphantly, glancing back at her Clanmates, who were staring at her, strung out behind her along the shore.

Bristlefrost nipped off a few stems of borage with her teeth and made them into a bundle so that she could carry them back. But as soon as she launched herself back onto the ice, she heard a sharp crack, and the ice where she had landed began to tilt. Dark water, painfully cold, welled up over Bristlefrost's legs as she scrabbled vainly at the slick surface in an attempt to keep her balance. Letting out a terrified screech, she plunged deep into the icy lake.

I've done it now . . . I'm going to die . . . , Bristlefrost thought as the water closed over her head. She didn't expect that her Clanmates would be able to save her. They'd be risking their own lives. . . . When she had saved Rootpaw, he had been close to shore, and rescuing him had been easy. And he had been an apprentice. . . .

I'm a warrior, old enough to know better.

Bristlefrost thrashed her paws helplessly, but the cold was sapping her strength. She had lost her sense of direction; she didn't know where the surface was. Then something hard struck her on the shoulder. Instinctively she grabbed at it and sank her claws into wood. A moment later her head broke the surface, and she saw Spotfur on the more solid ice nearby, hauling her to safety at the end of a long branch.

Scrambling up onto the ice, Bristlefrost collapsed at Spotfur's paws, coughed up a mouthful of water and ice, and looked up at her Clanmate. "Thank you!" she gasped. "I thought I was dead for sure."

She noticed that Spotfur's fur was disheveled and she had a tiny trickle of blood over one eye. Bristlefrost realized that she must have plunged into the gorse and brambles to get the branch, and then ventured out onto the same treacherous ice that had just given way under her own paws.

"We'd better get you to a medicine cat right away," Spotfur meowed. "You must be freezing."

Bristlefrost shook the ice crystals out of her pelt, beginning to shiver as she recovered enough to feel the cold. "I'm so sorry," she mewed, as the rest of her patrol gathered around, concern in their eyes. "It was a stupid thing to do. I put you all in danger—especially you, Spotfur. You were so brave."

And now I can understand what Stemleaf sees in you, she added to herself. *You're a brave cat, and a loyal Clanmate.*

"I'll tell Squirrelflight it was all my fault," Bristlefrost promised. "I won't let her blame any of you that we didn't get the borage."

"There's nothing to apologize for," Spotfur assured her. "We're all worried about Bramblestar, and that puts us all a little on edge. Besides, there's no need to worry Squirrelflight about any of this. You did get what you came for!"

For the first time, Bristlefrost realized that a few stalks of borage were lying just in front of her, at her paws, where she had coughed up the ice and water she had swallowed. Her eyes widened and laughter bubbled up inside her.

"I got it after all!" she exclaimed.

Stemleaf padded up to her and rubbed his cheek against hers. "I should have known you could do it," he told her. "You can do anything!"

Bristlefrost staggered to her paws, embarrassed by Stemleaf's praise, and yet happy too. She carefully collected the stalks of borage and waved her tail to gather the patrol together.

I can't do everything, she thought as she led the way back to camp. *But at least I did something.*

Her paws numb from patrolling the border, Bristlefrost limped across the camp toward the medicine cats' den. She was chilled through and exhausted, and she wanted nothing more than to curl up in her nest for a well-deserved nap, but she knew she wouldn't be able to rest until she found out whether Bramblestar was responding to the borage treatment.

When she had returned to camp the previous day, carrying the few precious stems, Alderheart had chewed them up and trickled the pulp and juices between Bramblestar's jaws, while Jayfeather massaged the Clan leader's throat to encourage the Clan leader to swallow.

"Now there's nothing to do but wait," Jayfeather had mewed grimly.

Reaching the den, Bristlefrost poked her head around the bramble screen. In the dim light she could barely make out Bramblestar's dark tabby shape, half buried in the moss and bracken of his nest. Alderheart sat beside him, close to his head, and as Bristlefrost watched, he reached out and laid one paw on his father's neck. His eyes were troubled, and he let out a faint sigh.

Jayfeather appeared from the back of the den. "Any change?" he asked.

Alderheart shook his head. "No . . . he might even be growing weaker."

Bristlefrost felt her belly cramp with apprehension. *This isn't supposed to happen! Why isn't the borage working?*

"It wasn't much of a chance," Jayfeather murmured, almost as if he were answering Bristlefrost's unspoken question. "And now . . . there's nothing more that we can do."

"We can't give up!" Alderheart's voice was anguished. "There must be a way to save him. We have to talk to Shadowpaw again."

Jayfeather let out a hiss of fury. "I've told you before, we are not listening to that useless ShadowClan lump of fur! Tigerstar is using him to—" He broke off suddenly and swung around to face Bristlefrost. "What are you doing here?" he demanded. "Eavesdropping?"

How did he know I was here, unless he has eyes in his tail? Bristlefrost wondered, until she remembered that though

Jayfeather was blind, his other senses were extraordinarily sharp; he would easily have picked out her scent among all the others in the den.

"I only wanted—" she began.

Alderheart interrupted her, his voice suddenly filled with authority. "This isn't our decision to make," he told Jayfeather. "Bristlefrost, fetch Squirrelflight."

Bristlefrost drew back from the den and pelted across the camp toward the tumbled rocks that led up to the Highledge. Before Bristlefrost had climbed halfway up, Squirrelflight appeared at the entrance.

"What is it?" she asked, her voice tight with strain.

"Alderheart wants you," Bristlefrost gasped, her paws skidding as she turned back, so she barely saved herself from falling.

She heard a choking sound from Squirrelflight before the Clan deputy bounded down the rocks, overtaking Bristlefrost as she raced back toward the medicine cats' den.

When Bristlefrost slipped, panting, back into the den, she found the two medicine cats where she had left them beside the Clan leader. Squirrelflight had joined them, and stood gazing down at Bramblestar, her green eyes filled with pain.

"So the borage didn't work," she mewed; Bristlefrost could tell how much effort she was making to keep her voice steady.

"No," Alderheart responded. "There's only one way to save Bramblestar now."

Squirrelflight's eyes narrowed as she glanced at him. "Shadowpaw's treatment?"

Alderheart nodded silently.

"You're flea-brained if you even consider that," Jayfeather snapped, working his claws into the moss and bracken in the floor of the den.

"Squirrelflight." Alderheart's voice still held that ring of authority, as if he were a much older and more experienced cat. "Bramblestar is dying. And we have no idea what will happen when he loses a life, seeing that no cat can make contact with StarClan—except, maybe, Shadowpaw. Trying his treatment would at least give Bramblestar one last chance."

Jayfeather let out a huff of annoyance and turned away. "Don't expect me to go along with this," he snarled.

Alderheart met Squirrelflight's gaze steadily. "It's your decision," he told her. "What do you want to do?"

CHAPTER 20

❧

"Let all cats old enough to catch their own prey join here beneath the Pinebranch for a Clan meeting!"

Shadowpaw poked his head out of the medicine cats' den to see his father sitting on the pine branch above his den, from which he always addressed the Clan. His paws were tucked underneath him, and his tail dangled. His father's expression was grave.

Worry prickled beneath Shadowpaw's pelt. "Now what's happening?" he wondered aloud. *I just hope I'm not at the center of it, for once. . . .*

"Listen and you might find out," Puddleshine told him, giving him a shove from behind. "But I'd bet a moon of dawn patrols it's something to do with your visit to ThunderClan."

Great. Shadowpaw thought that his mentor must be right. He cringed when he thought of how Squirrelflight had denied that Bramblestar was sick, and how no cat had believed him when he'd told them what to do to save their leader. *They thought I was trying to kill him! They really thought I could be that . . . evil!*

He padded out of the den with Puddleshine a paw step behind him and found a spot to sit near Lightleap and

Pouncestep. Cloverfoot and Tawnypelt turned away from the fresh-kill pile and joined Dovewing near the bottom of the tree. Cloverfoot looked apprehensive; Shadowpaw guessed that Tigerstar had already confided in his deputy what he was going to say.

Oakfur emerged slowly from the elders' den and plopped down just outside it, raising one hind leg to give himself a vigorous scratch behind his ear. Cinnamontail and Berryheart appeared from the warriors' den with more of their Clanmates behind them, to form a ragged circle beneath the Pinebranch where Tigerstar was waiting.

The Clan leader let his amber gaze travel around his Clan before he rose to his paws and spoke. "Cats of ShadowClan, once again we have been the victim of a grave deception! A fox-hearted betrayal!" He paused. Murmurs of shock and disgust wormed their way through the crowd, but Shadowpaw felt only surprise.

Tigerstar lifted his head. "Therefore," he went on, "I've decided that my only choice is to close our borders. So we'll be doubling our patrols, and renewing our scent markers twice as often. And I'm sure I don't need to tell you what to do with any cat who dares set paw on our territory. From now on—"

"Just a moment," Tawnypelt interrupted, her ears flicking up indignantly. "What happened? You can't do this without telling us why. That would be mouse-brained."

Tigerstar narrowed his eyes as he gazed down at the tortoiseshell she-cat. Shadowpaw winced at the way she was addressing her Clan leader, then reflected that as Tawnypelt had once been deputy, she was used to expressing her opinion. Not to mention that she was the leader's mother. *And a pretty outspoken cat.*

Before Tigerstar could respond, Oakfur paused in his scratching. "Things didn't exactly go well when WindClan and RiverClan decided to close their borders recently," he pointed out. "They just helped Darktail and his Kin to grow more powerful."

"That's right!" Snowbird agreed. "We need to know more before we do this."

A chorus of yowls broke out, as more cats demanded that Tigerstar explain himself. Finally the Clan leader had to raise his tail for silence.

"I've just learned that the other Clans have banded together to defile the Moonpool by trying to break the ice," he explained. "Their scheme failed, which is no great surprise . . . but, needless to say, I am disgusted by this snubbing of our Clan. The other Clans have tried to cut us off from the Moonpool because they don't trust Shadowpaw," he went on. "They don't trust that a ShadowClan cat could have such a connection with StarClan. But they're wrong about that! I know it, and soon the other Clans will know it, too. Shadowpaw has special powers. . . ."

Shadowpaw hunched his shoulders in embarrassment as his father continued to proclaim how sensitive he was, how many visions he had had, and how valuable his link to StarClan would prove for his Clan.

I'm not like that at all. I'm just a medicine-cat apprentice, and I don't know what's going on, any more than any cat!

Worse, he worried that his Clanmates didn't agree with their leader. He caught the doubtful glances they were casting at him. Even Puddleshine was looking at him thoughtfully. His mentor had defended him before, but was he regretting that now?

Strikestone cleared his throat to speak first. "Shadowpaw is unusual," he began. Tigerstar shifted and cast an angry glare at the white tom. But Strikestone lifted a paw, indicating he wasn't done. "But he's ours—and in my mind, there's no doubt that a ShadowClan cat could be singled out by StarClan."

To Shadowpaw's surprise, this time murmurs of agreement hummed through the crowd. Yarrowleaf purred, looking at him with fond eyes. "Shadowpaw is good," she agreed. "He and my kits grew up together. Maybe it's unusual for StarClan to communicate with only one cat, but why shouldn't it be Shadowpaw?"

This time cats were nodding, meowing their agreement. Other cats spoke up in support, but Shadowpaw's mind wandered. The certainty in their voices only made him feel more unsure. He knew they loved ShadowClan . . . but did that make him right? The visions he had received were so clear, just as if he were talking to a living cat. Shadowpaw knew that StarClan didn't usually communicate like that. But what other way was there to explain it?

If I'm not being given these visions to save the Clans, Shadowpaw wondered, *then why am I having them?* He remembered Spire-sight, whom he had met when he was a kit living inside the big Twoleg den, and remembered too how Spiresight had been treated by the other cats who lived there. Dovewing had said that Spiresight was a medicine cat in a group that didn't understand medicine cats. The cats who lived at the Twoleg den saw his visions as crazy and believed there was something wrong with him.

Even if my Clan believes me . . . it's not a long distance from "medicine cat" to "crazy furball," Shadowpaw reflected. *What if I am imagining it? Spiresight was right sometimes, but he talked a lot of nonsense, too. . . .*

"Exactly!" Tigerstar's loud, assertive voice jerked Shadow-paw out of his reflections. "I'm glad we all agree. Cloverfoot, please set the new border-patrol schedules and send out hunt-ing patrols."

The Clan leader leaped down from the branch and disap-peared into his den, leaving his deputy to carry out his orders. Meanwhile, most of the warriors drew together in little groups, talking with their heads together and glancing over their shoulders at Shadowpaw.

As he turned away from them, wanting to be alone, Shadowpaw caught Puddleshine's eye. His mentor looked curious but didn't call to him. *He could stand to be rid of me for a while,* Shadowpaw mused. *Let him get some real medicine-cat work done, without worrying about me, and all the trouble I'm causing.*

Leaving the camp behind him, Shadowpaw headed out into the forest. Clouds lay low over the tops of the pine trees, and the light underneath them was dim, though it was not long past sunhigh. The surface of the snow glimmered eerily in the dusk, unbroken by any traces of prey. Shadowpaw's paws and

legs grew numb with cold as he broke through the crusty surface into the powdery snow beneath.

Eventually he came to a tall rock where wind had scoured
most of the snow away, and he leaped to the top of it to get
away from the freezing flakes for a while. From here Shadowpaw could just make out the lake, and parts of the other
territories in the distance.

"I don't want to hurt any of you," he murmured. "Even I
don't know if my visions are real. I wish I did...."

As Shadowpaw sat there, tucking in his paws and his tail to
make himself as small as he could against the cold, the view
in front of him began to change. A red stain spread over the
icy blue of the lake, the color intensifying until the surface
was blazing with scarlet fire. Shadowpaw felt himself being
lifted up, as if he were a bird, passing beyond the trees until he
could look down on the whole of the lake and the territories
around it.

The fire raged more fiercely, spreading out into long lines
that followed the boundaries of the Clans, until each Clan
was separated from the others by leaping walls of flame. Then
the fire began to creep inward, greedily devouring the trees
and undergrowth as it encroached on the camps.

"No...," Shadowpaw whispered, his eyes wide with horror.

There was no way for the cats to escape. Shadowpaw
couldn't see them, but he could hear their wails and screeches
of terror. He could smell the smoke and hear the crackle of
the flames as they roared around the rock where he crouched,
trembling with fear. His head swam, and darkness swirled in

front of his eyes. He coughed as ash caught in his throat and filled his lungs, gasping for breath as his senses spiraled away.

Before Shadowpaw could lose consciousness, the vision ended as quickly as it had come. Shadowpaw took in huge gulps of cold, clean air, gazing stunned at the forest, which was peaceful, snow-covered, unharmed. The lake was still frozen; even the smell of smoke had vanished.

The fire is coming, and the flames will scatter the Clans! he realized. *I have to tell them!*

"Oh, it definitely means something." Tigerstar's tones were grave. "And that 'something' is not good."

Shadowpaw was sitting with his father just outside the Clan leader's den. He had raced back to camp as soon as he had recovered from his vision, and at once Tigerstar had called his senior warriors around him: Cloverfoot, Tawnypelt, and Dovewing, along with Shadowpaw's mentor, Puddleshine.

"I'm most concerned about the Clans being scattered," Puddleshine meowed. "The fire might not mean real fire; StarClan often uses symbols when they send messages. But it sounds like they're warning us that the Clans will be torn apart and destroyed by . . . maybe some outside force."

Shadowpaw noticed that Tigerstar was staring hard at Puddleshine as the medicine cat was speaking. Puddleshine noticed it, too. "What?" he asked.

"You just said that StarClan uses symbols," Tigerstar pointed out. "So do you finally believe that Shadowpaw is getting these messages from StarClan?"

Puddleshine frowned painfully, then nodded. "I'm not sure there's any other explanation," he admitted. "Shadowpaw's visions have always been . . . unusual. But this one seems like a clear message."

Every hair on Shadowpaw's pelt tingled with satisfaction. *At last!*

"So we have to warn the other Clans," Dovewing meowed.

"I've half a mind to keep the information to myself," Tigerstar growled, his gaze fixed straight ahead to where the forest trees crowded close. "The other Clans have made it clear they don't want listen to us anyway."

"But—" Dovewing tried to interrupt, but Tigerstar ignored her.

"Don't forget," he continued, "the other Clans have so little trust in us, they tried to break through to StarClan without us. They attacked the ice on the Moonpool! Maybe the reason Shadowpaw has been able to talk to StarClan is that we're the only Clan StarClan isn't angry with."

Cloverfoot blinked thoughtfully. "This latest vision showed that the fire was dangerous to all the Clans," she mewed. "That surely means we'll all suffer if we're torn apart—including ShadowClan."

"Yes," Tawnypelt agreed. "Hasn't StarClan told us before? The Clans are strongest when we stand together. Our experience with Darktail taught us that."

Tigerstar still looked undecided, flexing his claws and twitching his tail-tip irritably. "I still don't see why we have to be responsible for saving the other Clans, after the way they've treated us," he huffed.

Dovewing gazed at Tigerstar with clear green eyes. "Be-cause we're warriors," she responded. "We're loyal to Shadow-Clan, but we still have a code. We have honor."

Tigerstar let out a long sigh, then nodded reluctantly. "What do you think we should do?" he asked his deputy.

"If I were you, I wouldn't worry about closing our borders. Instead I would call an emergency Gathering," Cloverfoot replied. "The other leaders need to know this, and we all need to discuss what to do about this latest vision." She turned to Shadowpaw, warmth in her gaze. "This message is so clear, even the most stubborn Clans won't be able to ignore it—whether it comes from ShadowClan or not."

Tigerstar rose to his paws, looking decisive once more. "Good. We'll do it. Cloverfoot, please send out messengers to the other Clans."

It felt strange to Shadowpaw to be approaching the Gath-ering island in the dark. There was no full moon, and in any case the cloud cover was so thick that very little light could penetrate it. Shadowpaw could hardly see his own paws in front of him as he made the crossing on the tree-bridge.

His belly fluttered nervously as he padded over to join the other medicine cats in the clearing, but at least he had Puddle-shine by his side, and this time he knew his mentor would support him. He'd already met with the other medicine cats, just prior to this meeting, to explain Shadowpaw's vision and what he thought it meant. All the others, even Jayfeather, greeted him when he sat beside them, and their wide eyes, the way they dipped their heads respectfully to him, suggested to Shadowpaw that at least they were willing to listen.

But the warriors aren't going to like the content of my message, he realized with a jolt of apprehension. *What if they turn even more hostile?*

The Clan leaders took their places in the Great Oak. They were barely visible among the branches, except for the gleam of their eyes as they looked down at the assembled cats. Shadowpaw noticed at once that there was no sign of Bramblestar; Squirrelflight leaped into the tree to join the leaders of the other Clans.

"Bramblestar is feeling unwell," she explained. Shadowpaw caught a hint of awkwardness in her voice. *Bramblestar's illness is more than "feeling unwell"!* "I will be representing ThunderClan tonight," Squirrelflight finished.

As soon as every cat was settled, Tigerstar rose to his paws. "I have called this emergency Gathering," he began, "because Shadowpaw has had another vision from StarClan. Shadowpaw, please tell every cat what it was you saw."

Shadowpaw's legs felt wobbly as he stood up to address the Clans. He was aware of some muttering after Tigerstar's announcement.

"You mean we've all been dragged out here in the pitch dark to listen to an apprentice?" Berrynose of ThunderClan demanded.

Shadowpaw did his best to ignore the criticism. Catching a glimpse of Rootpaw, sitting erect with his gaze firmly fixed on him, he felt heartened knowing that at least one cat wanted to hear what he had to tell. He made his voice ring out clear and steady as he began to speak.

"I was sitting on a rock in the forest. . . ." Shadowpaw described how the lake had turned red with fire, and how the fire had spread, separating each Clan from the others and devouring the forest, the camps, and the cats themselves. "I know it was a warning that the Clans might be destroyed," he finished. "We have to do something about it."

Shadowpaw was encouraged by the murmurs of agreement that came from some of the other medicine cats, but the feeling died almost immediately when Harestar spoke.

"I still don't understand why StarClan would only communicate through an apprentice. Why him, and not a real medicine cat?"

Shadowpaw's pelt grew hot with anger, but he didn't dare argue with the WindClan leader. To his surprise, it was Jayfeather who responded, his tone edged with sarcasm. "An apprentice *is* a real medicine cat, thank you very much. And it's not for us to tell StarClan where to send their messages."

"That doesn't help us much, though," Leafstar commented. "Even if this is a genuine message, it doesn't tell us what we should do about it. If we're not careful, we could be bringing on the destruction, not preventing it."

"That's true," Mistystar responded, her pale blue-gray pelt glimmering among the branches of the Great Oak. "But this vision makes sense to me. StarClan warned us after we got rid of Darktail that it was important for all five Clans to stay together."

Squirrelflight moved to the end of her branch so that she could look down at Shadowpaw. He gazed up at her, nervous but managing to meet her green gaze.

"Did StarClan say anything?" she asked.

Shadowpaw shook his head. "No, not a word."

"And the fire came from the lake? Not from any one of the Clans?"

Not from ShadowClan, Shadowpaw wanted to reply, guessing what Squirrelflight was getting at. "From the very center of the lake," he mewed aloud. "And the flames seemed to reach every Clan at the same time."

"I see . . ." Squirrelflight let her voice die away, and when she spoke again, it was with new decision. "Bramblestar supported you at the last Gathering," she told Shadowpaw. "I confess I'm not entirely convinced that you've had a true vision, but for the time being I'll take you seriously, for Bramblestar's sake."

"We all believe in Shadowpaw's vision." Willowshine rose to her paws and spoke for her fellow medicine cats. "And we think that it couldn't be more important. Whether the fire is real or symbolic, it could destroy all our Clans."

"I won't argue with that," Jayfeather added. "But all the same, I think there's something . . . something not quite right about this vision. Oh, I don't think you're lying or making it up, Shadowpaw. I just think we have to go forward very carefully."

"Right or not, it's all we have to go on," Alderheart reminded his Clanmate, letting his tail rest for a moment on Shadowpaw's shoulders. "The rest of us have tried, and failed, to make contact with StarClan for a couple of moons now. Shadowpaw's vision is the only direction we have."

Shadowpaw felt that most cats were moving toward accepting what he had told them. But then Tree rose to his paws from where he was sitting with a few of the other SkyClan cats.

"Yes, that's all very well," the yellow tom meowed. "But what exactly does it mean to believe Shadowpaw? What are we supposed to do?"

"And is this vision connected to what Shadowpaw told us last time?" Harestar asked. "About the darkness in the Clans?"

Shadowpaw looked up at his father, remembering the other part of his vision, about the codebreakers, and the shock he had felt when his vision showed him his mother, Dovewing. But Tigerstar stared straight ahead, not meeting Shadowpaw's gaze. Shadowpaw tried not to let his expression give anything away. He decided to say nothing; he sensed that the other Clans were still a little hostile to ShadowClan and its leader.

"There is something more I must say," Squirrelflight announced, still keeping her position at the end of the branch. She hesitated, taking a deep breath, as if she was making a momentous decision. "I have a confession to make. I lied to the Gathering."

Gasps of shock and disbelief came from the cats in the clearing. *I knew it!* Shadowpaw thought.

"For that, I ask your forgiveness," Squirrelflight went on. "The truth is that Bramblestar is sick—very sick. Our medicine cats have tried everything, all the usual herbs and treatments, and they have been unable to make him better. He is close to death, and without StarClan he may not be able to return to take up his next life, as a Clan leader should."

Her words were greeted with a heavy silence among the Clans.

Shadowpaw could feel Squirrelflight's gaze fixed on him as she continued. "Shadowpaw had an idea for a very unusual treatment. StarClan told him that it would make Bramblestar worse before he got better, but it would save him."

"And you want to go ahead with this?" Jayfeather asked. "Squirrelflight, are you sure?"

The ThunderClan deputy nodded resolutely. "It's Bramblestar's only hope," she meowed. "Whatever Shadowpaw's connection with StarClan may be, none of the rest of us can reach them. And that means we can't be sure what happens to a leader when he loses a life. I know the chance that Shadowpaw's treatment will save Bramblestar is a slim one, but we've tried everything else. A slim chance is still a chance—and it may be the only one Bramblestar has."

"Are you sure you've tried everything?" Mothwing asked. "I'd be happy to come and look at Bramblestar, if you want me to."

"So would I," Frecklewish offered, and the other medicine cats added their agreement.

Shadowpaw narrowed his eyes as he glanced at his fellow medicine cats. *It sounds like they still don't trust me,* he thought.

"Squirrelflight said *everything*, and she meant it," Alderheart retorted. "I'd be delighted if we could find another way, but there isn't one."

"And what happens if the treatment kills Bramblestar?" Reedwhisker asked, his voice filled with anxiety.

Squirrelflight heaved a long sigh. "I don't know," she admitted. "But without it, Bramblestar is going to die. We can't make things any worse if we try. Shadowpaw, will you come to ThunderClan?"

"Of course I will," Shadowpaw replied, then added instantly, "if Tigerstar and Puddleshine give permission."

"You have mine," Puddleshine mewed, while Tigerstar announced, "It's what I've wanted all along."

"And if he recovers," Harestar put in, "then we can decide what is meant by this vision of fire, and by the 'darkness in the Clans' Shadowpaw told us about before. And more important, how we can drive the darkness out."

No cat added any objections, so Tigerstar announced that the Gathering was over. As the cats began to disperse, Squirrelflight leaped down from the Great Oak and padded up to Shadowpaw.

"Will you come with me now?" she asked. "Bramblestar may not have very much time. I'll get warriors to help move him up onto the moor, wherever you like. We'll do whatever you tell us."

"We're on our way." It was Tigerstar who spoke, appearing suddenly at Squirrelflight's shoulder. "I'll be joining you." Squirrelflight glanced at him as if she was about to object, but the ShadowClan leader gave her no chance to speak. "I'm bringing Puddleshine and Dovewing, too," he told her. "No cat knows exactly what will happen, and I must consider my own Clan's safety."

A shiver passed through Shadowpaw as he realized what his father meant. Even he was afraid that the treatment wouldn't save Bramblestar, and that if Shadowpaw failed, he might be in danger from angry ThunderClan warriors.

Shadowpaw swallowed hard as he followed Squirrelflight toward the tree-bridge. *StarClan, guide my paws,* he prayed.

CHAPTER 21

❧

Shadowpaw smoothed down the ThunderClan leader's fur and tucked his paws beneath him. The walls of the den that he had carved out in the snow rose a tail-length above Bramblestar's inert body. Following his vision, he had led the ThunderClan warriors to an exposed place on the moor, close to the WindClan border. Now, as he looked down at the sick leader, a shudder passed through him that had nothing to do with the biting cold: it was pure panic.

He looks so close to death. How can he survive this?

Shadowpaw hadn't finished with his medicine-cat training, but he knew this was a terrible thing to do to any cat, let alone one as sick as Bramblestar.

But StarClan said . . .

As he stepped back, leaving the ThunderClan leader inside the den, Shadowpaw saw Alderheart standing nearby, looking tense and uncomfortable. Jayfeather was beside him, even more unhappy than usual, his face set in the most sour grimace Shadowpaw had ever seen.

Squirrelflight had insisted on the ThunderClan medicine cats being present for this attempt to cure Bramblestar.

She herself had stayed behind in camp to take up her duties as temporary Clan leader, saying that if there was no news by dawn she would come to see for herself. Shadowpaw had guessed that part of her was relieved not to have to witness her mate's ordeal.

Once he was sure that Bramblestar was settled, Shadowpaw left the snow den and went to sit beside his mother. Dovewing draped her tail protectively over his shoulders. Shadowpaw could see the worry in her eyes; it hadn't been long since she had been a ThunderClan cat, and Bramblestar her leader.

Then Shadowpaw remembered his mother's face in the vision he had received of the codebreakers. She and Tigerstar had broken the warrior code by becoming mates. Dovewing had abandoned her Clan.

Will StarClan ever forgive her?

Moonhigh came and went, and Bramblestar only seemed to be getting worse. His chest barely moved with each shallow breath. Alderheart, who was sitting beside him in the snow den, was growing more panicked with every moment that passed. Shadowpaw wished that he could reassure the ThunderClan medicine cat, but fear was growing inside him, too: the fear that he had been terribly wrong, and that his treatment was only hastening Bramblestar's death.

"He's too cold!" Alderheart cried out. "Isn't there anything we can do to warm him?"

"No," Shadowpaw responded. "The cold is supposed to cure him, letting the sickness work its way out." He hoped that he sounded more confident than he felt.

Glancing around at the other cats, Shadowpaw could see his own doubt and anxiety reflected in every face. Even Puddleshine was looking uncomfortable.

"We took an oath as medicine cats," Jayfeather growled. "How can we sit here and watch a cat die? Knowing we're making him worse?"

"But we knew what would happen here," Puddleshine replied; Shadowpaw could tell what an effort his words were costing him. "It's just like when Alderheart cured my infection using deathberries. Bramblestar will get worse before he gets better—isn't that what the vision said?"

Shadowpaw nodded firmly. "Yes, it did."

"Then we must trust this young cat, as we all agreed," Puddleshine meowed. "As Squirrelflight—your own deputy, Jayfeather—agreed."

Jayfeather's only response was a scowl, but he made no move toward the den where the ThunderClan leader lay dying.

Shadowpaw closed his eyes, willing StarClan to send him more: another vision, another detail, anything to help convince him that this was right. *I'm supposed to help cats avoid death,* he thought. *But this time, am I chasing a cat toward his death?*

Behind his closed eyelids he saw a huge star exploding over the lake, splintering into countless glittering shards, which hung in the sky for a heartbeat and then faded into darkness. *There is a darkness in the Clans,* he repeated to himself.

Shadowpaw started as he felt some cat jostling him in his

side. He opened his eyes to see Puddleshine staring at him. "Are you asleep?" his mentor asked.

Blinking, Shadowpaw realized that the moon was lower in the sky than when he had last seen it. *I was asleep—and that must have been a dream.*

Jumping up, Shadowpaw padded into the snow den to check on Bramblestar. When he stretched out a paw and laid it gently on his chest, he felt that the ThunderClan leader was as cold as before.

Then an even deeper cold spread beneath Shadowpaw's pelt and invaded his whole body.

Bramblestar isn't breathing!

Shadowpaw let out a gasp. Forcing back panic, he rested his paw on Bramblestar's muzzle, then thumped his paws down on his chest, as if he might startle him back to life. But Bramblestar never stirred. Shadowpaw felt as though all the air had been sucked out of the tiny den, and an agonizing pain pierced his chest, as if claws were trying to rip him apart from the inside.

I killed him—I killed Bramblestar!

Forcing his legs to move, Shadowpaw backed out of the den and turned around. *I never thought I would kill him—I never thought he would die! StarClan didn't warn me. . . .*

Puddleshine was standing nearby, searching Shadowpaw's gaze. Shadowpaw could see his mentor read his expression, and flinched as the hope in Puddleshine's eyes changed to disappointment.

"Is he gone?" Puddleshine whispered.

Shadowpaw tried to speak, but he found he couldn't make the words come out of his mouth. *But StarClan . . .*

At that moment, he wished he had never come here, never poked his paws into ThunderClan's business. He felt like more than a failure; he felt like a murderer. As long as Bramblestar had been safe in ThunderClan's medicine-cat den, there had been a chance that he would have gotten better.

But now we'll never know.

Puddleshine brushed past Shadowpaw into the den, then a moment later slowly crawled out. By now all the other cats had realized that something was going on and had gathered around, all watching curiously as Puddleshine straightened up and let his gaze travel carefully over each of them.

"Bramblestar has stopped breathing," he announced.

Alderheart drew in a choking breath, while Jayfeather swung around to face Shadowpaw, his tabby pelt bristling in anger. "How did this happen?" he demanded. "You never said that Bramblestar would lose a life!"

"I didn't know—" Shadowpaw protested.

Jayfeather wasn't listening. "He was supposed to get worse and then better, right? If he was going to lose a life anyway, we didn't need to try this stupid plan. We could have just let the sickness run its course, and he could have died in his own nest." He gazed around, lashing his tail in frustration. "Whatever made any of us think it was worth following an apprentice with such a mouse-brained idea? Unless . . . unless this was part of ShadowClan's plan all along?"

At his words Tigerstar leaped forward, putting himself between Shadowpaw and the furious ThunderClan medicine cat. "Wait!" he ordered. "This may not be what we thought Shadowpaw's vision implied, but when has StarClan ever been precise? Perhaps this is what they meant to happen. Bramblestar has more lives, yes?"

Alderheart, who was looking as stunned as Shadowpaw felt, gave a brief nod.

"Then we must simply wait," Tigerstar continued. "Bramblestar will visit StarClan, and then return to begin his next life."

"That isn't what Shadowpaw said would happen," Jayfeather growled.

Tigerstar turned to him, his lips drawn back in the beginning of a snarl. "I have no reason to doubt my son," he stated. "Why don't we all sit back and wait?"

Grudgingly the other cats agreed and settled themselves outside the makeshift den. Shadowpaw's heart was racing, and he fixed his gaze on the dark tabby curve of Bramblestar's back, all he could see among the piles of snow. But there was no movement from the den.

"How long does it take?" Dovewing asked, her whiskers twitching nervously. "I know how it was for Tigerstar, when he died and was made leader. But that was different. Usually . . . if a leader loses a life . . . how long?"

"Every time I've seen a leader lose a life, it's been quick,"

Jayfeather replied. "Sometimes so quick that you might not even realize that a life was lost. The cat simply breathes out the last breath of one life and gasps the first breath of the next one. Sometimes there's a brief pause, but . . ." He hesitated, then went on more briskly, "If Bramblestar has gone to StarClan's hunting grounds, they will greet him, give him any messages they want him to bring back to his Clan, and return him to life. He should be back any moment now."

All the cats resigned themselves to waiting. Shadowpaw couldn't feel anything, not even his mother's comforting nuzzle, as he stared at the snow den. He desperately wanted to believe that Bramblestar would come back, but this wasn't how he had imagined it would happen. And something was nagging at him, like an ant crawling through his fur.

What if the voice I've been hearing was wrong? What if the older medicine cats were right to doubt me this whole time? What if I don't have a connection to StarClan at all, but am just a foolish, strange cat . . . a foolish cat who has led darkness into the Clans?

Moments dragged by, seemingly endless. Every cat was silent, their tension clear in their twitching tails and bristling fur. Every cat seemed to know that it was taking too long for Bramblestar to return, but Shadowpaw guessed that no cat wanted to be the one to say so.

Finally a gray light began to spill over the moor, showing the medicine cats' faces growing more and more despairing. The sun rose, red and angry.

As if at a signal, Jayfeather rose to his paws and strode over to the den, moved his head from side to side to scent the air, then turned back to face the others.

"Bramblestar is dead," he announced. "For good. StarClan has forgotten us."

"No!" Alderheart wailed. "No, he can't be!"

He pushed past Jayfeather into the den and crouched down beside his father's body.

Shadowpaw watched him, stunned, then turned to Tigerstar and Dovewing, who were staring at each other, their eyes wide with consternation. "We have to leave," Tigerstar meowed.

Puddleshine ducked into the den to check on Bramblestar one last time, while Tigerstar scraped the snow with his claws in agitation. "We should go," he continued. "We should go now." As Puddleshine reappeared he signaled to him impatiently with his tail. "Come on. Hurry."

"I'd like to wait and speak to Squirrelflight," Dovewing protested. "I know my sympathy won't do her much good, but still . . ."

"No, it's not safe," Tigerstar retorted. "The ThunderClan cats might turn on us. We're on unfamiliar territory, and if they come up from their camp, they'll outnumber us. We need to leave now. You're ShadowClan, Dovewing; don't forget that."

Dovewing stared sorrowfully at her mate, but didn't argue. The ShadowClan cats were turning to leave when Shadowpaw heard a terrible wailing.

"No! I came back for you, and you left me!"

Squirrelflight had arrived, flinging herself into the den beside the body of her mate.

Shadowpaw felt as though he would shatter into tiny pieces, like the star over the lake in his dream.

What have I done?

CHAPTER 22

Bristlefrost felt as though the sun had fallen out of the sky. She couldn't imagine ThunderClan without Bramblestar as leader: strong and brave, and wise enough to guide his Clan through every danger and hardship.

And he must have had many lives left, she thought. *He should have been able to lead us for season after season.*

Bristlefrost's whole body was numb with shock; though she knew she was lying on her belly, she couldn't feel the ground beneath her, or remember settling into that position. She watched as some of her Clanmates clustered around Squirrelflight, who sat slumped near the entrance to the warriors' den. She had returned from the moors to give her Clan the news of Bramblestar's death, and since then she had hardly spoken.

Bristlefrost remembered how Squirrelflight's sister, Leafpool, had died only a few moons before, and how Squirrelflight herself had spent time in StarClan. It was hard to imagine what Squirrelflight must be feeling now, to have lost her mate. *She must be so lonely. . . .*

Wondering if there was anything she could do to help, Bristlefrost rose and padded closer.

"Surely StarClan will contact you, if you go to the Moonpool," Whitewing was meowing as Bristlefrost came within
earshot. "We can't know why this is StarClan's will, but if you
go there and show deference—show that you accept what's
happened—then surely they'll give you your nine lives and
make you our leader."

"Yes, you must go," Sparkpelt, Squirrelflight's daughter,
urged her, pressing herself against her mother's side. Her kits
were tumbling about with Sorrelstripe's outside the nursery,
where Sorrelstripe kept a weary eye on them. "You can't truly
become our leader until you receive your nine lives."

Squirrelflight raised her head. "What good did nine lives
do Bramblestar?" she snapped. "He's dead!"

"But you're still alive," Birchfall pointed out. "And your
Clan needs you."

Squirrelflight's voice dropped to a low growl. "I'm not
going anywhere until I've mourned Bramblestar."

The cats around Squirrelflight exchanged anxious looks.
Bristlefrost knew what they were thinking as clearly as if they
had spoken aloud. *Our leader is dead, when he should have survived,
and our deputy is too crazed with grief to take his place.*

Oh, StarClan, Bristlefrost thought. *What will become of Thunder-
Clan now?*

Sunhigh was approaching when Bristlefrost plodded up the final stretch of moorland toward the snow den
where Bramblestar's body lay. Twigbranch, Rosepetal, and

Thornclaw accompanied her, to bring their leader back to the camp for his vigil that night.

When the cats stooped over Bramblestar to draw him out of the den, Bristlefrost could hear their sharp intakes of breath as they realized that his body was almost frozen solid. When she and her Clanmates lifted him, she was surprised to feel how light he was, and saw her own surprise reflected in her Clanmates' faces as they settled Bramblestar on their shoulders to carry him back to their camp. His illness had drained so much of his strength.

What cat allowed this to happen? Bristlefrost wondered, feeling like a fool. *I trusted Shadowpaw. I thought his advice would save our leader. And now our leader is dead.*

Despair crept up on Bristlefrost like a hunter stalking its prey as she helped carry Bramblestar's body back to the stone hollow. When the patrol maneuvered their burden through the thorn tunnel and emerged into the camp, every cat in the Clan was out in the clearing. Several of them broke into anguished wails at the sight of their leader's ice-crusted body.

Bristlefrost glanced around to see Jayfeather and Alderheart crouched close together at the entrance to their den. The elders, whose task it would be to bear their leader away for burial, stood waiting by the fresh-kill pile. Squirrelflight had not moved since Bristlefrost had left the camp, with several warriors still clustered around her. Even the kits were aware that something was wrong, and they burrowed into their mothers' fur with tiny whimpers of grief.

The assembled cats parted as Bristlefrost and her Clan-mates paced forward and laid Bramblestar's body down at the paws of the elders. With her task finished, Bristlefrost wasn't sure what to do. Glancing around, she spotted her mother and father, Ivypool and Fernsong, watching with sorrowful expressions, and ran over to them with a low cry of relief.

Fernsong nuzzled her close. "Are you all right?" he asked.

Bristlefrost leaned into her father's familiar embrace, thinking how lucky she was to have two parents who loved her. *I should have remembered that when I was heartbroken over Stemleaf.*

"I will be," she replied to Fernsong. "But what happens to ThunderClan now?"

No cat could answer her question.

"I remember how much Bramblestar taught me when I was a kit and an apprentice," Lionblaze meowed. "I believed he was my father then." His voice caught in his throat, and it was a moment before he could go on. "He was the best father a cat could have."

Darkness had fallen, and all the cats of ThunderClan had gathered to sit vigil for their dead leader. Alderheart sat clos-est, smoothing his father's fur with one paw. Sparkpelt was beside him, and Squirrelflight on their leader's other side, her head bowed. Lionblaze and Jayfeather sat nearby. Bristlefrost crouched in the circle of cats who surrounded them, listening to the tributes his Clanmates offered to Bramblestar.

"I remember when we made the journey to the sun-drown-place." Squirrelflight's voice was low, but clear enough to reach the ears of every cat. "Bramblestar—he was Brambleclaw then—was our leader. He was so brave and sensible. Without him we would never have made it there, much less survived to return to our Clans and give them Midnight's message."

A shiver passed through Bristlefrost as she heard Squirrel-flight speak of that long-ago journey, the story Ivypool had told her when she was a kit in the nursery. *Squirrelflight was actually there,* she realized, *and she and Bramblestar helped to bring the Clans to our home beside the lake.*

"Don't forget the Great Storm," Graystripe put in. "Bramblestar was a new leader then, but he kept our Clan safe until we could return to our home here in the stone hollow."

"And he guided us through the struggle with Darktail," Alderheart added. "When the other Clans drew away, or gave in to evil, ThunderClan never did. And that was because of Bramblestar." He bowed his head and his next words were choked out. "He was my father and I loved him."

Sparkpelt pressed herself closer to her brother's side. "We all loved him. Every cat in the Clan. And he was worthy of it."

A desolate silence fell, broken after a few heartbeats by Jayfeather, who rose to his paws from where he sat near Bramblestar's head. "Bramblestar was—" he began, then broke off, shaking his head helplessly as if the words wouldn't come.

A moment later he rounded on Squirrelflight, his shoulder fur bristling and his neck stretched out. "Why did you let Shadowpaw kill him?" he hissed. "Where is ThunderClan now? We have no leader, and without a leader we have no future. Did you learn nothing from your time in StarClan?"

A murmur of protest arose from the surrounding cats at Jayfeather's harshness toward a cat who was grieving. Bristlefrost didn't understand how he could be so hostile to a cat he had once thought was his mother.

Bristlefrost could see the hurt in Squirrelflight's eyes, but the deputy remained calm, raising her head to confront the angry medicine cat. "My time in StarClan is no cat's business but my own," she snapped. "And we weren't much better off when Bramblestar was so ill. I believed he was going to die. I had to make a choice, and I made it. And I will continue to do so as acting leader of this Clan."

"*Acting* leader?" Jayfeather sneered. "What good will that—"

"I believe that when this leaf-bare ends, we will hear from StarClan again," Squirrelflight interrupted. "And they will tell us what to do to make all this right."

Jayfeather looked as though he might say more, then closed his mouth with a snap and sat down again. Bristlefrost tried to find hope in Squirrelflight's words, but all she could see was a bleak future.

Bramblestar will still be dead. . . .

The vigil continued, with more cats offering their tributes to Bramblestar. Bristlefrost was one of the last cats to speak, wondering what she could contribute when she had known the Clan leader for such a short time.

"He made me a warrior," she meowed at last. "It was the proudest day of my life. I will honor his memory by being the best warrior that I can be."

Finally all the cats had spoken. A deep, reflective silence

fell over the camp. Bristlefrost realized that she could make out her Clanmates' faces more clearly; the sky was beginning to grow pale with the first light of dawn. A whole day had passed since they'd first learned that Bramblestar was dead.

The elders roused themselves, rising to stand around Bramblestar's body, ready to carry him out of the stone hollow to the burial place. Jayfeather rose too, moving closer to Bramblestar's head.

"May StarClan light your path, Bramblestar." His voice was steady now, its anger gone. "May you find good hunting, swift running, and shelter when you sleep." Then he nodded to the elders. "It is time."

The elders stooped to take up their burden, but before they could touch it, a faint ripple passed through Bramblestar's body. Bristlefrost gasped, hardly able to believe what she had seen. *I'm so tired. . . . I must be seeing things.*

But around her, all her Clanmates were staring too. At first Bristlefrost could see they shared her disbelief; then, after a moment, they began to look at each other, a gleam of hope kindling in their eyes. "Did you see that?" some cat muttered.

"It . . . it could just be his body settling," Alderheart stammered.

Another ripple, stronger this time, passed through Bramblestar. Bristlefrost crouched, frozen, hardly daring to breathe. Some cat whispered, "This can't be . . ."

Bramblestar blinked and raised his head, his eyes vacant. After a moment he rolled onto his belly, and as he turned his head to gaze at his transfixed Clan, his eyes gradually focused.

After a few more heartbeats, he rose slowly to his paws.

Every cat stared at him, stunned by what they were witnessing. Some of them backed away in alarm and confusion, while others took a wary step toward him, as if he were a predator who might lash out at them without warning.

"What's happening?" Sparkpelt whispered.

After a moment Bramblestar stretched out his forepaws and arched his back in a long stretch, as if he had just awoken from a deep sleep. *It wasn't death,* Bristlefrost realized. He looked healthier, too, not so emaciated, and his fur seemed to grow fuller, more sleek, as Bristlefrost watched.

Shadowpaw said he would get worse before he got better, she remembered. *Is he finally getting better?* Yet Bristlefrost was hardly able to believe what she was seeing. *What happened to him? He looked like he was dead, for so long. . . .*

Bramblestar padded across to Squirrelflight and dipped his head toward her. "Greetings," he meowed. "It's good to be with you again."

Squirrelflight pressed herself against him and twined her tail with his. She was purring too hard to reply.

Bristlefrost exchanged a shocked, wondering glance with Ivypool. "He's alive!" she exclaimed. "StarClan hasn't forsaken us!"

CHAPTER 23

❧

Puddleshine was already up, busily sorting herbs, but Shadowpaw still lay in his nest as dawn light grew in the ShadowClan camp. He glanced up listlessly as Snowbird appeared; a thorn in her bedding had scratched her nose.

"I'll fetch you some herbs," he mewed, beginning to force himself to his paws.

"Oh . . . no, it's okay," Snowbird stammered. "Thanks anyway, but I see that Puddleshine has already got some horsetail over there."

Shadowpaw let out a grunt and flopped back into his nest. Snowbird gave Shadowpaw a wary look as she passed him, and she seemed happy to deal with Puddleshine as he treated her and then sent her back to her warrior duties.

A trickle of cats followed Snowbird as the morning light strengthened, all of them with minor problems, and all of them reluctant to even look at Shadowpaw. Snaketooth actually let out a faint hiss, pointedly turning away. *Like I care,* Shadowpaw thought, watching morosely with his nose on his paws.

They're afraid of me, he realized. *And they have good reason to be. I killed Bramblestar, at the bidding of . . . who? Or what?*

The day before, Tigerstar and Dovewing had tried to comfort him, but there wasn't much that they could say. Shadowpaw could see in their faces that they too had begun to doubt his connection to StarClan. They knew StarClan wouldn't direct him to kill a leader.

What made it worse was that Bramblestar's sister, Tawnypelt, had barely moved since the news was brought to her. She remained crouched in the clearing even when snow started to fall, lazily dappling her tortoiseshell fur. Shadowpaw longed to comfort her, remembering how she had taken him to the Tribe of Rushing Water in the hope that they might cure his seizures. Tawnypelt had been there for him when he needed her, and now he longed to be there for her. But he knew that nothing he could say would help her now.

Grief is spreading from one end of the lake territories to the other, all because of my mistake.

Shadowpaw was still hunched in his nest, gloomily asking himself if there was anything he could have done differently, when he was disturbed by raised voices in the camp outside. He looked up, but he couldn't rouse himself to go and find out what was happening. The voices sounded surprised rather than hostile, anyway; the camp wasn't under attack.

Puddleshine hurried out, then reappeared a moment later. "Come on," he urged Shadowpaw. "Some ThunderClan warriors are here, and they want to speak to you."

Shadowpaw raised his head, as wary as if he had scented a fox in a thicket. *I don't want to speak to them.*

Puddleshine must have realized his nervousness, for his expression softened. "They say they've come in peace, Shadowpaw; they're not angry. And even if they were," he added, "you're in the heart of ShadowClan. There's no way Tigerstar would let anything bad happen to you."

Slowly Shadowpaw rose to his paws and shook off scraps of moss and bracken from his pelt. Confusion made his movements clumsy. *Why wouldn't ThunderClan be angry?* he wondered. *These are the cats whose leader I killed.*

Shadowpaw ventured out of the den, blinking in the stronger light outside. Lionblaze and Fernsong were there waiting for him, with Tigerstar and Dovewing a couple of tail-lengths away. Both his parents looked tense; Tigerstar had extended his claws, as if he was ready to fight.

As soon as the ThunderClan cats spotted Shadowpaw, they stepped up to him with tails held high in the air and eyes shining with joy. Seeing them like that made Shadowpaw even more bewildered. Tigerstar and Dovewing, and the other ShadowClan cats who were beginning to gather, exchanged confused glances. *They don't know what to make of it, either.*

"We've brought good news!" Lionblaze announced, his voice warm with happiness. "Bramblestar is alive. Your treatment worked, Shadowpaw."

Yowls of surprise and excitement exploded from the cats standing around, while Shadowpaw caught looks of pride and respect from Tigerstar and Dovewing.

"We're so sorry for doubting you." Fernsong was finding it hard to make himself heard above the joyful clamor. "Maybe you can see things other cats can't, or maybe StarClan sent you these weird messages so you would have the courage to try something no other medicine cat would have dared. We want you to know that ThunderClan doesn't bear you any ill will."

"Quite the opposite, in fact," Lionblaze added.

Shadowpaw stood still, completely stunned by the praise that every cat was heaping on him. *I'm not sure I really did anything....* It was hard to accept that StarClan really was guiding him. *If they are, they've chosen a very odd way to do it.* He was still shaken, though he tried to hide his doubts; he didn't want to spoil the joy of the ThunderClan warriors.

"Bramblestar has called another emergency Gathering for tomorrow night," Fernsong continued when the noise had died down. "He wants to discuss Shadowpaw's other visions, and the way forward for all five Clans."

Tigerstar dipped his head. "ShadowClan will be there," he promised.

The ThunderClan warriors turned back to Shadowpaw, thanking him and congratulating him again, then took their leave. Once they were gone, his Clanmates crowded around him.

"Good job!" Sparrowtail exclaimed. "I always believed in you, you know."

Right. And hedgehogs fly, Shadowpaw thought.

"We're really lucky!" Snaketooth mewed. "StarClan has chosen just one cat to receive their messages—and he's in our Clan!" Remembering how Snaketooth had hissed at him in his den, Shadowpaw felt wryly amused at how quickly the tabby she-cat had changed her opinion.

Shadowpaw bowed his head, murmuring thanks for his Clanmates' praise, but he felt more and more uncomfortable with each passing heartbeat. As soon as he could, he escaped back to his den.

Puddleshine followed him, gazing at him with mingled curiosity and confusion. "I'm beginning to doubt myself," he told Shadowpaw. "I examined Bramblestar, and I didn't think there was anything to be done for him. But you—my own apprentice—saw a way. Clearly you're the one whose paws are guided by StarClan." Shadowpaw wanted to protest, but his mentor went on. "Your connection with them isn't like any I've seen before, but I won't doubt you again."

A rustling sounded at the entrance to the den, and Tiger-star stepped inside. "I'd like a word with my son in private," he meowed with a nod to Puddleshine.

Once Puddleshine was gone, Tigerstar padded up to Shadowpaw and touched noses with him. "I always knew you were special," he announced. "We don't know yet what your destiny is among the five Clans, but what I do know is that you will change things."

Shadowpaw listened uneasily. He wasn't sure that he wanted to hear what his father was telling him. *Why has Star-Clan chosen me? Why can't I be an ordinary medicine cat, like Puddleshine?*

Tigerstar's expression became more serious, and he rested his tail on his son's shoulder. "Still, you mustn't tell the other

Clans about the message you received about codebreakers. Not yet, anyway," he added hastily. "Not until we're sure what it means . . ."

Shadowpaw glimpsed apprehension in his father's eyes; he realized that Tigerstar was worried. He and Dovewing had broken the code. What would happen to them if the message was revealed? "I won't," he promised, feeling that he had no choice but to obey his father.

Relief spread across Tigerstar's face, and he gave Shadowpaw's ear an approving lick. "Get some rest; you've had a tough time," he advised before he padded out of the den.

Shadowpaw was thankful to be left alone, but he felt more uneasy than ever. *If I am the Clans' only connection to StarClan, how can I be loyal to all of them, and to my parents, at the same time?*

Shadowpaw had expected an atmosphere of rejoicing at the emergency Gathering; every cat should be glad and relieved that Bramblestar had returned from the dead, proving that StarClan had not forsaken the living Clans. Instead, as soon as ShadowClan thrust their way through the bushes into the clearing, he was aware of suspicious glances, shoulder fur rising, with here and there a hiss of hostility.

Tigerstar ignored it all, holding his head high as he crossed the clearing and leaped into the branches of the Great Oak. The other Clan leaders were already there. Cloverfoot joined the rest of the deputies on the tree roots, while Shadowpaw, with Puddleshine beside him, padded over to sit with their fellow medicine cats. He kept his head lowered, not wanting to meet any other cat's gaze.

Once every cat was settled, Bramblestar announced, "Let the Gathering begin."

Risking a glance upward, Shadowpaw saw the Thunder-Clan leader standing strong and proud at the end of a thick branch that jutted out into the clearing. This time there was enough moonlight to see him clearly: his muscular body, his sleek tabby fur and gleaming amber eyes. Shadowpaw could hardly believe that this was the same cat who had lain, scrawny and unmoving, in the snow den. The ThunderClan leader was gazing around him, his expression filled with wonder, as if he too was finding it hard to believe that he was still alive.

"I'm pleased to see you all again," Bramblestar continued. "I've called this Gathering to discuss what happened to me, and the messages Shadowpaw has received from StarClan. Would any of the Clan leaders like to begin?"

"I will," Harestar responded at once, rising to his paws on a branch a little way above Bramblestar. He gazed down at Shadowpaw, his eyes warm and appreciative. "I'm impressed with what I've heard," he meowed. "I know Tigerstar believes his son has a unique connection to StarClan, and after what he did for Bramblestar, I think he might have a point."

Shadowpaw relaxed a little when he realized he had at least one supporter from another Clan, but his belly clenched with nervousness as Kestrelflight rose to speak from the group of medicine cats. There was a doubtful expression in his eyes as he looked at Shadowpaw, then turned to address all the assembled cats.

"Does any cat think it's strange that only ShadowClan can communicate with StarClan now?" he asked. "After all, if you think back, a lot of our problems started with ShadowClan. They allowed Darktail in, and that caused their Clan to fall apart, so that for a while they had to merge with SkyClan."

Murmurs arose from among the SkyClan cats as Kestrelflight spoke, and a few of them cast unfriendly glances toward the warriors of ShadowClan.

Mothwing moved to join the WindClan medicine cat. "Kestrelflight has a point. And it was ShadowClan who wanted all their old territory back," she added. "That almost caused SkyClan to leave, against the wishes of StarClan."

Jayfeather turned toward Mothwing, the tip of his tail twitching. "What do you know?" he snapped. "You don't really believe in StarClan, anyway."

Gasps of horror came from the cats in the clearing. Shadowpaw looked around, realizing that none of the warriors had been aware of Mothwing's disbelief.

Mothwing looked as if she could hardly believe Jayfeather had said this in a Gathering. "I don't believe that's relevant," she hissed.

Jayfeather twitched his tail in irritation. "It couldn't be more relevant. And it's obvious to every cat, every time you open your mouth to talk about StarClan."

By now all the cats were staring at Mothwing, uneasiness or plain hostility in their eyes. But Mothwing remained calm. "Actually," she began, "as I've already told you, after some thought, I can no longer deny that StarClan exists. But it's strange that they're only communicating with Shadowpaw, who is just an apprentice."

Clamor erupted around the clearing, some cats yowling in support of Shadowpaw, while others voiced their suspicions of him.

"He saved Bramblestar!"

"What are the other medicine cats doing for us?"

"This is all a ShadowClan plot!"

Shadowpaw squeezed his eyes shut and tried to shrink himself into the smallest space possible. He wished that he could flee out of the clearing and run back to his home in the ShadowClan camp. He hated to feel every cat's gaze on him and listen to their voices screeching about his visions and his loyalty.

Finally he heard his father's voice raised loudly above the rest. "Quiet! This is no time for arguments!"

Gradually the noise began to die down. As soon as he could make himself heard without yowling, Tigerstar continued. "What does it matter if Shadowpaw is the only cat who can receive messages from StarClan while the Moonpool is frozen? It's probably because his connection to our ancestors is so strong."

Frecklewish let out a disdainful snort. "Do you really believe that?"

"I do believe it," Tigerstar mewed emphatically. "All I know is a leader was brought back to life. That should be enough for every cat gathered here."

Shadowpaw relaxed a little, daring to look up again; he was

grateful for his father's support, though he could still hear uneasy muttering among the warriors.

"There is one way to settle this," Jayfeather stated. "If Bramblestar could tell us what he saw when he visited StarClan . . ."

The gaze of every cat turned toward Bramblestar, who still stood on his branch, his head raised as he stared out above the heads of the cats assembled below. A few moments passed before he startled, seeming to notice the silence, as if he didn't realize that every cat was waiting for him to answer a question.

"Could you tell us what you saw when you lost your life?" Jayfeather repeated. "Were you in StarClan?"

Bramblestar seemed to gather himself, as if the question needed some thought. Finally he nodded. "Yes, I'm quite sure I was."

"Did they speak to you before you took up your next life?" Harestar asked.

"They did."

"And what did they say?" Mistystar spoke for the first time, in a voice full of anxiety. "Did they give you any guidance you can pass on to the rest of us?"

Bramblestar turned toward her, his amber gaze unfriendly. "Mistystar, you are a Clan leader. You know as well as I do that what passes between us and StarClan is not to be spoken of to any cat. It is private, and I for one prefer it to stay that way."

Mistystar dipped her head apologetically. "I know, Bramblestar. I'm sorry."

"StarClan restored me," Bramblestar went on, "and that's all that matters, surely. And why wouldn't they? I'm a cat who has always honored the warrior code." His glance raked across the other leaders where they sat near him in the branches of the Great Oak. "Why are you questioning me?" he demanded.

For a few heartbeats there was an awkward silence while the other four leaders looked at one another. Shadowpaw braced himself for more argument or accusations.

"We're not. We believe you, Bramblestar," Leafstar meowed eventually, speaking for them all. "But—"

"Then, for now, we accept that Shadowpaw is our connection to StarClan," Bramblestar continued, cutting off whatever Leafstar would have said. "At least until the ice on the Moonpool thaws."

Murmurs of relief arose from the warriors in the clearing. Most of them seemed glad that a decision had been reached, though Shadowpaw was still aware of a few mistrustful looks.

He was hoping that the Gathering might end now, so that he could get away from the crowd, when Tree rose to his paws from where he sat among a group of SkyClan cats.

"Other cats besides medicine cats get visions too," he pointed out. "We shouldn't assume they're making it up if they say they've received a message from StarClan. And it doesn't mean that they're dangerous."

Why does Tree have to bring this up now? Shadowpaw wondered.

He caught the eye of the apprentice Rootpaw, who was sitting beside his father. He could see that Rootpaw was giving his chest fur a few embarrassed licks, even though most other cats were for once grunting in agreement with Tree.

But Shadowpaw couldn't forget that Tree was one of the cats he had seen in his vision of the codebreakers. *Maybe StarClan isn't as okay with "different" cats as we are.*

"Thank you, Tree," Bramblestar mewed. His tone suggested that he didn't want to hear any more from the SkyClan tom. "And now we must discuss the way forward. Shadowpaw, you had a vision about darkness in the Clans. Is there any more you can tell us?"

A deadlier cold than the chilly air of leaf-bare crept over Shadowpaw. He hadn't wanted even to think about this now, let alone in front of so many other cats. Besides, Tigerstar had ordered him not to say anything about his vision of the codebreakers. "No," he lied, staring at his paws. "That's all I know."

"Then can any cat suggest what a 'darkness within the Clans' might be?" Bramblestar continued. He glanced in Shadowpaw's direction, and Shadowpaw stared at his paws, suddenly cold. *He can't know, can he?*

After the moment had passed, Shadowpaw looked up to see the Clan leaders exchanging bewildered glances. "I could have answered that when Darktail was among us," Mistystar responded at last. "But he's gone now, and good riddance. Unless any Clan has taken in rogues or loners since we last met?"

"Like we're that stupid," Tigerstar muttered.

"Has any cat seen traces of the Dark Forest cats?" Harestar asked. "Would they dare to attack us again?"

"I doubt it," Kestrelflight, the WindClan medicine cat replied. "They learned their lesson in the Great Battle. And in any case, that wouldn't be a darkness *within* the Clans."

Shadowpaw began to breathe more freely, hoping that the whole question could be set aside, when Mosspelt, a River-Clan elder, heaved herself to her paws.

"I wonder if this message has something to do with the warrior code," she began. "Bramblestar is right; he is a cat who has always honored it. But not every cat follows the code as strictly as they could. Not like it was in my younger days . . ." Breathing heavily, she sat down again.

Shadowpaw forced himself not to flinch as Mosspelt's words struck at the heart of the truth. *Mosspelt is wise. . . .* He stole a look at his father, and saw that Tigerstar had grown utterly still.

"A good point, Mosspelt." Bramblestar dipped his head respectfully to the RiverClan elder. "That does sound like a possibility."

"Then does any cat want to confess to breaking the warrior code?" Harestar asked, gazing out across the crowd of cats. "Maybe if we admit our wrongdoing, it will ease the way back for StarClan."

Shadowpaw spotted many of the cats giving one another uneasy glances, but no cat spoke up. He could feel the tension in the clearing as if a thunderstorm were about to break. The silence was deafening.

"Well, then," Bramblestar continued, when several moments had passed, "does any cat know of another cat who has broken the warrior code? Would you like to name that cat?"

Yowls of outrage rose in the clearing at the ThunderClan leader's words. Mistystar's voice cut through the clamor; her blue eyes were like chips of ice as she glared at Bramblestar.

"What are you trying to get at?" she demanded. "Do we want to live in Clans where cats throw accusations around?"

While she was speaking, Shadowpaw noticed that Bramblestar's sister, Tawnypelt, was staring at her littermate, mingled betrayal and shock showing in her face. Shadowpaw remembered the story Dovewing had told him in the nursery, of how Tawnypelt had been born in ThunderClan but had left it to join her father, the first Tigerstar, in ShadowClan. *She changed Clans, just like Dovewing,* Shadowpaw realized. *That makes her a codebreaker, too. But is Bramblestar really encouraging some cat to report his sister?*

"Not at all," Bramblestar responded to Mistystar, his eyes wide and innocent. "All I want is to drive out the darkness that is threatening the Clans. And how can we do that, if we can't even speak about it openly?" He paused and then continued, his tone deeper and more serious. "All of us keep talking about our connection with StarClan being broken by the cold, as if we're assuming we'll hear from our warrior ancestors again when the Moonpool thaws. But how do we know that will happen? It hasn't been long since they told us they wanted us to draw closer to them. Have we done that? Have we even tried? What if StarClan isn't ignoring us because of the cold?

Who's to say they haven't turned away from us because too many cats aren't following the code anymore? Maybe this 'darkness' is what has severed us from StarClan. Maybe that's what's causing this dreadfully cold leaf-bare."

Tigerstar was gazing at Bramblestar, and Shadowpaw was alarmed at how meek his voice sounded, as if he was frightened even to speak. "Is that what StarClan told you when you lost your life?"

Bramblestar looked up at the dark sky, his muzzle twisted as if he was pondering what to say. "What StarClan told me is no cat's concern but mine," he replied in a low, cool voice. "I'm just posing some questions that I feel the Clans need to consider."

Shadowpaw felt a wave of relief that Bramblestar hadn't been told to drive out any codebreakers—especially not Tigerstar and Dovewing—but the silence that followed still made him uneasy. Every cat seemed unsure what to do.

"Don't forget Shadowpaw's other vision," Bramblestar added after a moment. "The lake of fire that destroyed the Clans. That could be telling us what will happen if we get this wrong."

A shudder passed through Shadowpaw as Bramblestar reminded him of that terrible warning. He could see fear in the eyes of every cat as they gazed at him and then turned aside to mutter to one another.

"It makes sense that StarClan might be upset about the code being broken," Harestar meowed at last. "We've had some troubled times, so maybe we've been more forgiving than in the past. And if that's the case, then we'd better not be so forgiving in the future."

"Then the only way to draw closer to StarClan is . . . what?" Mistystar added. "Find cats who are breaking the code and stop them? Punish them?" She didn't sound as if she was looking forward to the prospect.

Shadowpaw thought that all the cats in the clearing seemed uncomfortable, too, but before any of them could argue, Bramblestar spoke again.

"We will take it one paw step at a time," he meowed, his voice warm and reassuring. "All of you should think about the warrior code, and how it is being followed in your Clan, before we meet again at the next full moon." He gave a swish of his tail. "The Gathering is at an end."

As Bramblestar leaped down from the Great Oak, the meeting began to break up. Shadowpaw watched as many cats from all the Clans ran up to the ThunderClan leader, congratulating him on his recovery.

"It's great to see you back, Bramblestar."

"The forest wouldn't be the same without you."

Bramblestar seemed uncomfortable with all the attention, shifting his paws and flattening his ears. "There's no need for grown warriors to act like excitable kits." His voice was a low growl. "Have you never seen a leader come back from the dead before?"

He thrust his way through the crowd and headed toward the tree-bridge, followed by his Clanmates.

Shadowpaw spotted his mother and father looking uneasily

at each other—and more ShadowClan cats looking uneasily at them. He knew that his parents had broken the warrior code by becoming mates, because they were from different Clans. *My very existence breaks the warrior code,* he thought miserably. But if that were true, Shadowpaw added to himself, then why would StarClan have chosen him to save Bramblestar?

He knew that he ought to feel happy, even triumphant, because of the way he had helped ThunderClan. Instead, as he trailed after his parents on their long march back to Shadow-Clan territory, all he could feel was apprehension.

What have I done?

CHAPTER 24

❧

Rootpaw had just finished carrying in fresh bedding for Fallowfern in the elders' den when he heard his sister, Needlepaw, calling for him from outside in the camp. Dipping his head to Fallowfern, he padded out of the den. "What's the matter?" he asked Needlepaw.

"Violetshine and Tree want to talk to us," Needlepaw replied. "Tree says it's important."

Rootpaw glanced around, but he couldn't see either of his parents. At the same moment, Needlepaw gave him a shove.

"Out in the forest," she mewed. "Tree doesn't want any cat to overhear what he has to say."

Rootpaw rolled his eyes. *What now?* It was just like Tree, he reflected, trying not to show his irritation as he followed his sister through the fern barrier. So many cats had come back from the Gathering relieved that Bramblestar was alive again, but Tree couldn't just let cats be happy. He had to be weird and find some way to bring every cat down.

When he and his sister found Tree and Violetshine under a tree just outside the camp, Rootpaw noticed that his mother was looking bemused at Tree's serious look. His eyes were troubled as he gestured with his tail for the two apprentices to come closer.

"I was unsettled by the Gathering last night," Tree announced, when Rootpaw and Needlepaw had burrowed into the pine needles by his side.

"Why?" Violetshine asked. "Everything seemed fine to me. Bramblestar is back!"

Tree gave her a stunned look, as if he couldn't believe what he was hearing. "Didn't you hear what Bramblestar was calling for?" he asked. "He said cats should start accusing one another of crimes that could get them expelled from their Clans."

Violetshine still looked bewildered. "Why are you afraid? You follow the warrior code, don't you?"

Tree's whiskers arched in shock. "I can't believe you said that!" he exclaimed. "Have you forgotten Darktail? Didn't you tell me that he would manipulate the rules to punish cats he was unhappy with?" He hesitated, then added, "Like Needletail?"

Violetshine's expression was suddenly flooded with horror, and though she was clearly struggling to speak, no words came. *What just happened?* Rootpaw thought, seeing how upset his mother looked, and he wondered who Needletail was. *Is that where Needlepaw's name comes from? And why does mentioning Needletail make my mother look so devastated?*

Rootpaw had heard stories about Darktail and his Kin, and how they had nearly destroyed ShadowClan. And he knew that for a while his mother had been part of the Kin, and that she had eventually helped to destroy it. But Violetshine had always refused to talk about it.

Too raw, too painful, Tree had explained to him and Needlepaw.

"That was Darktail's Kin," Violetshine responded eventually to Tree. "It had nothing to do with the Clans."

"Not then," Tree meowed. "Not yet."

Violetshine turned her head away, unable to meet his gaze.

Tree reached out with his tail and gently laid the tip on her shoulder. "I just need you to understand why I'm suggesting this," he told her. "Should we go and be rogues again? I know how to find food wherever we go. I would keep you safe."

Rootpaw exchanged a shocked glance with Needlepaw. He felt every hair on his pelt prick with apprehension at the thought of setting out into the unknown.

"Leave the Clans?" Needlepaw asked, a dubious look on her face. "You can't be serious!"

A wave of relief surged through Rootpaw as his mother shook her head. "I can't do it," she meowed. "I worked too hard to find my kin. I could never leave Hawkwing."

Though Rootpaw could see regret in Tree's eyes, his father nodded understandingly. "I was afraid you would say that, so I have another idea. Maybe we should try to persuade Leafstar to go back to the gorge. SkyClan could live on its own again, like we planned before the big storm."

Rootpaw's relief was swallowed up in anger. *Trust Tree to make things difficult!* "The gorge?" he exclaimed. "But Needlepaw and I have never even been there! And I like having the other Clans around."

And it would mean leaving Bristlefrost.

Immediately Rootpaw pushed that thought away. The ThunderClan she-cat had made it clear that she didn't feel the same way about him. *And maybe it's just as well. The last thing the Clans need just now is another pair of mates breaking the code!*

Again Violetshine shook her head. "I would never go so far away from my sister, Twigbranch."

"I don't want to leave the other Clans, either!" Needlepaw put in. "And StarClan wants us all to live together."

Tree flicked his ears in irritation at the mention of StarClan. "Okay," he sighed. "I accept that I've been outvoted. But can we promise, as a family, that we'll keep our eyes open? If things get bad in the Clans, we'll go—with SkyClan or without them."

"Okay," Needlepaw mewed.

Rootpaw nodded in reluctant agreement with his sister, but he still didn't understand what his father was meowing about. *Surely it's a good thing if cats obey the warrior code?*

"Very well," Violetshine murmured, still clearly unhappy about the decision. "But we have to make the decision together. That's only fair."

Tree heaved an even deeper sigh. "Fine."

The meeting over, Rootpaw didn't return to the camp. Instead he headed out into the forest. Even though he knew he was due to meet Dewspring for hunting practice, he needed some time alone to clear his head.

Snow still covered the forest floor, and icicles hung from the trees. Rootpaw was so used to his paws being numb from cold and the chilly wind that probed into his fur that he had almost forgotten what it was like to be warm. But he still loved the forest, liked to feel that he was learning every paw step of it. He didn't feel that anywhere else could really be his home.

My apprenticeship is going really well now, he thought. He was eager for the day when Dewspring would decide that he was ready for his assessment. *Why would I want to leave? I might never become a warrior. Seriously, what's wrong with Tree?*

Rootpaw wondered what it would be like to have normal parents. Violetshine was pretty normal, he supposed, always calm and collected—except over Needletail. *What was all that about?* When Tree had mentioned that name, Violetshine had reacted as if he had clawed out her heart.

Lost in his thoughts, Rootpaw jumped, startled, when he spotted a dark brown tabby tom standing at the other side of a clearing. "Oh—sorry!" he gasped, hoping that he hadn't disturbed him.

The tabby tom looked up when he heard Rootpaw, angling his ears toward him. Rootpaw let out a gasp as he recognized him. "Bramblestar!" *But what is he doing on SkyClan territory? And why didn't I scent him?*

Rootpaw opened his jaws to taste the air, but he still couldn't pick up the least trace of ThunderClan. *What kind of cat has no scent?*

Bramblestar began to pad toward Rootpaw, who let out another gasp of mingled disbelief and terror. Rootpaw could see the trees at the other side of the clearing through Bramblestar's body. It reminded Rootpaw of all his father's stories of seeing dead cats.

But I don't have that power. And Bramblestar isn't dead!

Whatever the Bramblestar thing was, it was still coming toward Rootpaw. Gripped by claws of pure panic, Rootpaw whipped around and raced back to the camp, his belly fur brushing the snow and his tail streaming out in the wind of his passing.

Behind him, he could hear a fading voice, calling out to him. "Wait! You have to help me! Please!"

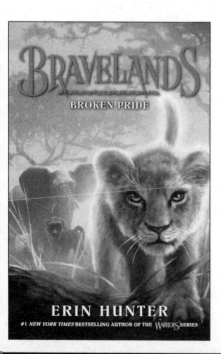

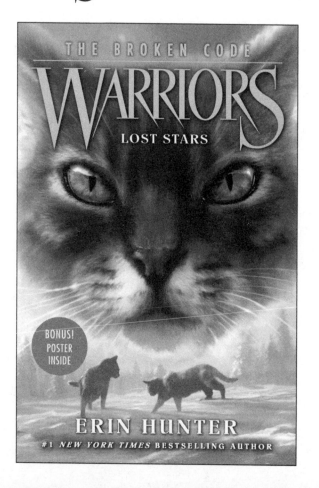

WARRIORS

How many have you read?

Dawn of the Clans
- ○ #1: The Sun Trail
- ○ #2: Thunder Rising
- ○ #3: The First Battle
- ○ #4: The Blazing Star
- ○ #5: A Forest Divided
- ○ #6: Path of Stars

Power of Three
- ○ #1: The Sight
- ○ #2: Dark River
- ○ #3: Outcast
- ○ #4: Eclipse
- ○ #5: Long Shadows
- ○ #6: Sunrise

The Prophecies Begin
- ○ #1: Into the Wild
- ○ #2: Fire and Ice
- ○ #3: Forest of Secrets
- ○ #4: Rising Storm
- ○ #5: A Dangerous Path
- ○ #6: The Darkest Hour

Omen of the Stars
- ○ #1: The Fourth Apprentice
- ○ #2: Fading Echoes
- ○ #3: Night Whispers
- ○ #4: Sign of the Moon
- ○ #5: The Forgotten Warrior
- ○ #6: The Last Hope

The New Prophecy
- ○ #1: Midnight
- ○ #2: Moonrise
- ○ #3: Dawn
- ○ #4: Starlight
- ○ #5: Twilight
- ○ #6: Sunset

A Vision of Shadows
- ○ #1: The Apprentice's Quest
- ◐ #2: Thunder and Shadow
- ◐ #3: Shattered Sky
- ○ #4: Darkest Night
- ○ #5: River of Fire
- ○ #6: The Raging Storm

Select titles also available as audiobooks!

HARPER
An Imprint of HarperCollinsPublishers

SUPER EDITIONS

- ○ Firestar's Quest
- ○ Bluestar's Prophecy
- ○ SkyClan's Destiny
- ○ Crookedstar's Promise
- ○ Yellowfang's Secret
- ○ Tallstar's Revenge
- ○ Bramblestar's Storm
- ○ Moth Flight's Vision
- ○ Hawkwing's Journey
- ○ Tigerheart's Shadow
- ○ Crowfeather's Trial

GUIDES   FULL-COLOR MANGA

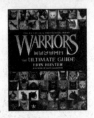

- ○ Secrets of the Clans
- ○ Cats of the Clans
- ○ Code of the Clans
- ○ Battles of the Clans
- ○ Enter the Clans
- ○ The Ultimate Guide

- ○ Graystripe's Adventure
- ○ Ravenpaw's Path
- ○ SkyClan and the Stranger

EBOOKS AND NOVELLAS

The Untold Stories
- ○ Hollyleaf's Story
- ○ Mistystar's Omen
- ○ Cloudstar's Journey

Tales from the Clans
- ○ Tigerclaw's Fury
- ○ Leafpool's Wish
- ○ Dovewing's Silence

Shadows of the Clans
- ○ Mapleshade's Vengeance
- ○ Goosefeather's Curse
- ○ Ravenpaw's Farewell

Legends of the Clans
- ○ Spottedleaf's Heart
- ○ Pinestar's Choice
- ○ Thunderstar's Echo

HARPER
An Imprint of HarperCollinsPublishers

www.warriorcats.com • www.shelfstuff.com